A SAVAGE NEW WORLD

Ben's radio crackled. "Those . . . people out there?" Ben picked up on the emphasis on "people." "They're dressed in animal skins. They got feathers and other crap stuck in their hair. Damnedest lookin' bunch of savages I've ever seen. I'm watchin' them from the rooftop of the old service station."

"How are they armed?" Ben radioed back.

Before he could get an answer, the old front door to the house shattered open. A man dressed in animal skins stood in the doorway, a huge spiked club in his right hand. He yelled at Ben and charged him, the club raised over his head. . . .

BLOOD
IN THE
ASHES

WILLIAM W. JOHNSTONE

PINNACLE BOOKS
Kensington Publishing Corp.
http://www.kensingtonbooks.com

PINNACLE BOOKS are published by

Kensington Publishing Corp.
850 Third Avenue
New York, NY 10022

All Kensington Titles, Imprints, and Distributed Lines are available at special quantity discounts for bulk purchases for sales promotions, premiums, fund-raising, and educational or institutional use. Special book excerpts or customized printings can also be created to fit specific needs. For details, write or phone the office of the Kensington special sales manager: Kensington Publishing Corp., 850 Third Avenue, New York, NY 10022, attn: Special Sales Department, Phone: 1-800-221-2647.

Pinnacle and the P logo Reg. U.S. Pat. & TM Off.

ISBN-13: 978-0-7860-1960-1
ISBN-10: 0-7860-1960-3

First Pinnacle Books Printing: September 1997

10 9 8 7

Printed in the United States of America

To: Charles & Bobbi

They that can give up essential liberty to obtain a little temporary safety deserve neither liberty nor safety.

Ben Franklin

If a nation expects to be ignorant and free, in a state of civilization, it expects what never was and never will be.

Thomas Jefferson

PROLOGUE

The bullet spider-webbed the windshield and knocked a hole in the interior of the truck before exiting out the rear of the cab. Gale screamed and ducked to the floorboards, her hands over her ears. She said some very unladylike words, just audible over the rattle of gunfire.

From the direction the slug took in entering the cab of the pickup, Ben knew it had been fired from his right, from the south side of the highway. Ben spun the steering wheel.

A six-wheeled V-300 roared up beside Ben's pickup. It passed the truck and wheeled about in the cracked and pitted highway, its twin Browning M2 .50-caliber machine guns yammering, spitting out death, clearing the thick underbrush by the roadside of all living things. An APC had rolled up beside Ben's pickup, on the south side, a buffer of protection for the general and his lady.

Rebels sprang into action. They were Gray's Scouts, and they knew their jobs, performing without any wasted motion. Small arms fire rattled over the thick timber.

A few screams were heard. Then a quiet settled over the area. The screaming ceased.

Ben's radio crackled. "All clear, sir. We got them all."

"Stay in the truck, sir," Colonel Dan Gray said, appearing by the driver's side of the pickup. "I've got teams working the north side of the highway." Gunfire came from the north side. "I suspected as much. Very sloppy ambush. Not professional at all."

Ben smiled. Dan was an expert at ambush. "Who were they, Dan?"

"Just another band of rabble and outlaws, sir," the Englishman said quietly. He was very calm. This was his job. "More and more of them appearing as conditions continue to deteriorate. I think it's going to get much worse."

"Yes," Ben agreed.

"We're under attack and you guys sit there discussing fucking politics, for Christ's sake," Gale said, crawling back on the seat. "What a bunch of characters." She looked down at Ben. "I'm hungry."

"She's pregnant," Ben explained.

"Yes, sir," Dan said blandly.

"It's a desperate time, Dan," Ben said. "What's left of the nation is reeling, with no direction, no leadership, no organization. The scum of humanity is surfacing."

Dan smiled. "Quite, sir. A strong man needs to take over."

BOOK ONE

ONE

The long convoy bivouacked between Lebanon and Cookeville, Tennessee, near a small town named Buffalo Valley. It was a dead town, with no sign of any living beings. Only the scattered bones in the streets gave testimony to that which once was.

Many of the towns the convoy had either driven through or bypassed on the interstate appeared dead, but Ben had detected a definite air of hope in the men and women and children in the long column that had snaked and threaded and picked its way from southern Missouri. Other columns were on their way to north Georgia, coming from Louisiana and Arkansas.

Yet another move for Raines' Rebels.

Hopefully, Ben thought, as he lay beside Gale in their tent, the last move.

But as he lay waiting for sleep to take him, Ben pondered over what he considered to be the somewhat mysterious behavior he had detected from his close circle of friends: Ike, Cecil, Doctor Chase, Juan, Mark and Colonel Gray. Something was in the wind. But what?

"Are you asleep?" he whispered to Gale.

Silence from her side of the double sleeping bag.

But her breathing had changed. Ben knew she was awake.

"I asked if you were asleep," Ben persisted.

She sighed, turning to face him, dark eyes shining in the dim light filtering through the open flap of the tent. "I was," she said sarcastically. "Despite your tossing and turning and snorting like a water buffalo."

"I do not snort like a water buffalo! Have you ever seen a water buffalo?"

"What's that got to do with it? Ben, *what* do you *want*?"

"Do you get the impression that Dan and his people are becoming a bit overprotective lately?"

"You woke me up to ask me that? Good God! And I was having such a nice dream. Do you wanna hear about it?"

"No. I am not in the least interested in hearing about your slumbertime sexual fantasies. Just answer the question."

"Sexual fantasies! I was dreaming about a hot roast beef sandwich, with mashed potatoes and lots of gravy. How in the hell can you make anything sexual about that?"

"Just answer the question."

"Yes, master. They're just trying to keep you alive, that's all. You're such a klutz."

Ben smiled in the darkness. "Wanna play?"

She looked at her watch. "At two o'clock in the morning?"

"Well, there is that old saying. I forgot about that."

"What old saying?"

"Warmed up coffee and woke up pussy."

14

"Good God! How crude." She rolled over and went back to sleep. But she was smiling.

Ben thought: I wonder if she knows more than she's telling? Whatever *it* is, maybe she's in on it, too? Damn! What I don't need is a mystery. Not at this time.

He put his arms around her and she turned to face him.

"He's not going to like it," Juan Solis said. "I can tell you all that right up front."

The group of men were meeting not far from the main bivouac area. Dan Gray, Cecil Jefferys, Juan Solis, Mark Terry, Ike McGowen, Doctor Chase.

"I think he'll see his way to do it," Ike said. "Once we lay it out for him. But Ben's gonna take off for a while before he does it. He wants some time alone on the road."

"He said it himself," Dan said. "This morning after the firefight. 'The nation is leaderless, with no direction, no organization.'"

"Ben is tired," Dr. Lamar Chase said. "Not to imply his health is bad," he quickly added, catching the alarmed looks on the faces of the men around him, "for he's in better physical shape than most men fifteen years younger. He's just tired. Good God, people, the man has been building and rebuilding *nations* for more than a decade. That would tell on a god. And he's worried about many of these new people that have joined us. And I am too."

"Yes," Cecil spoke. "Ben has talked with me about them. Captain Willette and his bunch especially. We

15

have no way of checking their stories, no way of knowing where their true loyalties really lie. Ben is leery of many of them. But they've done nothing out of line."

Ike said, "I'm with Ben about these new people. Some of them rub my fur the wrong way. I get the same feeling I had back in '88, just before the balloon went up."

"All we can do is keep an eye on them," Juan said.

"We'd better," Mark said. "You all notice how they're singling out the younger troops to talk with? I don't like that. I get the feeling something . . . evil is in the wind."

"I'm with you, partner," Ike said.

"When do we tell Ben?" Dan asked.

Ike looked at him. "When we get to Georgia. No point in gettin' him all stirred up now."

Ben experienced a form of mild depression as his eyes swept the land on either side of Interstate 24. The scene greeting him was one of almost total deterioration. Ben knew living beings were out there, knew many had survived not only the bombings of '88, but also the plague and the horror that followed a decade later. But the survivors did not appear to be *doing* anything.

Ben thought: How in the hell do these people expect to pull anything out of the ashes of destruction and despair if they just sit on their butts and do nothing?

Gale glanced at him. As if reading his thoughts, she said, "They don't have a leader, Ben. Someone to

16

put their faith and trust in."

Ben shook his head. "Uh-huh, and hell, no, lady. Not again. Not this ol' boy. I've had my shot at running the show."

"Then why are we moving to Georgia, Ben?" she challenged him. "Just to see the countryside?"

"It's one thing to build a small following of people, Gale. It is quite another to try to pull together an entire nation. I thank you, but no thank you."

She thought about that. She stuck out her chin. "You did it before," she reminded him.

"No," Ben contradicted her. "I *attempted* to do it. And for a very brief time, if you are speaking of my short tenure as president of this battered nation."

"Ben—"

"No, Gale. No. Another Tri-States, perhaps, something on that order. Perhaps, Gale, if I—we—could do that, and make it work, then others would follow our example. That is my hope. But only time will tell."

"All right, Ben." She knew that particular subject was, for the time being, closed. She gazed out the window. Nothing moved, no sign of human habitation, much less human progress toward rebuilding. "It just looks so . . . barren, Ben."

"It is, to some degree. But it's a dangerous illusion, Gale. I think many of the survivors have formed pockets of defense around the nation. Probably many have slipped back to the medieval fortress/village type of existence."

"This nation—or what is left of it—put people on the moon. We were reaching for the stars.

17

Now—this."

"It was inevitable, Gale. All people had to do was study history to find out where any nation is heading. Unfortunately, most people were too busy protesting this or that—whatever served their own special interest group or union—or were too busy glued to a television set watching the most asinine pap ever made for insulting the human intelligence. In short, the majority didn't give a shit."

"That's harsh, Ben. Perhaps too harsh."

"I don't think so. It isn't too harsh for me to say the nation's morals slipped to zero. It certainly is correct to say in our courts it became not a matter of guilty or innocent, but guilty or not guilty—and *not guilty* came, more often than not, as a result of some minor breach of technicality. Fuck the victims of crime and turn the punks loose. And as for my remark about TV, after a time, I just quit watching television."

"Come on, Ben—what did you watch? Stuff with a lot of violence, I'm sure."

"No. I bought a VCR and watched screw movies," he said with a grin.

"*Come on*, Raines! Get serious."

"What is this, Gale—psychoanalyze Ben Raines time?"

"I would like to know a little bit about the man I'm living with," she said, adding primly, "and the guy who got me pregnant."

"Takes two, you know?"

"Give, Raines."

"I watched what I personally enjoyed, Gale. High drama or low shoot-'em-up-and-stomp movies. I watched good comedy—as I define 'good.' Most of the comedians I enjoyed never used one word of profanity in their routines. A good comic doesn't have to. Just like a good actor doesn't have to rely on gimmicks. Their very presence emanates talent. And dancing should be graceful, Gale. Not leaping about like a pack of savages in the throes of a pre-sexual orgy."

"Ah-*huh*!" Gale whirled on the seat—and cracked her noggin on the sun visor. "Shit!" she said, rubbing her head. "I always knew you were a closet bigot. Admit it, Raines."

"I'm not a closet anything, Gale. How's your head?"

"Don't change the subject."

"You asked for my opinion, Gale—I gave it. Others are entitled to theirs, as well."

"I know," she said, smiling. "I just wanted to see if I could get a reaction out of you." She glanced at his strong profile. "I read every one of your books I could find, Ben. I didn't like some of them, but I read them. You really got down on the American people. I used to think what you wanted was a nation of clones, all patterned after yourself."

"And now?"

"I was wrong."

"My God! Let me stop and find a hammer and stone tablet. I want to preserve that last remark for posterity."

Gale stuck out her tongue at him.

"How's the kid?" Ben asked.

"Plural, Ben. Two. The twins are doing just fine,

19

thank you."

"In nine months I'm going to prove you wrong, Gale."

"You really know a lot about the reproduction system, don't you, Raines? Where are you getting this 'nine months' crap? Try about six and a half months."

He looked at her midsection. "I can't tell any difference. You look just as skinny and malnourished as ever."

"Thanks a lot, Raines. I've gained a few pounds. Hey! Look over there." She pointed.

Ben looked. He radioed the column to a halt and got out of the truck. Uncasing his binoculars, he focused them and then began cussing. "Bastards," he said. "Dan! Over here."

The Englishman appeared at Ben's side. "Sir?"

Ben handed him his field glasses. "Take a look, Dan."

Dan's face went white with rage. "Damned barbarians."

"What do you make of it, Dan?"

"They seem to have constructed some sort of miniature Stonehenge, General. And they are burning someone alive in the open center of it. My word! What has this nation come to?"

"It'll get worse, Dan," Ben said. "I assure you of that. Let's go take a look."

"Ah . . . General? Why don't you just let me take a team over there? We'll—"

The look on Ben's face stopped Dan. Ben said, "I believe I said *let's* go take a look, Dan."

"Right-oh, General," Dan replied cheerfully.

"You will permit me to lead the way, I hope?"

"Carry on, Colonel. Oh, Dan?"

The Englishman turned. "Thanks for your concern, Dan. But when I require the services of a nanny, I'll want one who's a hell of a lot better looking than you." Ben softened that with a smile.

Dan laughed, taking no umbrage at Ben's remark. "I certainly can't blame you for that, sir. I am a bit worse for wear."

"Be careful, old man," Gale called from the truck.

Ben waved at her and followed Dan and his scouts across the rocky field. The screams of the man being burned alive at the stake grew louder as the Rebels approached. The smell of burning flesh was offensive to them all.

"Jesus Christ, Ben," Ike said.

"I know, Ike," Ben said, then cautioned them. "You people step easy now. We don't know what we're facing here. Whatever these people represent, they're armed." He could see the man chained to the stake was not much more than a boy.

"That is far enough!" a robed and hooded man called from the outer fringe of the circle of stone. Other robed and hooded men joined him. They were all armed, most with sawed-off pump shotguns, a few with M-16s and AK-47s. All carried sidearms belted around their waists.

"Stand ready!" Colonel Gray barked the order. A dozen bolts on automatic weapons were pulled back. A stocky Rebel with an M-60 machine gun, belt ammo looped over his shoulders, leveled the light machine gun at the knot of strange-appearing men.

The guards quickly re-evaluated their position.

"We want no trouble, gentlemen," one of the older guards said. "But you are interfering in a matter that is none of your concern."

"Seems like to me you're giving that boy—" Ben's eyes touched the young man chained to the stake, his lower body now completely engulfed in flames—"more trouble than he deserves. What has he done to warrant this?"

"That is none of your concern," Ben was told. "Stay out of it."

"Colonel Gray?" Ben said. "Would you be so kind as to put that young fellow out of his misery?"

"My pleasure, sir." The Englishman lifted his rifle and shot the burning boy once in the head, forever stilling his hideous screaming and ceasing the agony from the fire.

A low grumble of anger sprang from the crowd. It was a mixed group, Ben noted. Men and women and some teenagers.

"Whoever you are," a woman spoke from the crowd of robes and hoods, "you do not have the right to interfere with justice."

"Justice is one thing," Ben said, his eyes searching the crowd for the source. "Torture is quite another. My name is Ben Raines. Now you know my name, what is yours?"

The crowd looked at one another. A tall, stately, middle-aged woman stepped from the inner circle. She walked out of the stone circle to within a few feet of Ben. The odor of burning flesh clung to her robes. She had the eyes of a fanatic.

The woman stared at Ben for a moment. "We were told you were dead," she finally said. She seemed disappointed to learn Ben was still alive.

"As you can see," Ben said with a smile, "paraphrasing Mark Twain, the reports of my death have been greatly exaggerated. I am very much alive and doing quite well."

"So I see," the woman spoke. Her eyes were like a snake's stare: unblinking. "I am called Sister Voleta. I am a princess in the Ninth Order."

"Fuckin' loony, is what she is," a Rebel muttered.

The woman heard the comment. Her dark eyes narrowed. The odor of unwashed bodies mingled with the sweet smell of human flesh.

These people, Ben thought, don't believe much in bathing.

Ben's peripheral vision picked up movement from the north, along the timberline that bordered the open, weed-filled field.

"I see 'em," Ike muttered. He lifted his walkie-talkie and spoke quietly.

At the interstate, mortar teams began setting up by the side of the road.

"If those are your people," Ben told the robed and hooded woman with the dark, evil eyes, "you'd better pull them up short before I give the orders to have them annihilated."

The woman's eyes never left Ben's face as she spoke. "Very well," she said softly, speaking so only Ben and those near them could hear. "You win this small battle. But I assure you, there will be a next time. You have made a serious error by interfering. It will not be forgotten." She smiled strangely as her gaze swung to the long column behind Ben. She raised her voice. "Tell our guardians to halt. We are too few against many. This time," she added.

A woman lifted her arm and waved the group of men to a halt. She lowered her arm and the men squatted in the field.

Ben pointed to the charred, bloody remains of the dead young man. "What had that boy done?"

"He violated the rules," Sister Voleta said. "That is punishable by death."

"Must have been a serious violation."

"He bred with an outsider. That is not permitted in our society."

"An outsider? Where is she?"

"She will be stoned to death at dusk. That is our law."

"Get her and bring her here." Ben's words were harsh.

"You do not give orders on this land, Ben Raines. Your words are meaningless here. For as far as you can see and beyond, all that is land claimed by the Ninth Order. You are trespassers. Do not tempt the gods, Ben Raines."

"We take her easy, or we take her hard. Your choice." Ben threw down the challenge.

The woman made no attempt to hide her hate or her anger. Her eyes flashed venom at Ben. "The Ninth Order is powerful, Ben Raines. Your interference this day will neither be forgotten nor forgiven."

"I'm scared out of my wits," Ben said. He barked, *"Get the girl."*

The robed and hooded woman trembled with rage. She glared at Ben. Finally she said, "Bring the godless slut here."

A young girl, no older than her middle teens, was dragged from the inner circle. She had been forced to watch her lover burned and ultimately shot in the head. She had been savagely beaten. One eye was closed. Her face and arms were bruised. Blood leaked from her mouth. She was naked from the waist up. Her breasts were bruised.

"They took turns raping me," she said to Ben. "They hurt me."

"She is a fornicator," Sister Voleta said. She enjoys it. How could it be rape?"

Ben shook his head. "Lady—and I use the term as loosely as possible—you people are weird." He looked at a Rebel. "Take the girl to the convoy, to Doctor Chase. If anyone interferes, shoot him."

A jacket was placed over the girl's bare shoulders. She was led away. No one tried to stop them.

Ben looked at Sister Voleta. "I haven't the vaguest idea what the Ninth Order might be. I don't really care. I strongly suspect it is another of the pagan, barbaric groups that are growing like fungus to join the other nuts and kooks around this country. But I warn you—all of you. If you people cause any trouble for me, or for those who travel with me, I promise you I shall return and wipe you out to a person. And do not take my words lightly, *sister*."

"We are not afraid of you, Ben Raines," the woman spat her words at him. "For the Ninth Order stands on the word of God."

"Horseshit!" Ben returned the venom. "You people twist and profane God's word to suit your own perverted whims. You're no better than Emil Hite and his nuts down in Arkansas."

"We have been in contact with Father Hite. We might join forces with him."

"Father Hite!" Ben laughed at her. "All right, lady, you do that. It's just as easy for me to cut the string on two yo-yos as one."

"It is not over, Ben Raines. Rather—it has only begun."

Walking back to the column, Ben wondered what in the hell that last bit was all about.

The going got slower on Interstate 24. The convoy was forced to call it a day just south of Manchester, near what had once been the Arnold Engineering Development Center. The complex now lay in ruins.

Ben ordered the young woman taken from the hands of the Ninth Order to be brought to him after the evening meal.

"Go easy with her, Ben," Doctor Chase cautioned. "She's had a rough time of it. She was raped fore and aft."

"Nice people," Ben muttered.

"Dangerous people," Chase commented, then left Ben's quarters.

"What is your name?" Ben asked.

"Claudia." She looked much different from the first time Ben had seen her. She had bathed, dressed in clean clothing, and fixed her short hair.

"Claudia . . . ?" Ben prompted.

"I have no last name. I . . . think I am fifteen years old. But I'm not sure. I was born—I think—in the state of Michigan. I do not remember anything about my parents."

She was looking at Ben very intently, her eyes serious, mixed with fear. Her direct gaze made Ben uncomfortable.

"Why are you looking at me in that manner, Claudia?"

"Because Sister Voleta says you are evil. She says you are the greatest threat on the face of the earth. She says Ben Raines thinks he is a god, that you want to return to the old ways."

"I'm not a god, Claudia. But I sure would like to return to the old ways. If the old ways she was referring to meant hard work, honesty, ethics, and everything else that once made this nation great."

"I know nothing of the old ways you speak of. I remember only hunger and cold and running from gangs of evil men."

Of course, Ben thought. This child was maybe two years old when the world blew up in our faces. Only two. He shook his head.

Is everything I want to see accomplished before my time is through hopeless?

Ben sighed.

"How much schooling do you have, girl?"

"I . . . I can read some words. I can figure some, too. But I can write my name!" she said brightly.

That's more than a lot of young people your age can do, Ben thought. "Tell me about the Ninth Order, Claudia. And don't be afraid of me. I won't hurt you. I promise."

"I believe you, Mister Raines. The Ninth Order is all around us. Sister Voleta is the princess of the Ninth Order. They worship both Satan and God. They are not nice people."

Still a writer at heart, Ben had to fight to hide his smile. Obviously, brevity was Claudia's forte. "What do you know about us, Claudia? About what my people are trying to accomplish?"

"Nothing. But I do know you have traitors among your ranks. People who wish to replace you as leader of the Rebels."

TWO

The young girl could not or would not, probably the former, tell Ben any more concerning her statement of traitors among his ranks. She knew only that she had overheard it from men and women of the Ninth Order. That news did not come as any surprise to Ben. So many of the old group was gone. So many of the original people who gave their sweat and blood to build the old Tri-States. Long dead. And with them, some of the fire and passion and longing for justice and freedom and peace.

Ben sent the girl back to her quarters and sat in his tent alone, mentally reviewing some of the new people who had joined the Rebels just recently. And they numbered several hundred.

Lieutenant Dick Carter had joined the group just after the battle in Missouri with the Russian, General Striganov. So had Sgt. Charles Bennett and Capt. Tom Willette and his company of soldiers. And the three men had made friends almost immediately. Coincidence? Ben doubted that. But there was absolutely no way of checking any of the stories the men had told. They had to be accepted at face value. They were all good soldiers, no doubt about that. They knew their stuff. Ben could not fault them as soldiers. They took orders without a gripe, and carried those orders out.

Many of his younger Rebels liked the trio of newcomers. They were easygoing, and . . . glib, the word came to Ben. Glib. And very slick.

Ben had heard a lot of the rumors attributed to Carter and Willette and Bennett. But none were *bad* things. Nothing that would constitute any lack of respect for Ben. Things like: "Ben should retire, put his feet up, and enjoy his position." And: "The man is a living legend." And this: "General Raines has certainly earned his rest. He needs to be in a fine office, with a general staff around him. I'm worried about him out in the field. God! What if something should happen to the general? Christ! What would we do?"

Ben smiled ruefully. All the remarks that had filtered back to him were spoken solely out of love and respect for the man—so it would appear. But Ben could see, now, the silent insidiousness behind the seemingly loyal words.

What to do?

He didn't know. Yet.

"I tell ya'll what," Captain Willette said to a mixed group of Rebels after evening chow. "General Raines sure scared me this afternoon. Does he *have* to go out into the field taking chances like that? Damn! Look, I don't want you folks to think I'm trying to run things around here—you know that's not what I want. I'd die for General Raines. All of us would. But I'm worried about General Raines. Somebody has got to convince him to start delegating some of the more dangerous tasks to other people. He's just got to do that.''

Many of the younger troops under Ben's command were beginning to vacillate, leaning toward Captain Willette's views. Even some of the older Rebels, men and women who had been with Ben for years, wanted Ben to retire from the field. They wanted Ben to remain in charge, certainly, but to do so from an office, and when he traveled, to do so with a contingent of bodyguards. Not just with Buck Osgood and a couple of Rebels.

All agreed, mentally if not vocally, General Raines would have to start taking more precautions. If he didn't do so willingly, then . . . Well, they would just have to think about doing something. It was a touchy situation. No doubt about that.

At Ben's orders, Colonel Gray sent a team into Chattanooga the next morning with orders to check out as many survivors as possible, find out what, if any, organization they had and what, if anything, they had planned for the future. If they were willing, they could link up with Raines' Rebels.

Skirting the city of Chattanooga, Ben's convoy slipped into north Georgia at mid-morning, staying on two-lane country roads. The column slowly made its way east, heading for Interstate 75. When the scouts reported the interstate just ahead, Ben halted the convoy. He had made up his mind to bring the smoldering whisper campaign into full flame. He didn't know what else to do. If he allowed it to continue, he knew it could destroy what he had built. He didn't feel he had any choice in the matter.

"Ike," Ben said. "Take them on east to Base Camp. Link up with Captain Rayle. I'll maintain radio contact daily."

"Where are you going, Ben?"

"I'm taking a platoon and visiting Atlanta. Haven't been there in a long time. I want to see what is left. Who knows, we may find something worth salvaging."

"Ben . . ."

"I'll see you in a few days, Ike," Ben cut off any further conversation on the matter. "James!" he yelled. "Get your team together. Let's roll."

James Riverson, the senior sergeant in the Rebel army, a man who had been with Ben for many years, nodded and began pulling supplies. At a slight nod from Ben, James began pulling a lot of supplies. The sergeant knew they would be gone much longer than a few days.

Ike opened his mouth to yell his protests at Ben's actions when Colonel Gray touched him on the arm.

"Relax, Ike," the Englishman said. "I anticipated this yesterday, saw him studying maps of the city and the Atlanta area. I sent teams of LRRPs out last night. They'll intercept him about fifty miles north of the city and stay with him. Ben won't like it. He'll know who did it. But there won't be a damn thing he can do about it."

Ike grinned. "You're a sneaky bastard, Dan. You know that?"

"But of course," Dan said, returning the smile. "Besides, with Ben gone, we can get a more accurate picture as to the next moves from Carter, Willette and Bennett. Those three and their followers are up to no good."

"Like I said, Dan. You're a sneaky bastard." But it was all an act on Ike's part. Ben had confided in him the night before.

Ben had told only a few of his plans. Dan had been out of pocket when Ben had made up his mind; but Ben knew the Englishman would put it together very quickly and probably have teams of Scouts and LRRPs out in the field to intercept him before he reached Atlanta.

So Ben didn't go to Atlanta.

He cut east of the interstate at Highway 20 and stayed with it, edging south with the highway, skirting Atlanta. Gale didn't argue with Ben, but she was curious as to what he was doing. She grew even more curious when she noticed a mischievous little smile playing at the corners of his mouth.

It finally reached the point of irritation.

"Ben, *what* in the hell are you *pulling*?"

"We're taking a vacation, Gale. Just the two of us. Along with a platoon of bodyguards, that is."

She looked at him. "I think you are positively bonkers, Raines. The entire world is crumbling around us; there are gangs of bandits all over the place; nuts and kooks and crazies are worshipping everything from toadstools to titties—and you want to take a vacation. I worry about you, Ben. I really, really worry about you."

"Thank you for your concern. However, there is

another reason for my devious behavior."

She waited for an explanation. She looked at him. "Well?"

"You noticed Cecil didn't object to our taking off?"

"Yeah. So what?"

"There are three people who know why I'm doing this," Ben explained. "Cecil, Lamar and Ike. We agreed we've got a coup building within the ranks, Gale. It's still small. So I'm going to drop out of sight for a few weeks and see where it goes in my absence. I'm just going to have to play it by ear for a while. I think, Gale, it's shaping up to be a bad one."

"That's why you've been so tense the past couple of days."

"Yes. What I'm doing may not be the best way to go—I don't know. I do know a few of the people behind the whisper campaign. Willette, Bennett and Carter are the leaders. And there is this Ninth Order business. I got some strange vibes talking with that woman. I want to ramble around some. Test the water, so to speak."

"All I wanted was a nice man to fall in love with," Gale said. "I would have liked a nice home, a couple of kids. A new dress every now and then. Jesus Christ! I had to go and pick Ben Raines, of all people. Now I'm wandering all over the country like a damned gypsy, with a man who blows things up for a hobby." She looked out the window. "Ku Klux Klan is probably waiting for us right around the next bend in the road," she muttered.

Ben laughed at her. "What did I do for laughs before I met you, Gale?"

"Laughs? I suppose *you* think the Klan is amusing?"

"Yes," he replied with a chuckle. "I've always thought them funny. Ever since my dad showed me a picture of them all decked out in bed sheets and pillowcases. They tried to organize around Marion when I was just a kid. Tried to get my dad to join. Dad told them to go to hell. Dad wasn't a liberal, by any stretch of the imagination, but he was no bigot, either. They came back about a week later. Tried to burn a cross on Dad's south field. Dad was waiting for them with a twelve-gauge shotgun, loaded with rock salt." Ben laughed at the memory. "Dad shot several of them right in the ass. I never saw so many bed sheets flapping in the breeze in all my life. You talk about steppin' and fetchin'. Those rednecks had their sheets up around their knees and I mean some kind of *gettin'* it across that field. One of them got all tangled up in a barbed wire fence and started bellowing like a calf in a hailstorm. Dad was laughing so hard he couldn't see to shoot."

Gale had to practically stick her fist in her mouth to keep from bursting out laughing. She turned her head away and sat giggling, looking out the window.

"You see," Ben said, laughing at her antics. "You think it's funny the way I described it. Right?"

"Yeah, but Ben—come on! the KKK preaches hate against minorities. Jews included, I might add. In that respect, it ain't so damned funny. But you wouldn't know about that."

Ben grinned and put the needle to her. "Oh, come on, Gale. Stop postulating. And knock off wearing your heritage like a thorny crown."

She cut her eyes at him. "Very funny, Raines. Ha ha. And what the hell do you mean: postulating?"

"You want me to explain the word?"

"You want a fat lip? I know what postulate means."

"You are assuming I don't know where you're coming from because I haven't been where you're going, right?"

She thought about that for a few seconds. "Weird way of putting it, but yeah, I guess so."

"Wrong. That's like saying I can't feel for a starving child because I'm not a starving child."

"Oh, crap, Ben. Your analogy is all twisted. That's not—"

A hard burst of gunfire stopped Gale in mid-sentence.

Ben twisted the steering wheel hard left and cut into the driveway of an old farmhouse.

Gale hit the floorboards. "I am getting very tired of this," she said.

"We shall continue this scintillating conversation at a later date," Ben said.

"I am in the company of a fucking madman," Gale muttered, as gunfire blasted the quiet afternoon.

Lead sparkled the windshield, showering both of them with glass.

"I don't think those people like us very much," Ben said. "Did you forget your deodorant this morning, dear?"

"Will you for Christ's sake do something!" Gale shouted.

"Calm yourself," Ben said. He took his old Thompson SMG from the clips built into the dashboard and the floorboard. "Stay low," he told her.

"That just has to be one of the most useless instructions I have ever heard," Gale said.

Ben slipped from the truck. "Where away, James?" he called over the rattle of gunfire.

"That grove of trees to the northeast, General. They won't be there for very long, though," he added.

.50-caliber machine guns began yammering from the rear of the six-bys in the short column. 40mm grenade launchers began lobbing their payloads into the brush on the slope. Mortars began plopping and popping from the tubes.

Ben's Rebels began flanking the hidden assailants, spraying the area with automatic weapon fire. WP grenades blasted the brush, setting it on fire. Men leaped up and tried to run from the burning brush and timber. The Rebels cut them down, offering no quarter or mercy.

Ben called for a cease fire. It was quiet except for the moaning and crying of the wounded. "Finish them," Ben ordered.

In five minutes it was over. No prisoners.

"Gather their weapons and fan the bodies for anything intelligence might use. Leave the bodies for the animals. We'll head for the nearest town and see about a new windshield for my truck."

The wounded outlaws put out of their misery, James walked to Ben's side. "Sorry looking bunch, General. Trash and no-counts."

"Weapons?"

"Some of them in pretty good shape. Nothing intelligence could use."

"Let's roll it."

The entire ambush, firefight, mop-up and victory, had taken less than fifteen minutes. Raines' Rebels were known for their fierceness in battle.

"Just to take off like that," Sgt. Charles Bennett said. "Leaving all of us behind to worry about him. OK. I know. I'm going to make some of you mad. Can't be helped. It just isn't right. Maybe General Raines is . . . Naw. Couldn't be that."

"Couldn't be what?" a Rebel asked.

"Skip it," Bennett said. "It's just something I heard, and I ain't gonna repeat none of it. Even if it is true."

"At least tell us where it came from."

Bennett shook his head and turned to go. He looked back at the group. "You won't tell anybody where you heard it?"

"Not a soul, Charles. But if it involves the general, I think we all have a right to know."

"Yeah," Bennett said. "I guess that's right. OK. I'll just do this, and if you pick up on it, fine with me." He tapped the side of his head, temple area, and made a circling gesture. He walked away.

After several moments of arguing among themselves, the Rebels came to this conclusion: Ben needs a long rest. He deserves it.

All agreed with that. More Rebels joined the group. They agreed that Ben was probably more tired than anything else, that he was mentally exhausted. But how to get him to take that much-deserved rest?

"Let's ask Captain Willette. He's pretty sharp.

He'll know what to do."

Ben stopped the small convoy in Monroe, Georgia. After some searching, a windshield was located, popped out, and the bullet-shattered glass in Ben's pickup was replaced.

"No safety inspection," Ben joked. "I'm likely to get a ticket."

"Beg pardon, sir?" a young Rebel looked at him, not understanding what Ben said.

"Never mind, son," Ben said. "All that was before your time."

A lot of things were before your time, Ben thought. He looked at the young Rebel and shook his head. They will never be the same. From now on, it's pure survival.

"Let's head for Monticello and the Oconee National Forest," Ben said, after looking at an old map of Georgia. "We'll hole up there for a few days. Keep our heads down and out of sight. Cec is supposed to contact me tomorrow, at noon."

James Riverson, the huge ex-truck driver from Missouri, spoke his mind. "I don't know about this move, General. Personally, I'd like to go back to the convoy and kick the ass off Willette and his bunch. This move could backfire on us."

"He's right, General," Buck Osgood expressed his opinion.

Some Rebels agreed with Buck, others weren't sure. While Ben demanded rigid discipline from his people, anyone could express an opinion. When Ben was in the active U.S. military, he had detested chickenshit units. In his outfit, officers pulled their weight just like everyone else.

Surprising James and Buck, Ben agreed with them. "I know that, boys. But I've got to know how many of our people are with Willette and his crew. Let's face it: None of the three, Carter, Bennett or Willette, or anyone aligned with them, has said anything treasonous about me. If I confronted them now, what would I confront them with? This is the best way, I'm thinking. There is an old adage about giving a person enough rope to hang himself. That's what I'm doing."

All the Rebels knew that when Ben made up his mind, that was it. End of discussion.

They would lay low for a couple of weeks, see what developed.

Monticello contained a half dozen survivors. They had survived, but though they were survivors—in one sense of the word—they were pitiful in Ben's eyes. No one appeared to be in charge. No organization. No one had planted a garden or done anything else constructive. The people just seemed to be existing. Their children were dirty and ragged. There was no type of school. The adults had worked out no plan of defense against the many gangs of thugs and outlaws and paramilitary groups that now roamed throughout the land.

Ben dismissed the families in Monticello from his mind. They might have survived thus far, but not for much longer. They would be easy prey. God alone knew what would happen to the children when that occurred—and Ben knew it would happen. For the scum—who for some reason seem to survive any holocaust—were surfacing, to rape and ravage and kill.

"Wind it up," Ben ordered. "We're moving on. Losers don't impress me."

The convoy moved a few miles down the road, to what was left of a small village. The Rebels had what was left of the hamlet to themselves. Only a few scattered bones lay in white, silent testimony to that which once was.

The Rebels began setting up camp, first cleaning out a few stores and homes. Ben waited by the communications truck for Cecil's call.

When the radio crackled, Ben answered the first signal.

"How's it going, Cec?"

"We're in place and setting up," Ben's second in command replied, his voice popping from the speaker. "Now the rumor is you are suffering from a mental disorder; you need a long rest. Even gods get tired. So on and so forth."

"So the power play is firming up?"

"It's beginning to have some consistency, yes. But nothing of any real substance. Willette is very smooth and very intelligent, Ben. He's shifted many of his people around. Has them in every unit except HQ's Company and Dan's LRRPs and Scouts. Dan and I have seen to that exclusion. Speaking of Dan, he's plenty miffed at you. I settled him down by telling him why you did what you did, and that you tried to find him to tell him yourself."

"That's fine, Cec. How are our people being

received by the mountain people?"

"Very well. Captain Rayle says the incidents of terrorism and brutality by the gangs of thugs and slime along the borders—all borders surrounding us—have picked up dramatically during the past month. The country is really going to hell in a bucket, Ben. I don't have to tell you to be careful out there in the boonies."

"I heard that, Cec. When do you want the next voice contact?"

"Day after tomorrow. Noon. We'll use the same frequency. Ben? You people keep your heads down out there."

"Ten-four and out."

Ben turned to Gale. "You heard him. So don't take it in your head to go out picking wildflowers. It's dangerous out there." He looked at the group of men and women gathered around the communications truck. "That goes for all of you. Travel in pairs and go armed at all times."

"You trying to give me orders, Raines?" Gale stuck out her chin.

"Let me put it another way; maybe I can get through to you that way. How would you like to get gang-shagged by a dozen men?"

"You just have to be the most tactful, literate person I have ever met, Raines."

"Thank you. I'm cute, too," Ben said with a grin.

Gale choked back a reply.

THREE

He had been christened Anthony Silvaro in New York City. That was in 1970. When he was fourteen years old, he left his parents' very comfortable apartment and became a street punk. Sociologists and psychologists had nothing tangible to blame for Tony's behavior. In this case they could not fall back on their universal catch-all and blame Tony's behavior on society. Tony's parents were both college educated, both professional, successful people who made a good living, loved their kids, and would not dream of anything even remotely close to child abuse. Their combined incomes placed them in the upper, upper middle class. Tony's two brothers and one sister were nice, normal, well-behaved young people. They made good grades in school, usually obeyed their parents, and all had plans to attend college. Tony—as he had been a good-looking boy—turned into a strikingly handsome man. He had never suffered the "embarrassment" of pimples, had no physical infirmities, had never been "picked on" by his teachers or by anyone else, and was very athletic.

Any streetwise cop knew Tony's problem.

Perhaps there is some chemical imbalance in the brain? the shrinks said, clutching at what few straws remained them.

The streetwise cop's reply was predictable. "Horse-shit."

Dyslexia, then.

"You have to be joking."

The shrinks swelled up like a puff adder. They knew what was coming.

"He's a punk. Period. He was born a punk. He will be a punk all his life. He will die a punk. He's just no good."

Tony was eighteen when the balloon went up in '88. He had been busy running his string of teenage whores and mugging old ladies and terrorizing old men over in Brooklyn when the rumors of war began. Tony didn't know from jackshit about survival outside the concrete canyons of the Big Apple, but he figured he'd damn well better learn. He also figured he'd better head for the wilderness.

He went to Paterson, New Jersey. I mean, Christ! How far out in the boonies do you have to go to be safe from The Bomb? *Paterson*, for Christ's sake.

It wasn't far enough, and Tony got out with only minutes to spare, driving a stolen car. He left the owner of the car dead in a puddle of blood. Just an old fart. Who gives a shit about old people, anyways? He got lost down in southern New Jersey, in the fuck-ing swamps. He managed to cross over into Wilm-ington, Delaware, just before the bridge became hopelessly jammed up with stalled cars and trucks.

He got on the JFK Memorial Highway and almost blew it with that move, only at the last possible exit veering off to the north before touching Baltimore. He was in southern Pennsylvania when the lid blew off the pot.

Tony sought refuge in a barn, coming face to face with a black angus bull. The first bull he'd ever seen up close. Tony had visions of a rib-eye, rare. He shot the bull four times in the head with his .38.

After making a large mess with a butcher knife, Tony gave up his dreams of a rare steak. He couldn't figure out how to get the hide off the ugly goddamn stinking brute. He found some chickens, only to have them peck his hands when he tried to grab some eggs.

"Motherfuckers!" Tony yelled in frustration. He blasted the hens with his .38. Maybe he'd have to settle for fried chicken. But how in the hell do you get the feathers off them?

Tony pilfered the farmhouse, looking for guns and food. He found both. Plus a very frightened twelve-year-old girl. Tony raped her several times. He'd always preferred young pussy. Liked to hear them squall when he stuck it in. But this one wouldn't quit hollering. Tony cut her throat. Stupid cunt. If she had cooperated, Tony reasoned and rationalized the issue in his punk mind, she could have made both of them some money. Guys like to make it with young chicks. A hundred bucks is nothing to a guy with a hard-on for young gash. Stupid cunt.

Tony couldn't believe the next few months. The whole fucking world went nuts. People running around like scared rabbits. And the broads. Christ! They'd do *anything* for protection from the gangs that began cropping up all over the place.

Tony had never had so much pussy in his life. Black pussy, brown pussy, yellow pussy, white pussy. It was all the same when the lights went out and a guy got it hung in there good.

Soon Tony had teamed up with a dozen other thugs, all about his age. In six months time, they had more than a hundred women of all ages. And a dozen boys for those who leaned in that direction.

President Hilton Logan almost screwed all that up for Tony, with Logan's police state and secret agents snooping around and relocating the citizens all over the goddamn place. But crime will out if it's worked right, and Tony was far from being stupid. He knew how to keep his head down and to roll with the flow. And who to pay off. And he knew to keep far away from Ben Raines' Tri-States out west. Ben Raines was fucking *nuts* on the subject of law and order. Screw up in Ben Raines' Tri-States and a guy's chances of getting much older dropped to damn near zero.

Tony kept his people far, far away from Tri-States. And he hoped Ben Raines' conception of crime and punishment wouldn't catch on nationwide. There wasn't just a little crime in the Tri-States. There wasn't *any* crime. Period.

By the time Tony Silver hit his twenty-fifth birthday, he was on his way to being an empire-builder. An empire built on pain and the suffering of others, to be sure, but still an empire. And Tony had learned his hard lessons about the true wilderness. He wasn't in Ben Raines' league yet, but he was learning. His gang was more than five hundred strong. He ran all kinds of scams, from whores to gambling to extortion to dope.

When Tony was thirty, the bottom dropped out. First came the mutants—ugly bastards—then the bugs and the rats and all that other gross shit. Tony had figured that if he could live through Ben Raines as president, with his high-handed tactics and methods of law and order, Tony could live through anything!

That bastard Raines was a law and order *freak*. Hadn't the dude ever heard of loopholes and technicalities and all that other good liberal shit?

Guess not.

Christ, Raines was putting people against the wall and shooting them just for rape. How unconstitutional. Hell, Tony knew all cunts liked it once a guy got it in. Everybody knew that.

Tony and his gang of thugs and slime and punks lived through Ben's short term as president of the United States by being very careful and keeping an extremely low profile.

But the fleas and the rats and the disease almost finished Tony's career in crime.

But not quite.

Tony Silver bounced back, bigger and stronger than before. He now ramrodded a gang of more than a thousand men. Over a thousand of the most undesirable and socially unredeemable assholes ever assembled.

And Tony controlled all of north Florida and south Georgia.

"When are we going to return to the group, Ben?" Gale asked.

Truth was, Ben really didn't want to go back. By nature, Ben was a loner, and the pull of the highway

47

was getting strong. What he really wanted to do was put Gale in the pickup and pull out, just the two of them. He wanted to be free of duties and responsibilities and overseeing rules and laws and regulations and moral conduct.

Ben sighed. He knew he could not turn his back on a group of men and women who depended on him. Even though he wanted to do just that. Wanted that so badly it was almost a tangible sensation at times. But maybe when his people were settled in and this power play concluded . . . maybe then.

"We head back when Cec gets word to me that the coup attempt is something firm. Gives me something I can sink my teeth into. That's all I can tell you at this time, babe."

"And when Cecil does that?"

"We go back and I take out Mr. Bennett, Mr. Willette and Mr. Carter."

"Take out?"

"Dispose of them."

"You're a hard man, Mr. Raines."

"Hard times, Ms. Roth," he said with a smile.

Ben knew his plans could backfire, knew he was taking a chance going at it by this route. But he had known for some time many of the younger Rebels in his command were unhappy at the way Ben was running things. Ben was, for the most part, a steady type of man, a man who tried to think matters through, very carefully, before implementing them. Many of the younger Rebels were not too happy about Ben's demands that they all receive some formal education. They reasoned that there were no more rocket ships to be built, no more searching for

48

the stars. If they were going to start rebuilding from scratch, it was more important to know how to build a house than to understand higher math.

Ben had told them he understood their feelings. He also added, "But you will have to know how to read a blueprint in order to build more permanent structures."

He got through to a lot of them. Some of them he did not reach.

But Willette had.

Most Rebels, of all ages, were really afraid of Ben. Afraid not to obey him. Rumor was the man was close to being a god. It not only confused them, it angered them, because if the man was a god, and everybody knew he was, kind of, then goddamn it, why didn't Ben Raines *behave* like a god? Why didn't he get himself a big ol' house, with people to wait on him, and just sit there with that old Thompson submachine gun by his side, and let those with troubles come to him so he could solve them?

And that old Thompson was something to be feared, too. Only a few would even touch the thing. That Thompson was synonymous with Ben Raines. A part of the man.

And then General Raines really pissed many of the Rebels off by saying when they received some education, they would then see he was no god, just a mortal being, just like the rest of them.

Well, that was a crock of crap and they all knew it. The young man from the east, Ro, said Ben was a god. The young man from the west, Wade, said Ben was a god. Travelers who came in to seek refuge said monuments and tributes and places of worship were

49

built all over the nation—all erected toward Ben Raines.

That had to prove something. And nothing Ben could say would make them believe otherwise. The man was a god. Sort of. But . . . maybe a *human* god. That way Ben could have human emotions and stuff like that. But he couldn't die. Everybody knew that. That was accepted as fact.

No, Captain Willette and Lieutenant Carter and Sergeant Bennett were right. Ben needed to be in some . . . special place. By himself. A place where he could just sit and hand down judgments and make decisions. But it would have to be a place befitting Ben Raines' stature.

And none of the Rebels involved with Willette were too thrilled about Gale, either. She wasn't right for Ben Raines. She just wasn't the right woman. Goddesses were tall and blonde and . . . what was the word? *Magnificent.* Yes. Grand in appearance.

It wasn't the fact that Gale was . . . well, not one of them. That wasn't it at all. Didn't have anything to do with it. That's what Willette told them. Very convincingly, too.

And nobody thought to mention that of all Captain Willette's followers, there were no blacks, no Jews, no Hispanics, no Orientals.

That came as no surprise to Cecil.

"This camp is being divided, Ike," Cecil told the ex-SEAL. "Invisible battle lines are being drawn. And I don't like it."

"If we could just get settled in one spot," Ike said. "If we could just have a couple of years to work it out, set up schools and get people working. I'm gonna tell

50

you something, friend: Ben isn't going to put up with much more of this," Ike prophesied. "And I wouldn't blame him if he just walked out and said to hell with it all. I've been reading the signs, and they're strong. If Ben can work this out here, I got a feeling he's gonna split for a year or two. After Gale has the baby."

"I hope you're wrong," Cecil said, a frown on his face. "Ben is the glue that is holding us together."

"I'm not wrong." Ike was firm in that. "Like Doc Chase said, Ben's tired. And if we don't bring this . . . present matter to a head pretty damn quick, Ben is gonna walk. Believe it."

"I know," the black man said glumly. "I see the signs, too. Ben never wanted the responsibility. We pushed it on him. Goddamn it!"

"That goes twice for me, buddy."

Ben and his small contingent of Rebels sat it out in the small town. Cecil contacted Ben every other day, but there was really no news to report that would prompt Ben to return, to personally take a hand in stopping the rumor mill. More and more, Ben entertained the notion of just taking off, of gathering up those he knew he could trust and just getting the hell out. He was fed up. Tired of paperwork and being chained to a desk, overseeing the several thousand lives in his command.

Gale picked up on his mood. "You really want to cut out, don't you, Ben?"

"Yes, I do, Gale. And I can't say it's a selfish move on my part. The Rebels have to be made to see they can survive without me. Will you come with me, Gale?"

She sighed. She loved him, but she was a realist. She had accepted the fact that no woman was going to hold Ben Raines for any length of time. Ben was a gypsy at heart. He was loving and gentle and kind to whatever woman shared his bed; but that woman had best be prepared for Ben's leaving, for that was inevitable. Take the good times while they were being offered, and accept the fact they would not be permanent.

"I don't know, Ben," she said. "I'm not a wanderer like you. We'll see."

Ben told her of his original plans, back in '88. Of just wanting to travel the country, writing of his experiences along the way, putting down on paper what had happened to the nation. And of how he had gotten sidetracked. He told her of Tri-States, of Salina, Jerre, the other women.

Gale was more amused than jealous, for she understood Ben much more than he realized.

He spoke to her at length, and she detected a longing in his voice. Ben was a master at survival, having recalled all his hard service training and put it to use. But he was still a writer at heart. Ben felt that someone should, for history's sake, chronicle the events leading up to and after the bombings of 1988.

And he felt he was probably the only one remaining who could do that job.

"I guess that makes me sound very arrogant, doesn't it, Gale?"

She felt somehow closer to him for his sharing his thoughts. She knew only too well just how private a man Ben Raines really was. But while she felt closer, she experienced a sense of loss as well. As if Ben, in his own peculiar way, was telling her their time together was getting short. She accepted it. She had anticipated it. "No, Ben, I don't think it makes you arrogant at all. I think it makes you a man who is determined to chart the events of this nation. I think you owe it to history to do so. And I think I would only be in the way. What do you think about it?"

He brightened, his mood lifting. "I think you're nuts, Gale. We'll go together. I'll put this little coup attempt to bed, and we'll take off. Just as soon as you have the baby."

"Babies, Ben, babies. I keep telling you. It's going to be twins. And I don't know if I'm going with you, or not."

"Twins, Gale. Right. Twins. And you're coming with me."

"We'll see, Ben," she said, patting his arm. She smiled. "How many offspring will this make, Ben?"

Ben muttered under his breath and Gale laughed at him. "I keep telling you, Ben: You keep this up and in a hundred years, half the population in America will be direct descendants of yours."

He sobered her abruptly by saying, "There is no America, Gale. And what is left of the nation is falling apart rapidly. And it just dawned on me, Gale. I can't pull it back together. No matter how much I might want that, I just can't do it alone. It's just too large a task for one man."

She touched his arm as she realized he was right. "Ben . . ."

James Riverson walked up. "Sorry to bother you,

General. But we got trouble coming at us. Scouts report armed men just rolled past their positions. 'Bout a platoon of them. We got maybe ten minutes 'fore they get here."

The survivalist in Ben quickly overrode the writer's side of the man. The warrior in him, never buried too deeply, leaped to the surface. The warrior rudely pushed the philosopher aside. A line from Ecclesiastes came to Gale: A time to kill and a time to heal.

"Stagger positions on both sides of the street," Ben ordered. "M-60s on top of that building and over there," he said, pointing. "50s set up there and there. Move it!"

Gale watched the man change before her eyes. He never failed to amaze her. He could shift personalities at the blink of an eye. And while she loved him, she was woman enough to let him go.

In thirty seconds the street was deserted. A slight breeze blew lightly through the old town. Paper swirled through the air, floating and bouncing on invisible wings. The sounds of engines reached the ears of the hidden Rebels. The nose of a deuce and a half edged around the corner. Two men in the cab. Half a dozen in the uncovered rear. The bed of the truck was piled with supplies. The men in the trucks were armed with automatic weapons and dressed in paramilitary fashion.

Ben had no idea who the men were, or what they represented. They might be like himself, people who were trying to put the nation—or what was left of it— back on an even keel. But Ben somehow doubted that. The men were unshaven and dirty. They looked more like pirates than soldiers. Something about the men nagged at Ben's mind, pulling at the shadowy reaches of his brain. Then some old bit of intelligence came to him. Colonel Dan Gray had said his LRRPs had reported that a man named Tony Silver was in command of a large group of thugs and goons down in Florida. And at that time—that was several months back—Silver's men were moving into south Georgia. They were terrorizing the citizens, robbing and raping and killing and turning the civilians into virtual slaves, the women into unwilling whores.

"Do we take them, General?" James' voice whispered out of Ben's walkie-talkie.

"No," Ben returned the whisper, his eyes on the passing convoy. "Let them through. I've got an idea. No one makes a sound. Hold your fire. James? Have a team maintain a loose contact on the column. Stay back and be careful. Keep in radio contact with me several times a day. I want to see where these men are heading. I've got a bad feeling about them."

The column rolled through the tiny village, the men in the trucks totally unaware of the eyes on them, the guns trained on them. Death could have reached out and touched them at any time.

"That's all of them, General," James reported from his vantage spot on top of the building. "Rear scouts report the road is clear."

"Team out," Ben ordered. "James? How many did you count?"

"Forty-odd. Supplies for a long time on the road. Well armed. General, are you thinking these people have something to do with Captain Willette and his bunch?"

"That was my gut reaction, yes. We'll wait for the team to report back. I think we'll find they're heading for a spot near where we've decided to settle. It wouldn't surprise me to learn this Sister Voleta and her Ninth Order is involved, as well. I got some strange vibes from that woman."

"That would seem like a strange pairing, Ben," Gale said. "Silver is a thug and the Ninth Order is supposed to be so religious."

"I think she's about as religious as a rattlesnake," Ben said. "That religious business is a front, I'm thinking."

"A front for what?"

"I don't know."

"Why don't we just let Colonel Gray and his people take them all out right now?" a Rebel asked.

"Because that way, we'd only knock off the tip of the iceberg. They'd rebuild. I want the entire chunk."

"Colonel Jefferys on the horn, General," the radio operator said. "He says it's urgent."

Ben walked to the communications truck and took the mic. "Go, Cec."

"One of our scouting parties was ambushed just inside the Chattahoochee National Forest," Cecil said. "We took some hard casualties. And Ben? Ike's missing."

FOUR

Ben tossed in his sleeping bag that night. He would doze for a few moments, then awaken to toss and turn once more. After several hours of fitful sleep, Ben threw back the sleeping bag cover and said, "Shit!"

Gale was silent. But Ben knew she was not asleep. He looked at her form in the darkness, her back to his eyes.

Gale sighed deeply after a few moments. "Will you quit staring at me?"

"Go ahead," Ben said. "Say it. Get it over with, Gale."

"Say what?"

"You've been pulling the silent treatment on me all evening. Now either knock it off or say what's on your mind, will you?"

She turned to face him, fixing her dark eyes on his face. "That was quite a performance you gave this afternoon. And in front of the troops, too. I must admit, I'd never seen anything quite like it."

Ben grunted. "Yeah. I thought perhaps that was it."

"You almost scared the pee out of those young troops, Ben. Some of them were actually trembling, listening to you rant and rave and carry on like a madman."

"I guess so. All right. I'll apologize to them in the morning."

"It *is* morning!"

"Oh. Really? Well . . . later on in the morning, then. Damn it, Gale, Ike *knew* better. He and Cec share the responsibility when I'm gone. He had no business taking off like that. This not only puts me in a bad situation, but just think where it leaves Cecil."

"Oh, Ben! Hell! Ike is just like you. He can't sit around doing nothing. He's got to be a part of the action. Just like you. So ease off Ike's case, buster." She softened her tone. "You're really upset about this, aren't you, Ben?"

"Yeah. But I shouldn't be, I guess. Ike can take care of himself." But the whispered reply held a note of concern. "We've been together a long time. Really, since the beginning, back in '88."

Gale waited.

"I met him down in Florida. Ike and four or five lovely young ladies. Ike married one of them, Megan. I told you about that." He laughed softly. "Let's see. There was Honey-Poo, June-Bug, Tatter, Angel-Face, Bell-Ringer. That was Megan's nickname. Juno was with me, then. The husky."

"Did you ever see any of those women again? I don't mean . . ."

"I know what you mean. No, I never did. I don't know what happened to them."

"You ever wonder?"

"Oh, yes."

"You two—three, really, counting Cecil—have been through a lot together."

"Yes. And Ike's not a young buck any longer. He's

58

crowding fifty awfully hard. Goddamn it!"

"Settle down, Ben." Gale slipped from the sleeping bag and came to him. She slipped slender arms around his neck and blew in his ear, "Watch your BP, old man."

He smiled and kissed her.

"Really, Ben, you can't blame Ike. In a sense you're doing the same thing."

"Oh?"

"Sure. We're sitting down here, a hundred miles away from the main group. Nobody wanted *you* to leave—right?"

"We might head back soon."

"No, we won't, Ben. Think about it."

His smile flashed white in the darkness. "You giving the orders, now, huh?"

"You want to return so you can lead the search for Ike," she said, pegging his thoughts accurately. "And that is dumb on your part. Very dumb. Think about it, Ben."

He was silent for a moment. Then he sighed. "You're right, Gale. Ike knows the policy. We won't sacrifice a dozen to save one. They were his rules, back in Tri-States. He wouldn't want them violated any more than I would."

"Get some sleep, Ben. We'll talk about it in the light."

He returned to his side of the big double sleeping bag and to the warmth of the woman.

Her fingers found him; his hands found her.

"Won't this hurt the baby?" he asked.

Her reply was at first a chuckle. "I really doubt it, Ben."

FIVE

"You can save yourself a great deal of pain," the voice came to him. "Tell us where General Raines is hiding."

"Don't know, partner," Ike said. "Ben is his own man. He goes where he damn well pleases. And he don't always tell us."

White hot pain tore into Ike's left arm. He bit back a scream as the electric charge lashed at him with invisible claws.

"You lie."

"Tellin' you the truth, partner," Ike gasped.

The pain left his arm. Ike sighed with relief. Then the pain shifted to his right leg as the wires were attached and activated by a crank. Ike chewed his lips bloody fighting back screams.

"Ben Raines is a false god." Ike heard the words through waves of hurt. "Only Sister Voleta and the Ninth Order is real. We have learned that to worship both God and Satan is the real way to happiness and contentment on this earth. We all have taken vows to destroy any who worship false gods. Where is Ben Raines?"

Ike looked at his torturers. "Fuck you!"

The pain came in waves.

SIX

Tony looked at the just-budding breasts and thin pubic hair of the young girl lying on his bed. Blood dotted the white sheet.

She had been a virgin. A real, honest-to-God cherry. Tony had begun to believe there weren't any of them left in the country. He'd wait a few minutes more before taking another whack at the kid. Been a long time since he'd had any pussy that tight. Like to have never got his cock in. Sure felt good once he did, though.

"How old are you, kid?"

"Twelve, I think," she whispered.

"No shit! You got some fine gash, baby. It got good to you, didn't it, sweets?"

The child hesitated for only a few seconds. Then survival took precedence over the pain between her legs. She knew all about Tony Silver. Everybody in north Florida and south Georgia knew about Tony Silver. The Man. She was young in years, but wise to the ways of staying alive. She was a survivor. "Yes," the child said. "I liked it."

Tony grinned. "Sure, you did, baby. Ol' Tony's been pleasin' the ladies for years. Now you roll over here and give ol' Tony some head. Get me all hard

61

again and we'll have some more fun."

The child named Ann did not hesitate. She was tired of being cold and hungry and afraid and always running for her life. This wasn't nearly as bad as all that. And she knew from talking with older women that it would get better as time passed.

She took him orally just as the door to the motel bedroom opened and a man walked in. He approached the bed, flicked his eyes to Ann's young nakedness, then shifted his hard gaze to the naked man.

"Raines' right hand man, Ike McGowen, was captured yesterday up in north Georgia. But he's a tough one. Voleta's people haven't been able to break him. Yet," he added.

"Don't kill him," Tony warned. He pulled Ann's mouth from his half erection and pushed her away. "Cool it, baby." He looked at the man. "This Ike guy was one of them Frogmen, or something like that—from way back in the wars. My guess is you ain't gonna break him with pain. Radio that stupid cunt, Voleta, and tell her to use mental shit on the guy. But first, tell her to tape record some of the guy's screamin' and hollerin' and send it to Ben Raines' headquarters. Let Raines hear his best buddy being tortured. That'll get the son of a bitch's attention, I betcha."

The goon looked confused for a moment. "But . . . how can we do that, boss? Don't nobody know where Ben Raines is at."

Tony's face reddened. *"Dumbass!"* he yelled, frightening the young girl. "I gotta think of everything around here, for Christ's sake? *Somebody* in that fuckin' camp knows where Ben Raines is. Bet

SEVEN

"Abe." The man sat down by Abe Lancer's front porch rocker.

"Rance," Abe Lancer said, looking at the man. "What's on your mind this mornin'?"

Abe was the unofficial and unelected leader of the mountain survivors. It was not a position Abe sought, or really wanted. As a matter of fact, he didn't like it at all. But rather like Ben Raines, he didn't know how to get out of it. But he thought about it. A lot.

"The new folks is settlin' in right well."

"That's good." Rance would get to whatever it was on his mind in his own good time. That was the mountain way. Wasn't polite to rush a body 'fore he got it clear in his head.

"Right nice day, ain't it?"

"Yep."

"How you likin' these new folk, Abe?"

"I reckon most of 'em is all right. Probably some is better than others. Just like us here in the mountains."

"That's the way I see it." Rance spat a brown stream of tobacco juice off the porch.

Abe grinned. "You kill my old woman's flowers

with that poison and she'll take a broom to your backside."

"Don't doubt that none at all."

"Nope."

"I like these new people. Hard workin' bunch of folk. Just jumped right in and started workin'. Ever'body pulled they weight. I think we gonna get along just fine."

"That's the way I see it myself."

"I ain't seen hide nor hair of President Ben Raines. You?"

"Nope. Way I hear it, though, President Raines got a good reason for layin' low. What do you hear 'bout it?"

"Same thing. I don't like that there Captain Willette. Not one damn little bit. He's got snake eyes on him. Distrustful of him. And I ain't alone in that, neither. My cousin from up to Tellico Plains sent word this mornin' them people that ambushed and shot them Rebels Colonel McGowen was leadin' had some of Willette's people mixed in with 'em."

Abe cut his eyes to the man. "How come your cousin knew that?"

Rance smiled, returning the man's gaze. "How much of what goes on in these mountains slips by you, Abe?"

Abe grunted. "Damn little, I reckon. Got folks usin' their eyes and ears for me."

"Same with Waldo. Most folks over there come to him with problems. Like we'uns do with you."

"I hope your cousin likes it more than I do," Abe said dryly.

Rance grinned. "Anyways, Waldo says they was all

65

tied up with and in this crazy damn Ninth Order business."

"That nutty woman calls herself Sister Voleta?"

"That's her."

"Shit!"

"That's the way I feel about her, myself."

"You tell your cousin to keep his eyes open. For now, let's go see Colonel Jefferys. I don't like the way this mess is beginnin' to stink."

"People watching us, General," James said. Late afternoon in central Georgia.

"They've been out there for about fifteen minutes," Ben said. "I spotted them when they started circling the town."

"Thanks for telling me, Ben," Gale said.

"No point in worrying you. Whoever it is out there is very wary of us. They—"

Ben's radio crackled. "General? Those . . . people out there?" Ben picked up on the emphasis on "people." "They're dressed in animal skins. They got feathers and other crap stuck in their hair. Goddamnedest lookin' bunch of savages I've ever seen. I'm watchin' them from the rooftop of the old service station."

"How are they armed?" Ben radioed back.

"A few got guns. Rest of them have spears and clubs and sticks and knives. Jesus, those are weird-lookin' people."

"They've made no hostile moves," Ben said. "But I don't like the idea of them watching us. Order them to disperse, James."

Riverson shouted out the command. The brush around the tiny village shook with movement.

"They're scattering, sir," the lookout reported. "That was the damnedest-looking bunch of . . . whatever-the-hell-they-are I've ever seen."

"Stay alert," Ben ordered. "I don't think they've gone far." He felt Gale's eyes on him, then answered her unspoken question. "I don't know, Gale. But there appears to be large numbers of subcultures popping up all over the land—probably the world. I told you about the cave people. They're called the People of Darkness. I don't know anything about this bunch." Ben's eyes were haunted for a few seconds, filled with concern and unnamed trouble.

"What is it, Ben?"

"How could people revert back to the caves in so short a time? In just slightly over a decade, we've gone from high tech to barbarism." He sighed. "Sometimes I wonder if Doctor Chase's theory isn't the correct one."

"What does he maintain?"

"That all this," Ben said, waving his hand, "is God's will. His doing. That He gave the human race opportunity after opportunity, and all we did was screw it up. Then He became angry and brought it all back to the basics. That this is our last chance to get it all together. If we don't . . ." He shrugged. "It's over. A long slide backward."

"Do you believe all that, Ben?" Her question was quietly spoken.

He took her hand. "I don't know, Gale. I do know the human race quite literally raped this earth—and for no other reason than our own greed. I am not a religious man, Gale. I have never professed to be something I am not. But I do believe very strongly in God. I *do not* believe all this—" again he waved his hand—"just happened. I do believe we evolved—because I don't know, and neither does anyone else, how many times God tried to create the human race and failed. I have no difficulty accepting both creation and evolution. At least to my satisfaction. If people choose to disagree—fine. That is their right." He looked at Gale and smiled ruefully. "And once again, Professor Raines mounts his soapbox."

She laughed. "When I get tired of it, Ben, I'll let you know."

"Right!" Ben cut his eyes and lunged at Gale, grabbing her up and tossing her to one side of the room just as a spear came through the broken window of the old house. The point of the spear imbedded in the wall. Ben jerked his .45 from leather and the room rocked with gunfire. A painted face, looking savagely at them through the window suddenly exploded as the heavy slugs hit the jaw, the nose and the forehead.

Gale screamed from her position in the corner as Ben's .45 roared again.

The tiny town roared and rocked with gunfire, as arrows and rocks and spears quivered and sang through the air. The Rebels reacted with lead and grenades.

The old front door to the house shattered open. A man dressed in animal skins stood in the doorway, a huge, spiked club in his right hand. He yelled at Ben and charged him, the club raised over his head.

Ben leveled his .45 and squeezed the trigger. The

slug struck the savage in the center of the stomach and doubled him over, dropping him to his bare knees.

The .45 was empty.

Ben grabbed his Thompson, clicked it off safety, and put two rounds in the savage's back for insurance. The half naked man jerked and howled as the slugs tore life from him.

Ben stepped to the door just as several painted-up men were climbing over the railing to the porch. Ben gave them a burst from the Thompson, blowing the men off the porch. They landed on the littered ground in a mass of torn flesh and gushing blood.

Ben heard a woman screaming. He ran to the corner of the porch. A painted man had a woman Rebel spreadeagled on the ground, her field pants off, her arms held by another painted and feathered savage. One man knelt between the woman's legs, trying to force his erection into her. She jerked her hips from side to side, frustrating penetration.

Sergeant Greene ran around the back of the house, picked up a spear from the ground and drove the point through the man's neck, the sharp head almost decapitating the man as blood sprayed from his mouth.

The near-naked man holding the woman's arms jumped to his sandaled feet. Ben's Thompson barked, a line of crimson holes appearing on the man's chest as he was flung backward.

Painted shapes ran from the tiny village, disappearing into the ever-growing forest and brush that had almost completely overgrown the town and the sidewalks.

The village grew quiet after the noise of battle. Only the moaning and occasional screaming of the wounded could be heard.

"Report!" Ben yelled.

Two Rebels dead. Five wounded. One of the wounded not expected to make it.

Thirty savages lay dead, scattered about on the streets. A dozen more twisted and moaned in pain.

"Just about wiped them out, General," James said.

"I hope," Ben replied. "Finish them, James."

"Yes, sir."

Gale walked to the safety of an old service station. Two Rebels accompanied her at a nod from Ben. Gale did not like this side of Ben, although she recognized Ben's order as being very necessary. The Rebels had taken prisoners from the gangs of thugs and misfits that had the misfortune to attack them from time to time. It had never worked out. Many had diseases that baffled Doctor Chase's medical people. The "viruses," as Chase referred to them—holocaust or not, anything that baffled doctors was still called a virus—did not respond to any known medication. Several Rebels had died from the strange illnesses.

Ben had been forced to send down the order, "No prisoners."

It also appeared that a form of insanity was cropping up among many of the survivor/victims of the aftermath of germ and nuclear warfare that had hit the world back in the late eighties. Chase's medical teams had performed numerous autopsies on the dead. Pockets of highly infectious pus were found in the brain of many.

"I don't know what is causing it, Ben," Doctor

Chase admitted. "I just don't. I don't understand it. But I can tell you this: this—" he grinned—"virus is very dangerous." He lost his grin and became very serious. "Ben, what makes it so dangerous is the fact—and it is a fact—that I don't know how to treat it. I can't find anything that will even arrest it, much less kill it. No prisoners, Ben. We can't risk it. It's for our own safety. Give my people time. They'll find something that'll work."

Single gunshots slammed the late afternoon as Rebels went to each downed man and put a bullet through the head.

"Face masks and gloves on when you handle them," Ben shouted. "Drag them into that building." He pointed to a shack on the edge of town. "We'll have a controlled burn. The rest of you get your gear together. When the burn is over, we're pulling out of here."

When the dead were stacked in the old building and fires were set, Gale walked to Ben's side.

He met her eyes. "I tried to question one of them, Gale. I couldn't get any sense out of him. He babbled first about the Bible, then about Satan, then about me being Satan's child. Only one thing he said made any sense."

She looked at him.

"He'd seen a man who called himself The Prophet."

Gale sighed. The old man she'd seen personally had come to haunt her.* "You think these people are insane?"

*Anarchy in the Ashes

"No. I think they're losers and savages. People who have given up and who are trying to justify what they've become by twisting the word of God all out of proportion. Hell with them."

James walked up. "We must have wasted one or more of the leaders," he said. "Some of the wounded screamed out that they'd be back, in force this time."

"We won't be here," Ben said. He looked toward the shack. The fire was almost out. The sweet smell of what certain cannibalistic tribes used to refer to as "Long Pig" filled the air. "Mount 'em up, James. Let's roll."

The small convoy rolled out on Highway 11. They connected with 129 and rolled south. About ten miles north of Macon, Ben pulled them off the road and they made a cold camp for the night. During the night, two of the wounded Rebels died. They were wrapped in blankets and at dawn were buried in a wooded area off the highway, with Ben speaking a few words over the unmarked graves. He then read from Ecclesiastes and from the Psalms.

Leaving the small gathering, Ben walked to the communications truck and called in to Cecil. He told him of the strange savage people who attacked them, and the loss of four Rebels. He concluded with, "What's the situation up there, Cec?"

"Stable, Ben. But we're unable to do much in the way of setting up shop, so to speak. I can't take the chance of spreading our people out too thin. Willette and his bunch have between five hundred and seven hundred followers ready to move. I don't believe they'll try anything violent; but I can't be sure of that. And I can't risk moving many of our regulars into the countryside to set up permanent bases. Not yet. And—" he sighed—"I've got teams out looking for Ike. No luck as yet, I'm sorry to report."

"I'm just about ready to come back and start kicking ass, Cec."

"Not yet, Ben," Cecil cautioned him. "I didn't realize just how slick Willette and his people were until yesterday. He's quick and he's smart. There is *nothing* I can pin directly on him. Not one damn thing. And Ben? I am afraid for you to return. I mean, *physically* afraid. Accidents happen, if you get my drift."

Ben got the drift. Hot anger filled him, rushing through his veins. "Yeah, Cec, I get the drift, all right. It was sure to happen someday. Well, that day is here. OK, ol' buddy. After we take a look at Savannah—if there is anything left of that city—I'm going to take my contingent and swing around to the east. I want you to quietly, and quietly is the word, assign me another full platoon. Have them link up with us at . . ." He scanned a map. "Well, just west of Clark Hill Lake. When we get close I'll contact them by radio as to exact location. Full combat contingent, Cec. And keep teams out looking for Ike."

"Long as you stay out of it, Ben."

Ben ignored that. "You have any idea who ambushed Ike and his party, or the reason behind the ambush, Cec?"

"Yes. But it's getting complicated, Ben. Abe Lancer—he's the unofficial spokesman for the mountain people of this area—says he got word it was the Ninth Order who grabbed Ike. He says they were working hand in hand with some of Willette's people. Now try to make any sense out of that."

"I figured as much, Cec." He told his second-in-command about the trucks of armed men they had seen and of the teams he had following them.

"Curious, Ben. Very curious. You think they're tied in with Willette?"

"It's a possibility we have to take under consideration. What about Abe Lancer and his people? How do they stand?"

"Abe is solidly with us. None of the mountain people trust Willette or any of his followers."

"Cec? Keep in mind this coup attempt might get bloody. And that we may have to fire on some of our own people."

"I try not to think about that, Ben."

"I know the feeling. OK. I'm about to read the riot act to the Ninth Order. Tell me, what new intelligence do we have, if any, on this punk named Tony Silver?"

"Not much new. Runs a paramilitary organization out of north Florida. Rapidly moving into south Georgia. Strong-arm stuff, slavery, forced work camps, prostitution. The whole filthy bag."

"We settle matters with Willette, we'll see about punching Mr. Silver's ticket, too. And it wouldn't surprise me in the least to find him mixed up with Willette and the Ninth Order."

"You getting your dander up, Ben?"

"Damn well better believe it, buddy."

EIGHT

"Got some survivors in Macon, General," the radio operator told Ben. "Scouts report they're in bad shape."

"Diseased?"

"No, sir. Susie didn't say that. Ragged, dirty, down on their luck. That type of bad shape."

"Losers."

"Yes, sir. I guess that's about it."

"We going to meet any resistance?"

"Negative, sir. Silver's bunch was there, on a fishing expedition, but they left after taking some of the women."

"Jesus Christ!" Ben said. "You mean the men just stood back and allowed Silver's bunch to kidnap women and girls?"

"That about it, sir. Silver's bunch took their pick and left."

"Too bad," Ben said with a grin. "I'm in the mood to kick some ass."

The radio operator flashed Ben a smile. She said, "Me, too, General."

Ben laughed. "That's the spirit. Christ, I wonder what happened to the men's guts?"

Gale stood by silently, listening. She had stopped

trying to convince Ben that all men did not have his will to survive, did not possess his skills at fighting, did not have his knowledge of weapons, had not spent time in one of the roughest military units ever formed.

Ben would look at her and reply, "What stopped them from learning the same things I know? Lack of guts, maybe?"

She would throw up her hands and walk away, knowing that to argue further would be futile. Once Ben Raines' mind was set, it was next to impossible to change.

"Who is in charge of this team of Scouts?" Ben asked the radio operator.

"Susie."

"Tell her to hole up. We're on our way."

The convoy approached Macon on Highway 129. The once-thriving city was no more than a hollow shell of what it had once been. Out of an original population—circa 1987 roadmap—of more than one hundred thousand, the Scouts were reporting perhaps no more than six to eight hundred people were left.

"Oh, Ben!" Gale said, upon sighting the first survivors.

They were a pitiful bunch, ragged and dirty.

"I feel so sorry for them," Gale said.

"Why?" Ben asked. "It's their own fucking fault. There is no excuse for them to walk around dressed in rags. I don't feel a damn bit sorry for the adults. It's the very young and the elderly who get my sympathy—and no one in between, who doesn't have some physical infirmity."

Her eyes were hot on him. "That's a pretty damned

selfish and arrogant attitude, Ben."

"I don't think so," Ben said, unruffled at her condemnation. "Gale, there were many of us over the years—before the bombings—who saw all this coming. We wrote about it; we yelled about it; we talked ourselves blue in the face advocating compulsory military training. Nothing came of it. I defy you, Gale—I *challenge* you to find one man in that bunch of losers who ever did time in a hard military unit. Odds of you finding one are very, very slim, my dear. And I challenge to find one, just *one* hard-line conservative in that pack of rags. I challenge you to find just one person, male or female, who practiced—before the wars—the art of survivalism. You won't find one, Gale."

She sat silently. It was at moments like these she experienced pangs of dislike for Ben, overriding her true feelings for him. No one likes to be told they are wrong. And Gale was no exception. What made it so bitter-tasting was the fact that she knew Ben was right.

"Honey, people who shared my feelings—male and female—beat their heads against the wall, verbally speaking, against the creeping cancer of liberalism. We tried to tell people in positions of power not to bend to the misguided whims of those pressure groups who favored gun control—for criminals *wanted* gun control. All gun control did was work in favor of the lawless and against the law-abiding citizens. We *saw* it all coming. We were laughed at and ridiculed.

"So-called *comic* movies and TV shows were made, belittling and ridiculing those who even

77

slightly practiced any type of survivalism. It was all great fun, Gale. See the funny people stockpiling food and weapons and other survival gear. Big joke. The nation's press showed us as ignorant buffoons and nuts. We expected that, since the national press was controlled and run by liberals. Print and broadcast. But we did try, Gale.''

Ben sighed. ''And we were laughed at. Probably by some of those very people right over there.'' He pointed. ''Those sad, sorry, naive bitches and bastards called us right-wingers, fascists, war-mongers, to mention only a few of the titles that were hung on us. We were laughed at, insulted, belittled and humiliated. The press had a field day with us. And you want me to feel sorry for those sacks of shit over there, Gale? No way, dear. Just *no damned way!*''

Totally liberated woman that she was, free-spirited and quick to speak her mind, Gale remained silent for this round, for she knew the ring of truth when she heard it. Like many reconstructed liberals, the truth had reached up and boxed her ears too many times for her to ignore it.

Ben pulled off the highway and drove up to a clump of unwashed citizens.

''Who is in charge here?'' he asked.

''Nobody in charge,'' a man said. ''I don't take orders from no one. Who are you people?''

Ben bit back an impulse to tell the man they were Snow White and the Seven Dwarfs. In drag. ''If no one is in charge, how in the hell does anything ever get done?''

''What is there to get done?'' the man challenged Ben. ''We're getting by. Isn't that all that matters?''

"Beautiful," Ben muttered. "What a bunch of losers." He raised his voice to a normal speaking level. "All right, tell me this: How are you people living?"

"Still lots of canned food left. We scrap around. What business is it of yours?"

Ben's eyes found a small knot of ragged and dirty kids, most of them very young, standing in a weed-filled lot, staring at the uniformed Rebels. "Where are the parents of those kids?"

"Who the hell knows," the man said with a shrug. "They're street kids. You see lots of them around. Damn nuisance is what they are."

Gale stirred beside Ben. He cut his eyes at her. She was getting angry and reaching that state very quickly.

Ben got out of the pickup, Thompson in hand. He faced the man. "I can see why Silver's people had such an easy time with his only opposition being you tigers. But I cannot believe you represent the majority of survivors in Macon. Where are the other people?"

The man would not meet Ben's eyes. Keeping his eyes averted, he said, "There's some folks over yonder." He pointed. "But we don't mess with them. They've got a lot of guns and they don't hesitate to use them."

"Go on," Ben prompted.

"What are you tryin' to get me to say, mister?"

"Those . . . other people, they have a leader?"

"Yeah."

"Everybody works in their society?"

"Yeah."

"They have schools for the kids and they raise gardens and maintain some type of law and order, is that right?"

"Yeah. All those things. So what?"

"And what you and these—" Ben's gaze swept the ragged, dirty crowd of men and women—"other people want is to lay on your lazy asses and do nothing. Is that correct?"

"Our business," the man's reply was sullen.

"Yeah," Ben said, the one word filled with sarcasm. He turned his back to the man. "Sergeant Greene! Get those kids and clean them up. Have the medics check them out. We're taking them with us."

"Yes, sir."

"What about us?" the dirty man said, a whine to his voice that grated on Ben. "Ain't you gonna give us some food or something? Help us out just a little bit?"

Ben lifted the muzzle of the Thompson, placing it under the man's chin. Ben saw fleas hop around on the man's neck. "Don't tempt me," Ben told him softly.

The man swallowed hard. "I get the message."

"I thought you might."

"Least you can tell me your name."

"Ben Raines."

The man's eyes glinted hard momentarily. His hatred overrode his fear of Ben. "Mr. President Raines, huh? That figures. Your time in office was cut kinda short, wasn't it? You was really gonna come down hard on some folks, wasn't you? Make everybody obey *your* law. Make everybody work, whether they wanted to or not. You weren't any better than a damned communist."

"Don't worry about it, sad sack," Ben told him. "You're not going to last much longer. Not unless you shape up. If thugs and punks don't kill you, disease will. You might last another year. Two if you're lucky. And if *I'm* real lucky, I'll never have to look at you again."

"You don't have any right to talk to me like that, mister."

"You may rest assured you have my heartfelt apologies for bruising your sensitive ego." Ben walked back to his truck and slid under the wheel. "Worthless son of a bitch!" he said.

"I could not agree with you more, Ben," Gale concurred.

They waited in the truck while the kids were rounded up and herded into trucks. The convoy shifted locations and the kids were checked out, bathed and dressed in clean clothes. They had all heard of Mister Ben Raines, and Ben was amused at the way they shyly looked at him. He felt sorry for them, for many told of being abandoned by their parents, left to wander alone, fending for themselves. They told of many of their little friends who had died, from the cold, from hunger, brought down by the many roaming packs of dogs gone wild. They said that Silver's men had taken several of the girls—after they had raped them.

In another section of the city, the scene was quite different. The streets were free of litter, the houses neatly kept. Gardens grew in every back yard. Block after block had been cleared and planted with all types of vegetables.

Ben stopped his truck in the center of the street, got out, and held his empty hands in the air. A gesture that he meant no harm to anyone. All the Rebels had been very conscious of eyes on them as they traveled from conditions that would make a pigsty seem attractive, to this well-attended section of Macon, Georgia.

Ben shifted his eyes left and right as heavily armed men and women appeared out of houses, to stand on well-kept front lawns.

"I'm friendly," Ben called. "We're just passing through, looking for survivors. To see how they're getting along. We mean no harm to anyone, believe me."

"You look familiar," a man called. "Who are you?"

"Ben Raines."

The men and women relaxed, lowering their weapons. "I thought it might be you," a well-dressed man said. "But none of us were certain. Have your people park their vehicles over there." He pointed. "You're all welcome here."

NINE

He did not know why the pain had suddenly stopped. But he was glad it had. His cuts had been cleaned and bandaged. He had been allowed to bathe and was given clean clothing.

Ike now sat alone in a small room. The door was locked from the outside. The room contained a cot, with blanket and pillow, a bucket of water, and a cane-bottomed chair. Nothing else.

He did not have any idea where he was.

But he sure as hell wished he was somewhere else.

He began making plans for escape.

TEN

Cecil knew Ben Raines as well as any man living, and Cecil felt certain Ben was going to pull out once Ike was found and the suspected coup attempt was put to rest. And Cecil really couldn't blame Ben. The man had never asked for the job. It had been pushed on him, beginning back in '88, in the old Tri-States. Ben had *never* wanted all the responsibility that had been piled on his shoulders. Big shoulders, to be sure, but lots of big problems, too. And Cecil knew Ben didn't want to break away on any permanent basis— he just wanted to take a rest, get away for a time.

Cecil knew the reins of government would be handed to him if Ben pulled out. And he wondered if he could handle all the problems that went with the territory.

He knew he had the respect of the Rebels. The Rebels were so racially mixed, that old issue never came up. People just did their jobs and nobody gave a damn what color they were. Ben wouldn't put up with blind race prejudice for five seconds.

But Cecil knew that while he had the loyalty and respect of the Rebels . . . he wasn't Ben Raines.

ELEVEN

He would really be king of the mountain if he could kill Ben Raines, Tony mused. He didn't know what had happened to that Russian bastard, Striganov, only that he had taken his people and headed out west. All that mess had been over and done with before Tony even knew what was happening. One had to rely on the infrequent broadcasts of ham operators for news, and they sometimes got it all screwed up.

Fuck the west! Tony thought. The Russian could have the west, Tony would take everything east of the Mississippi River. Maybe after he blew Ben Raines' shit away, he could arrange for a sit-down with General Striganov, work something out. Striganov. Christ, what a name. Sounded like something to eat.

Tony leaned back in his chair in the converted motel room outside Savannah. The young chick, Ann, was in the adjoining room, playing with *dolls*, for Christ's sake. Acted like she'd never seen a goddamn doll before. Tony shook his head in disgust. Cunt like Ann had on her and she plays with fucking dolls! Tony grinned. He knew Ann had been lying when she'd told him she got off their first time together. But Tony knew women, and after their fourth time together, he looked at the kid's face and knew she really was getting off. Now she couldn't get enough cock. His grin widened.

Women were all alike. Young or old. Kept their brains between their legs.

It had been a good move, coming up to south Georgia. He'd been friggin' tired of north Florida. He'd left a good man down there to run the operations, so he wasn't at all concerned about that.

Ben Raines concerned him.

All that garbage about him being some kind of a god. Shit! Goddamned law-and-order freak was what he was.

Wasn't no back-up in Raines. He just went in shooting. But he was a mortal; he bled just like anybody else. And Tony meant to be the one who pulled the trigger on Ben Raines.

Yes, getting rid of Raines would be quite a feather in his cap.

He'd definitely see about wasting Ben Raines. He had people in Raines' camp.

The son of a bitch!

TWELVE

It didn't take Dan Gray long to put it all together. He had looked around and found a lot of seasoned combat vets gone from camp. Probably gone to link up with General Raines.

He wondered if the general was going to make a move against those who grabbed Colonel McGowen. Probably, he concluded. Dan knew he had a bad reputation in a fight. But nothing to compare with General Raines' reputation as a bad ass. He felt very sorry for the Ninth Order when Ben Raines caught up with them.

The Englishman had detected a growing restlessness in General Raines lately. And he had pegged it accurately. When the Rebels were settled in, the problem with Willette and his malcontents solved— and it would be solved—and Ike found, dead or alive, Dan was certain Ben was going to take off. Probably after Gale birthed her babies. But he couldn't be sure of that, for Gale was one very astute person, and Dan had spoken with her at length many times. Gale knew Ben was getting restless, and she also knew no one woman held Ben for very long. Not since Salina. Gale just might insist Ben take off without her.

Dan didn't blame Ben for wanting to get away for a

time: a few months, perhaps even a year. Lord knows the man had been saddled with the problems of creating nations for more than a decade. It was time for a break.

Dan smiled. All right, General, he thought, take your hiatus—you've earned it. But before you do, *I* shall be equipping a new truck for you. And when I get through with it, I shall be able to track you and pinpoint your location no matter where in the ravaged nation you might decide to wander.

He was grinning and rubbing his hands together gleefully as he walked off toward the motor pool.

"I suppose, Mr. Raines," the spokesman for the Macon group said, "it would be a losing proposition for us to stay here. Is that the way you see it?"

"Yes," Ben replied without hesitation. "Mr. Harner, Tony Silver, so I'm told, has a small, but very well-equipped army. And he is pushing hard into south Georgia. His tactics are brutal. I've told you about them. I believe the only way civilization can endure is for people of like mind to band together. When that is done, perhaps others will join us and we can spread out. I've been entertaining the thought of outposts throughout the nation, small fortress/village types."

"Well-armed and well-equipped," Harner said, leaning forward. "Much like the old west days when the settlers were pushing westward. Yes. I like that concept, General. Count us in."

"Don't delay your move too long, Mr. Harner," Ben cautioned the leader of the Macon survivors. "I noticed you have a good communications system. I'll be in touch if I hear anything I think you should be informed of."

"We'll start the packing in the morning, General Raines. But we'll do it in a manner that will not be too obvious. We should be ready to pull out in two or three weeks."

"Good. I'll radio Colonel Jefferys and tell him to be ready to receive you, or to give you help, if you should need it."

"General? Are you, ah, aware of the, ah, manner in which many people view you?"

Ben smiled. "The rumor that I am more god than man? Unfortunately, yes. But every time I bring it up, it seems to make matters worse. Strengthens the rumor, so to speak. So I decided to just drop the subject."

"I see," Harner spoke softly. "But, General . . . have you ever given any thought to the idea the rumor might just hold some degree of truth?"

Ben shrugged that off. He'd heard it many times before. "Take care of the kids," he said.

THIRTEEN

The team following the convoy of armed men had reported the men headed into the mountains of north Georgia. They appeared to be skirting the Rebels' new Base Camp and heading toward the border of Tennessee.

Ben told them to break off pursuit and to head for Clark Hill Lake. Wait there for the other contingent to join them. Ben's convoy would meet them there.

Ben pulled his small convoy out of the Macon area at noon, pointing them east on Interstate 16. The going proved very slow.

They were heading for Savannah.

The nation's highways and freeways were rapidly deteriorating, Ben noted. Almost fourteen years of virtual neglect had dramatically taken its toll. Another fourteen years, and many roadways would be impassable. If he was to once more see the country, or what was left of it, with even some degree of access, he would have to do it quickly.

Gale picked up on his thoughts. She could do so by watching the expression on his face and the direction his eyes were taking over a period of time. That plus the fact that when deep in thought, Ben had a tendency to mutter. "The twins will be born around the last of February. I won't even consider taking them on the road until they are a year old."

"Hell, Gale, that's eighteen months," Ben said, frowning.

"My, how quick you are this afternoon."

He laughed at her. "Woman, thou hath a barbed tongue."

She slid across the seat and whispered vulgarly in his ear.

"Well . . . I suppose there might be a modicum of truth in that—putting it that way. I was speaking figuratively, however."

"No kidding! Did Cecil have any good news about Ike when you spoke with him?"

Ben shook his head. "No, nothing. He's got teams out looking. Ike will show up, unless he's dead. As soon as we take a quick looksee at Savannah, I think we'll head north, link up with the platoon at Clark Hill Lake, and then *I'll* join the search."

"You weren't listening to a word I said the other day, were you, Ben?"

He grinned at her.

"Shit, Ben!" She stared out the window for a few seconds. "I wonder if Ike is all right?"

Ben said nothing. He was wondering the same thing. He was worried about Ike, but not as much as Gale thought. Ben knew the ex-Navy SEAL—if he wasn't dead, and Ben didn't like to think about that—was busy planning and rejecting escape options. Given just a second's carelessness on the part of his captors, Ike would strike faster than a cobra and be gone.

After reviewing what he knew of the ambush in his

mind, going over it many times, Ben was almost positive Ike was being held captive in either the Chattahoochee, the Nantahala, or the Cherokee National Forest. Hundreds of thousands of acres of wilderness. More wilderness now than ever before. And that would be in Ike's favor, for he was survival-trained, and Ike knew where the hidden caches of guns and ammo and supplies were located, left behind by the Rebels a couple of years back. And God alone could help the Ninth Order if Ike escaped and found the caches. The ex-SEAL would not leave a one of them alive.

"Ike is all right," Ben said.

FOURTEEN

Ike thought he had it figured. Each afternoon, precisely at five p.m., a robed and hooded figure came to the door and knocked once. Ike replied. He was then ordered to stand away from the door, his back to the far wall. The door would open, a tray of food would be shoved in, on the floor, and the door would close.

Ike looked at the makeshift manlike figure he had constructed from pillow and blanket and wood from the chair. He had placed it in a shadowy corner of the large room. It would have to do. It might fool the guard for a few seconds. That was all the time Ike would need.

He hoped.

Although painful while occurring, his torture had left no serious physical problems. Had they continued, however, that would have been another story.

Ike hefted the chair leg, quietly smacking the heavy end against his open palm. "Come on, you son of a bitch," he muttered softly. "Just stick your hooded head inside that door."

He heard the sound of footsteps coming down the hall. One set of footsteps. They halted in front of his door. Ike smiled grimly. The smile of the hunter.

"Disbeliever!" the voice called.

93

That was Ike's cue. "Yeah."

"Step away from the door."

"All right, all right. Hurry it up, partner, I'm hungry."

"Stand back."

"Done."

The key rattled in the lock. The doorknob turned. The door swung slowly open. A tray of food was placed on the floor. The hooded man looked at the dim outline of the makeshift bundle of blanket and pillow and sticks. He grunted and placed the tray of food on the floor. Just as he once more lifted his eyes, eyes that now held suspicion, Ike stepped from behind the door, the club raised over his head.

"Overpass out just up ahead, General," the lead scout radioed back to the main column. "Three miles from your location." Late afternoon in Georgia, the fall air cooling.

Ben pulled up behind the Jeep. The support columns had been blown under the east side of the bridge, collapsing it.

"Now why would anyone want to do that?" Ben asked. He took a closer look. He could see weeds and brush growing amid the jumble of concrete and steel. "It wasn't done recently."

"Doesn't make any sense to me, General," a Rebel replied. "Another patrol went north to see if the access road to Highway 80 is clear. She'll be reporting back in a minute."

"Well," Ben said, "this might have been an accident. We'll see."

The radio crackled. "319/441 is blocked, Jerry. None of this is making any sense. 'Fore the general makes any moves, send a patrol to backtrack and check out this old Highway 257 into Dublin. I got an edgy feeling about all this."

James pointed at two Rebels in a Jeep. "Go," he told them. "Maintain radio contact and stay alert for trouble."

"Susie?" James spoke into the mic. "Stay loose and heads up."

"Ten-four, Sarge," she responded. "Rolling."

The Rebels waited in the cooling wind that blew from the north. Winter was not far away. Five minutes passed. The last recon team sent out called in. "Sarge? Highway 257 is blocked just off the interstate."

Ben took the mic. "This is General Raines. Backtrack to the interstate and head west until you intersect with Highway 338. That'll lead you into a small town named Dudley. Check it out and be careful doing it."

"Ten-four."

"Susie?"

"Sir?"

"You getting hinky about this?"

"Yes, sir. All senses tell me something is bad wrong."

"Back off about a mile and sit it out. Keep your head up, now."

"Yes, sir. Rolling."

"James? Have a Jeep jump the median and cut across that field. Swing back to the interstate then cut north on Highway 19. See if it's blocked. This downed overpass may have given someone a grim idea. All this is getting just a little weird to me."

"Yes, sir."

The minutes ticked slowly past. Ben tuned up the collar on his field jacket. He checked his weapons. The Scouts began calling in.

"Dudley is a ghost town, sir. Highway 338 is blocked on the east side."

"Hold your positions and stay alert for trouble," Ben ordered.

"Highway 19 is blocked, sir. Just off the interstate."

"Come on back. Susie? Come back in."

Gale looked at Ben. "Let me guess, Ben. We're going to visit Dublin, right?"

"Right on the money, honey," Ben replied with a grin.

She walked back to the pickup, muttering as she walked. "Man just can't mind his own business."

The Scouts who had jumped the interstate rolled back in. "Let's move it," Ben ordered. "Load those .50s and stay alert. We're probably heading into trouble up ahead. I hope not, but let's be ready for anything."

"You hope not!" Gale said as Ben dropped the pickup into gear. "Ben, you *thrive* on trouble."

"And if you didn't like it, you would have split a long time ago." He grinned at her.

"Just think," she replied. "I used to belong to the Youth for Peace movement."

"Did you have a little banner you waved about?" Ben asked.

"Very funny, Raines."

"Did you?"

"Yes!"

They backtracked the ten miles and cut north on 338. The small town was deserted and in ruin. It had been picked clean by looters. The Rebels rolled through what remained of the town and stopped several hundred yards from the barricade that stretched across Highway 80.

Ben got out of the truck and looked at the barricade through binoculars. "It wasn't put up to last any length of time," he said. "All right, knock it down."

Explosives were set in place. Sixty seconds later, the barricade erupted in a smoky mass of wood and brick and concrete blocks.

"Scouts take the point," Ben ordered.

Susie wheeled her Jeep through the smoking ruins, an armed Rebel riding shotgun, his M-16 ready. Another Rebel stood in the rear of the Jeep, ready with a mounted M-60 light machine gun.

"Roll it slow," Ben said.

The column moved out, all weapons held at the ready.

"What do you think is up ahead, Ben?" Gale asked. "And before you get smart-mouthed, I realize that is a stupid question."

"Several possibilities. One: a group of people—much like us—who have bunkered themselves in for personal safety. Two: a gang of thugs who have taken over the town for whatever reason. Three: the complete unknown."

"Mutants?"

"I doubt it. No mutant I've seen has the intelligence to build a barricade that well. Tony Silver's name keeps popping up in my mind. Sooner or later, we're going to have to deal with Silver."

"So it's the unknown thus far?" she said.

"Right. We'll know in about half a minute, I'm thinking."

"I can hardly wait."

"Your adventurous spirit is overwhelming, Ms. Roth."

"Just drive the damn truck, Raines." She looked at the 1987 roadmap. "Sixteen thousand people in Dublin. Back before the bombs, that is."

"Maybe one-tenth survived that. I doubt it was that high. The plague? I don't know. That may have finished the town. We'll soon see."

Susie's Jeep was stopped in the middle of the highway as Ben slowed and pulled up beside her, on the north side. The woman had an odd expression on her face.

Ben got out of his truck. "What's the matter, Susie?"

She pointed to the side of an old service station. "Look over there, General."

Ben looked. "Jesus Christ!" he blurted.

Bloated, naked bodies were hanging from a beam that stretched from building to building. Their hands were tied behind their backs, their faces were dark, tongues swollen and protruding.

Before anyone could say anything else, a hard burst of machine gunfire knocked the Rebel still sitting in the front of the Jeep out of his seat, the heavy slugs tearing away part of his face. The Rebel in the rear swung his M-60 and pulled the trigger back, holding it, spraying the area where the fire had originated. He fought the rise of the weapon on full auto.

Ben located the source of the firing and burned half a clip at the hidden machine gun emplacement by the side of an old house. Rebel rocket launchers cracked their explosive messages. The machine gun nest was blown into bloody bits.

"Teams on both sides of the road!" Ben yelled. "Clear it, house to house. Medics, up front, now!"

It was too late for the Rebel lying in his own blood in the front of the Jeep. The heavy .50-caliber machine gun slugs had torn the life from the young man.

Ben glanced at Susie. The young woman had tears in her eyes. "You all right, Susie?"

"I will be, sir," she replied. "In a minute." She turned her back to him and wiped her eyes. Facing him, she said, "General, Bert and I were engaged, sort of. We had talked of getting married." She looked at the young man named Bert, now being wrapped in a tarp. "I wouldn't want to leave here until his death had been avenged."

"We won't, Susie," Ben assured her. "I want to find out what in the hell is going on around this place."

Susie spat very unladylike on the ground. "Personally, I would rather burn the whole fucking town to the ground."

She walked back to her Jeep. She found a rag and began mopping up Bert's blood from the seats.

FIFTEEN

Ike both felt and heard the man's skull pop under the hickory club. He quickly dragged the robed and hooded man into the room and closed the door, after checking the lock. He damn sure didn't want to get locked back in with a stiff.

Ike stripped off the robe and put it on, grimacing as he did so. The robe stank of old sweat. Fanning the body, Ike discovered a .38-caliber pistol and a pocket full of cartridges. He found a package of cigarettes—Lord only knew how old they were—and a Zippo lighter. Even though Ike had been trying to quit smoking for years, he made up his mind he'd sure fire one up if he got out of this loony bin in one piece.

He smiled. After he wasted a whole bunch of these kooks, that is.

He slowly opened the door and looked up and down the dimly lit hall. Must be a gasoline generator producing the power, he thought. The hall was quiet and deserted. He slipped out into the hall, stood for a moment, trying to get his bearings, then walked in the opposite direction his guard's footsteps had always sounded. He passed a room that smelled strongly of kerosene. An idea came to him. He smiled grimly and entered the room.

He found two five-gallon cans of kerosene and a carton of rags. Ike saturated the room with raw kerosene and ran back to the room where he'd been held captive, leaving a trail of kerosene as he ran. He doused the dead man with kerosene, and threw the rest of that can of flammable liquid on the walls and floor. He lit a handful of rags and dropped them to the floor, backing out of the room.

He backed right into a breathing body.

"Brother Jake?" the man said. "Why . . . you're not Brother—"

That was as far as he hot. Brother whatever-in-the-hell-his-name-was felt his throat explode in pain as Ike ruptured his larynx with the knife edge of his hand. Brother Yo-yo hit the floor and began flopping around, slowly suffocating, gagging and making horrible choking sounds. Ike hastened death's touch by kicking the man in the temple with the toe of his boot. The man croaked once and was still. Fanning the body, Ike found another .38 pistol, more cartridges, and a long-bladed hunting knife in a leather sheath.

Ike took the seconds required to check both pistols. Fully loaded. He tossed Brother Yo-yo into the burning room, shut the door, and picked up the second can of kerosene. He ran down the hall, slopping kerosene on the walls and floor, the fire trailing behind him as he ran.

Smoke was rapidly filling the corridored building as Ike came to a dead end. A dirty window faced him. He unlocked the window and climbed out, closing the window behind him.

The outside air was clear and cold. Ike breathed

deeply, gratefully. It felt good to be free. Even better to be armed. Now to get his bearings and find some heavier weapons. Then to do some damage, draw some real blood.

He could hear the sounds of men and women yelling, some of the yelling pain-filled as the fire spread quickly through the old, wooden building. It had been some type of old warehouse, Ike guessed.

A man ran around a corner of the building, carrying an M-16. He ran toward Ike, crouched in the darkness. When the robed man passed the kneeling Ike, Ike jammed one end of the hickory stick hard into the man's gut. The air left him in a rush. Ike cracked the man's skull with the club and hit him again for insurance. He grabbed up the M-16 and tore the full ammo pouch from the man. He checked the M-16. It was one of the older models, manufactured long before the M16A2 came to be. This old baby was full auto.

Ike checked the clip. Full. The clips in the ammo pouch were all full, a mixed bag of twenty and thirty round clips.

"Now for a little fun," Ike muttered. "*My* kind of fun, kids."

Using the heavy brush around the burning building, Ike slipped into deep cover, edging into the prone firing position. He found a group of robed men and women standing about two hundred yards from the burning structure. He blew a full clip into them, knocking half of them sprawling, kicking and screaming on the ground.

"Bastards!" Ike growled.

The roaring of the fire completely covered the

stutter and crack of the M-16. Ike jammed home a fresh clip and began picking his targets.

He knocked the props out from under a half dozen more hooded and robed persons before deciding it was time for him to haul his ass out of that area.

One man came close to Ike's position and Ike shot him, one slug hitting the magazine of the M-16, the rounds exploding, mangling the man's belly and chest. Ike tore the ammo pouch from the man and ripped a pair of field glasses from around the man's neck. He ran into the woods.

Stopping once to check the stars, Ike got his bearings and headed southeast. He found a stream and followed it until he spotted a bridge looming dark in the early fall evening in the mountains.

Ike carefully reconnoitered the bridge and the grounds around it while remaining motionless in the brush. First chance he got, he was getting out of that stinking robe. It was insulting his nostrils. People of the Ninth Order must not believe much in bathing, he thought.

Cautiously, he made his way to the bridge. He followed the highway south by staying close to the timberline. He came to a highway marker. He was on Highway 60.

Ike searched his memory. The patrol he'd been leading had been ambushed just to the east of Highway 411, very close to the town of Chatsworth. So the members of the Ninth Order had carried him quite a distance to the east. He still couldn't quite figure out exactly why the Ninth Order had grabbed him. He thought all that questioning about Ben had been to throw him off.

Unless . . .

Yeah, he reflected sourly, that had to be it. Willette and his bunch were probably playing footsie with that gang of kooks. Christ! Ike had hoped they were all through with people like that when they left Emil Hite and his band of fruitcakes back in Arkansas.*

Ike had to softly chuckle at the memory of Emil Hite. Hite was more harmless hippie than anything else. The man had a scam working for him. But he wasn't dangerous—at least not like the Ninth Order.

The Ninth Order. Sister Voleta. What the hell did they want? Good Christ, there was surely enough land for everybody.

Ike just couldn't figure it.

He walked for half an hour before spotting an old house set off the road, almost completely overgrown with thick brush. He circled the house once before stepping up to the porch. Carefully, he tried the doorknob. It turned with a grinding, unused sound. M-16 ready, on full auto, Ike pushed open the door. It protested on rusty hinges. Ike stepped into a musty-smelling living room.

Something screamed an animal sound and came leaping at him in the darkness.

*Anarchy in the Ashes

SIXTEEN

"We're clean up to that point," the Rebel said, pointing to an intersection about a half mile from the first barricade just outside Dublin, Georgia. "Beyond that point, General, is the unknown. You want me to send teams in there?"

Ben nixed that quickly. "It'll be full dark soon," he said. "No point in risking more lives wandering around at night. They—whoever *they* might be— know the terrain. We don't. Let's backtrack a few miles for safety's sake. We'll hit the town in the morning."

"Whatever is in there," Susie said, "they're pretty good. I haven't seen any movement since we knocked out that machine gun emplacement."

"Either pretty good or pretty scared," Ben said. "Or pretty few." He turned to another Rebel. "What did you learn from inspecting the bodies at the machine gun nest?"

"Five white males," Sergeant Greene said. "Dirty. Unwashed. Bad teeth. All different ages. I'd say from twenty to forty-five. All wearing battle dress. None of them wore any type of unit crest or any other type of insignia."

"Odd," Ben said, more to himself than anyone

else. Once again, Tony Silver's name came to his mind. Suddenly, Ben thought about Ike. He shook that away. "OK. Let's pull back and get our camp set up for the night."

Gale touched his arm. "I get the uncomfortable feeling we are being watched."

"I imagine we are," Ben said. "From a safe distance."

Gale looked at the ten naked bodies hanging from the rafter across the street. Tortured and mutilated and grotesque. "What are you going to do with them, Ben?"

"Leave them for the time being. We'll cut them down and bury them in the morning. Twelve more hours won't make a bit of difference to them."

The Rebels backtracked to the interstate and set up for the night around an old motel complex. Ben posted guards on the roof and on both sides of the interstate.

"Heads up," Ben told his people. "We don't know how many of the enemy we're facing, much less *what* we're facing."

"Seems to me, General," a woman spoke from the ranks, "since we didn't make the first hostile moves to open this dance, those people back in Dublin—the ones who fired on us—are lookin' to get their asses kicked."

"That is precisely what we are going to do, Judy," Ben told her with an accompanying smile. "At first light."

"Good!" she replied. "I'm damn tired of people shootin' at me. Especially since all we're tryin' to do is be friends and help those who need it."

A low growl of agreement spread through the ranks of the Rebels.

"In the morning," Ben repeated, dismissing the Rebels.

"I'm hungry," Gale announced.

"I'm sure," Ben said. "You eat like a horse normally. Now you're eating for two."

"Three, Ben. Three." She looked at him. "A *horse*!"

SEVENTEEN

Ike sidestepped, tripped the man who came shrieking at him in the darkness, and got the guy in a hammer lock. Ike had dropped his M-16 and was just about to cut the guy's throat when his hand cupped a soft breast.

Ike squeezed gently. He grinned and squeezed again. Soft. Quite a handful.

"Perverted son of a bitch!" the woman said. "Are you gonna cut my throat or just feel me up?"

Not relaxing his hold on the woman, Ike said, "I might decide to do both." He squeezed again.

"Will you turn loose of my titty? And you're choking me, you bastard."

Ike eased off and stood up. The woman remained crouched on the floor. She rubbed her throat. In the dim light filtering through the dirty windows, Ike looked at her. She was maybe twenty-two or three, no more than that. Light brown hair, tanned skin. Old work shirt and faded jeans. She was built up nice and shapely. She met his gaze squarely, no back-up in her.

"What are you, a fat monk?" she asked.

Ike stepped back and pulled off the hooded robe.

He tossed the stinking garment to the floor. Ike was all muscle and gristle and bone. And he was strong as an ape.

Her eyes swept him from face to booted feet. She nodded her head.

"Did I pass inspection?" Ike asked.

"If that's what you want to call it. OK. So you're not fat. You're a fireplug. But *what* are you? Besides a pervert, that is."

"I am *not* a pervert. But you do have a nice set of titties." He grinned. "I'm Colonel Ike McGowen. Now who in the hell are you?"

"A *colonel*! Sure you are," she said sarcastically. "A colonel in what?"

"Raines' Rebels."

She opened her mouth to speak. Closed it. Blinked her eyes. She twisted around and sat on the floor, looking up at Ike. "General Ben Raines? I mean, *President* Ben Raines?"

"Yeah. Ben. I was leading a patrol a couple of counties west of here. Some nutty bastards that call themselves the Ninth Order ambushed us, grabbed me. I broke out several hours ago. That's it in a nutshell. What's your name?"

"Nina. Yeah, I know that bunch of crazies. Know them well. They killed my old man last month. They burned him to death," she added bitterly, almost spitting out the last. "Stripped him, tortured him, tied him to a stake, then burned him. Made me watch. The men holding me had a good time feeling me up. They told me what they were going to do to me. Real perverted. They were going to *screw* me to death. You

109

believe that? They *meant* it! I kicked one in the balls and split. Been runnin' ever since. Thought they had me a couple-three times, but I always managed to slip past them. Screw me to death. Caught me and my old man, ah, messin' around. Called me a sinner. So that was to be my punishment. Jesus! What a pack of nuts."

"I agree with you. Your old man? Your husband?"

"Kind of. We never got married, though. How about you?"

Vibrations passed between the man and the woman. Both of them picked up the other's silent message. Strong erotic messages. The meaning was very clear.

"How do you want me to answer that?" Ike asked her.

"The only way to answer it, Ike. By tellin' the truth."

"I'm married."

"Faithful to her?"

Something clutched at Ike's guts. "Up to now," he said with a grin, meeting her pale gray eyes. "You got anything to eat?"

She smiled.

Ike picked it up. He laughed loudly. The laugh felt good; he hadn't had much to laugh about the past few days. "Food, baby," he said, patting his stomach. "Sustenance for the bod."

"Yeah. I got a sack of army rations. I swiped it yesterday."

"C-rations?"

"I guess."

"Yuk! Well, let's eat. Then we'll get some rest and

head out at first light." Ike tossed her one of the .38s taken from the Ninth Order. "You know how to use that?"

Nina looked at the pistol. An odd look came into her eyes. She pointed the weapon at Ike and jacked back the hammer. "I sure do, sucker."

EIGHTEEN

"Hold her hands, baby," Tony said to Ann. He positioned himself behind the sobbing young girl. "You 'bout the same age, you two. So you tell this chick she fights me, she's gonna get hurt. I can work it in real easy, or I can tear her cunt up. It's all up to her."

"Believe him," Ann said to the naked, frightened girl. "It ain't bad once it's done to you two, three times. It gets to feelin' real good. Believe me. He'll treat you real good, too. Just don't fight him no more."

The young girl nodded her head. "OK." She pressed her face against the sheet on the bed. She was thin from years of extremely bad diet and from being on her own in a world rapidly filling with savagery and barbarism. Her name was Peg. She was twelve years old.

Tony ran his fingers over the girl's buttocks. He touched her anus, then his fingers touched her center and pushed inside her. The girl moaned at the sudden intrusion.

Tony said, "I can make it good for you, baby. Or I can hurt you. It's all up to you." He worked his finger in and out. Peg began weeping. "You tell me where your little buddy ran off to."

Ann stroked the girl's hair. "Tell him, Peg. It's better than being out there all alone. You won't have to fuck no one but Tony. Believe it. You'll have plenty of good things to eat. Dolls to play with. He'll get you pretty things to wear and a machine that makes musical noises come out of funny little round things."

"She ran off to our hiding place. On the waterfront. It's an upside-down number on the front of the place."

"What?" Tony looked confused.

"Can't you do numbers?" Ann asked.

"No."

Ann wrote a six on a piece of paper. She showed that to Peg.

"Yes. That's it. What number is that?"

"Nine," Ann told her. "Don't you have any schooling?"

Peg shook her head.

"Who gives a shit?" Tony said. He pulled away from the child. "I got to see a man. I'll be back later."

He left the motel room. He really didn't want sex now. That report he'd received from Dublin about his people there coming under attack had him a little worried. Tony stopped outside his motel room, an idea coming to him.

Who would be foolish enough to attack the army of Tony Silver?

Only one person. He had everybody else too scared of retribution.

Only one person.

Ben Raines.

Had to be.

"Well, I'll just be goddamned!" Tony muttered. "Ben Raines, right under my fuckin' nose all this time. Things are definitely beginning to look up for me."

Tony began laughing.

He motioned for one of his men to come over. "Paul, get a team together. 'Bout, oh, fifty guys ought to be enough to kick the ass off of Ben Raines. More than enough. A *god*!" Again he laughed, Paul joining in the laughter. "Goddamn joke is what Ben Raines is. I'll show the people who is really boss around this land. Me!"

"Right, boss," Paul agreed. "Everybody knows that. Everybody."

"Shut up, Paul. We'll be moving out first thing in the morning. 'Bout nine o'clock."

"Right, boss." The goon turned to leave.

"Oh . . . Paul?"

"Yeah, boss?"

"I want you to get some boys together and go down to the waterfront. Warehouse number nine. Do it quiet like, now. There's a young chick down there I want. Bring her back and have her cleaned up. And don't none of you guys even *think* about stickin' a dick in her. That's prime gash and it's mine."

"Sure, boss. Don't worry none about that. I'll see to it personal."

"All right. You bring her to my room when she's bathed. I'm gonna bust me two cherries in one night."

114

The man grinned, exposing rotten teeth. "Right, boss. I gotcha."

"Two tight pussies and Ben Raines. All within twenty-four hours of each other. Son of a bitch! My luck is on a steady roll."

"Right, boss."

NINETEEN

"All right, lads," Dan Gray spoke into the mic. "Thanks and take care." Breaking the connection, Dan smiled. Interesting, he thought. Big fire up near Blue Ridge Lake. Gunshots reported. Dan had ordered his scouts into the area at first light.

Shooting the place up and then burning it to the ground would be something the ex-SEAL would do if his feathers got ruffled. Ike was as randy as they came.

"Hang on, Ike," Dan muttered.

TWENTY

Ike looked at the loaded and cocked .38 in Nina's hand. She held it like she knew what to do with it. And had done it before.

"Now what?" Ike asked.

Nina grinned and eased the hammer down. She tucked the pistol behind her belt. "We eat—what else?"

Ike stared at her in the gloom of the darkened living room. "Would you mind telling me just what in the hell that stunt was all about?"

"I just wanted to see if you were as ballsy as you appeared to be."

"And?"

"You are." Nina found her knapsack and took out several cans of army rations.

Ike knew the rations well. He looked at the olive-green cans. He grimaced. "You sure you ain't got any dehyde?"

She shook her head. "Sorry, Ike. It's this or go hungry."

"Long as it ain't them gawdawful green eggs. What all you got in that bag?"

She chuckled softly in the gloom of the old house.

"Bacon and eggs."

Cussing under his breath, Ike found his little military can opener and began circling the rim of the can. "Least it's dark in here," he muttered. "Won't be able to tell if they're green or not." The odor hit his nostrils. "They're green," he said glumly.

TWENTY-ONE

Ben's walkie-talkie crackled softly. "Come on," he whispered into the AN/PRC-6T.

The most forward Scout said, "They're definitely waiting for us, General. They've set up an ambush on both sides of Highway 80. First big supermarket on the south side."

"Weapons?"

"Heavy machine guns and M-16s. That's it, sir."

"Hold your position and stay low. I'm sending teams to flank them."

"Roger, sir."

Ben gave James the coordinates. "Don't jack around with them, James. Use mortars and rocket launchers. I don't want any more casualties from this operation."

"Yes, sir. We'll stand back and blow hell out of the bastards."

"Go."

The paramilitary troops of Tony Silver knew the savage fury of trained and disciplined troops for only a few seconds before the M-60 machine gunfire, the mortars, and the 40mm grenades blew them into their own dubious place in the yet unwritten history of the aftermath of the most humanly destructive war ever waged on the face of the earth.*

The attacks were coordinated to launch within a second of each other. And the troops of Tony Silver, who thought they were so well-hidden, so tough, so professional and so feared by all, had only a maximum of five seconds to scream out their pain and fear before their unwashed bodies were torn to bloody strips of mangled flesh.

Ben watched grimly through binoculars as Tony's little army was creamed.

"Let's get the fuck outta here!" the man in charge of this contingent of Silver's army of thugs and goons and murderers and rapists shouted. "Them is regular army troops. Where the fuck did *they* come from? We're outclassed."

The "army" split. They tucked their tails between their legs and cut out, jumping into cars and pickups and vans and heading east on Highway 80, fleeing as if pursued by the devil.

They left behind them death, rape, torture, sexual perversion and hideous memories in the minds of the people in Dublin who had survived—thus far.

"Cut down those people over there," Ben said, pointing at the hanging bodies. "James, have Scouts follow those retreating for several miles; make certain they're really bugging out. Let's find out about the residents of this town."

Ben Raines and his Rebels soon discovered the aftermath of Silver's scurvy followers. The scene was sickening to them all.

Tortured and sexually abused men and women

*Out of the Ashes

and children began streaming into the littered streets of the town when they discovered the new troops were there not to harm them but to help them.

The Rebels broke up the mob of people into sections, for interviewing, for medical treatment, for food and clothing.

After a time, Susie came to Ben. "This Tony Silver's got to be stopped, General. I've talked with and seen little girls and boys not over nine or ten years old who were sexually assaulted and abused. It's pitiful, General."

Ben listened.

Sergeant Greene said, "One man told me a lot of the kids—mostly girls, ages twelve to fourteen—were taken out of this area. To be turned into whores for shipment around the country."

Ben nodded. But one question kept nagging at him: Why did the people left in the town allow it to happen? Why didn't they fight?

James said, "There isn't a female in this town, between the ages of nine and sixty, who hasn't been raped repeatedly. The men were sexually humiliated, in front of the women."

"Are these people residents of this town?" Ben asked.

"No, sir," a Rebel said. "Those I've talked to say Dublin was wiped out by the plague. These people are a mixed bag, from all over the state. They just got here 'bout six months ago."

"Why here?"

The Rebel shrugged. "They're some kind of religious order, sir. Don't believe in violence."

"No guns?" Ben said acidly.

"That's it, sir. Not a weapon in the whole town."

Ben felt anger wash over him. What had the young Rebel, Bert, died for? A group of dickheads so naive they believed all they had to do was hold up the dove of peace and it would be honored? Stupid, naive, out-of-touch-with-reality crapheads.

Ben brought his anger under control. "Tell them to read Ecclesiastes. Get their priorities in line."

"Sir?" the young Rebel asked.

"Never mind, Joey. Just talking to myself. All right," Ben said with a sigh. "Maybe it all ties in. I have a feeling it does."

"What, Ben?" Gale asked. She was sick at her stomach from what she had seen and heard this awful day. But she knew Ben had no patience with people who would not fight for their lives.

"The Ninth Order, Captain Willette, Tony Silver. The whole rotten, scummy bag."

"How does it tie in, Ben?"

He shook his head. "Hunch, Gale. That's all. Could be I'm wrong."

The Rebels gathered around him dismissed that instantly. The thought of Gen. Ben Raines being wrong about anything was something no loyal Rebel ever entertained. That would be unthinkable.

"Let's patch these people up and get the hell out of here," Ben ordered. "I feel sorry for the kids and the elderly—but losers don't impress me."

"You have no right to judge us so harshly, General," a man said.

Ben turned. The man facing him was dressed in a business suit. Ben found that just slightly less than ludicrous, considering the surroundings. "I lost a good man in your town, mister. And I'm not real sure his death was worth it—considering the fact that you people refuse to stand up and be counted in a fight."

"We are peaceful people, General Raines."

"That's fine, mister," Ben countered. "All well and good back when you could pick up a phone and call the police, back when law and order and rules and codes of conduct were the norm. That is no more. And I seriously doubt—except in isolated pockets of this world—it will ever be again. At least not in our lifetime. Now, mister," he said, lifting the old Thompson, "*this* is the law."

"We refuse to take a human life," the man said.

Ben frosted him with a look. "Then you're a god-damned fool. I'm not advocating mass murder, mister. Just telling you to protect yourselves."

"The Lord will provide."

Ben smiled grimly. "Then I suggest you find yourself the jawbone of an ass. Or, in your case, the backbone might be a better choice."

TWENTY-TWO

Nina lay in Ike's strong arms. The morning sunlight was beginning to filter brightly through the dusty windows of the old home. Nina's bare breasts pressed against Ike's naked chest. It had been quite a sex-oriented night. Ike smiled, recalling an old saying from his boyhood days down in Mississippi: Girl could do more with six inches of cock than a monkey with a mile of vines.

He laughed softly at the crudeness of the old expression.

Nina opened her eyes and yawned in his face. "What's so funny, Ike?"

He told her.

"Jesus! What an awful saying." But she laughed as she said it.

"What's for breakfast, Nina?"

"Canned eges and bacon."

"Thanks just the same, but I think I'll pass." Ike disengaged himself from her warm nakedness and dressed, conscious of her eyes on him.

"You got a few scars on you, Ike," she observed.

"More than my share, I reckon," he replied. "Got a few in Vietnam. Rest of them came from my days as a Rebel, following Ben."

"This really the first time you've been unfaithful to your wife?"

"Yep. Not countin' the mental times."

She laughed. "I can relate to that." She rose from the pallet on the floor, totally unashamed of her young lush nakedness. "Your wife been faithful to you, you think?"

"I think so," Ike said thoughtfully. "But I'll tell her about us. Even though I don't have to. She'd guess. She knows me pretty well."

Nina shook her head. "What is it with you people who follow General Raines? You're so . . . well, I guess, *dedicated* is the word. And Ben Raines . . . is he really a god like I've heard a lot of people say he is?"

"The Rebels?" Ike shrugged. "We're just kinda like that ol' boll weevil, I reckon. Lookin' for a home. Ben a god?" Again he shrugged. "I don't know. Sometimes," his reply was very soft, "sometimes I believe he really is. Others?" Ike shook his head. "How old are you, Nina?"

"I . . . I think I'm twenty-one, Ike. But I really don't know for sure. I was either seven or eight years old when the bombs came."

And I was in my mid-thirties, Ike thought. And already fought a war this girl has no memories of. "You get dressed," he told her, picking up his M-16. "I'm gonna check out the area."

"Ike?"

He turned.

"I'm very glad it was you who come along last night."

Ike grinned. "You did some of that yourself, Nina.

125

Last night."

She laughed. "Get outta here!"

Ike stepped out of the old house, using the creaking back steps. The mountains of north Georgia loomed all around him, the area thick with brush, having grown wild and unattended for more than a decade. It was a peaceful dawning, the birds singing and calling to one another, the calling a sound of joy, of being alive on this cool early fall morning in the mountains. And, Ike thought, shivering, winter is just around the corner.

"Got to find some clothing for the both of us," he muttered. "Damn feed sack would be better than that stinking robe."

Nina stepped out on the back porch, a can of C-rations in one hand, a spoon in the other hand. Ike looked at the contents of the can and shuddered.

"I just never *did* develop a taste for that crap," he said.

"I wish I had a real cup of coffee," Nina said wistfully. "And some bacon and eggs and toast. And some jelly."

"Smucker's?" Ike asked with a grin. He backed away from the odor of the eggs.

Nina cocked her head to one side. "I don't know what that means."

"Yeah? Well . . . it used to be a brand of jams and jellies."

"Smucker's? With a name like that, it had to be good, I betcha."

Ike laughed as the young woman pegged the company's old slogan right on the button. In the brightening morning, standing in God's light, Ike could see the young woman was really quite lovely. "Yes, that's true, Nina." He cleared his throat. Shook his head as he thought of all the things this young lady had missed out on: the fun of college, the Saturday afternoon games, the dances; the joy of living in the most affluent and powerful nation in the world; daily breakthroughs in medicine; fine perfumes and designer jeans. God! the list was almost endless.

Now she had only a world gone savage to look forward to.

Maybe he could help ease that transition.

"Let's get our gear together, Nina. We've got a long way to go."

"I'm with you, Ike."

James reported to Ben. The big sergeant had a disgusted look on his broad face. "These people want us to stay and protect them, General."

"What did you tell them, James?"

"I told them to forget it, sir."

"Good. Get the people ready to pull out." He looked at his watch. "Fifteen minutes, James."

"But you *can't* leave us!" a woman's voice came from behind the men. "You're our president. You have to protect us."

Ben turned to face the source of the complaint. The woman was in her late twenties, Ben guessed. Nice looking, a pixie with a dirty face, and a misguided view of reality.

"I am not your president," Ben informed her. "And I don't owe any of you a damned thing. You owe it to yourselves to learn weapons and how to protect yourselves."

"But that is against our religious beliefs!"

"Then I would say you people definitely have a problem."

Tears cut twin paths down the woman's grimy cheeks. "Do you have any idea what those animals did to us? No—how could you? They were filthy and perverted and evil and godless. And if you leave, they'll return. And this time, they'll kill us after they . . . use us as vessels of their depravity."

"Get a gun," Ben told her. "The first one who shows his head in this town, shoot him."

"We can't do that!" she screamed.

"Won't," Ben contradicted her. "How did you avoid being shipped out with the other younger women?"

She wiped her eyes. "I'm a nurse. They—those animals—had some medical problems. That's how. You can't just drive off and leave us here, defenseless."

"I am sorry to inform you, miss, but that is precisely what we intend doing. If you would like for us to show you weapons and how to use them, we'll stay and do that. The choice is yours."

The woman's eyes glowed with hate. "You're just as cruel and heartless as Silver's men. I hope Silver's people get you."

"They won't," Ben told her.

"You can't know that for a fact."

"Yeah, lady, I can. We're just something you people will never be."

"Oh? And what is that?"

"Survivors, ma'am."

"But we have a *right* to our religious beliefs!" she

128

shouted at Ben. "A God-given right."

"That is probably true," Ben agreed. "But you do not have the right to expect others to die for your lopsided beliefs."

"God will strike you dead, General Raines."

"Perhaps," Ben replied solemnly. "But I rather think God likes His warriors. 'Cause He damn sure made a lot of us."

"That's *blasphemy!*" the woman yelled at him.

The crowd of men and women began yelling threats at Ben, shaking their fists at him, calling him Judas.

Ben laughed at them and walked away, to his pickup, Gale by his side.

"You're a hard man, Ben," she said.

"Hard times, kid," Ben replied.

TWENTY-THREE

Tony's convoy met the men from Dublin on the interstate, one group heading west, the remains of Tony's Dublin contingent heading east as fast as they could go. The lead vehicle of Tony's group flagged them down.

Tony stood in the middle of the interstate, growing angry as the men tried to explain what had happened.

"What the fuck do you mean?" Tony shouted. "You mean you guys just cut and run out? What the hell does Raines have, trained tigers with him?"

"Uh, that's about the size of it, Tony," the leader of the Dublin contingent said. "Them Rebels is all trained better than us. They got them military weapons and they know how to use them."

Tony fought his temper under control. "Awright, awright," he finally said, clenching and unclenching his big hands. "Jesus, I don't wanna hear no more of your excuses. How many troops does Raines have with him?"

There was a lot of shuffling of feet and eyes that would not meet Tony's hard eyes. "Uh . . . 'bout forty, boss."

"*Forty*!" Tony screamed. "Forty fucking guys

caused you people to turn tail and run?"

"Uh . . . they wasn't all guys," a man said, making matters much worse. "There was some cunts with 'em, too."

"Cunts! Pussies?" Tony sputtered. "You mean to stand there and tell me you tough guys ran from a bunch of *broads*?"

"Jesus, Tony. These broads had guns!"

"I don't care if they had pussies that fired torpedoes!" Tony screamed, jumping up and down in the center of the highway. "A broad is a broad. *Shit!* Goddamnit. What is this gonna do to my image, you crapheads?" He once more fought his temper, finally winning. "Well . . . come on, then, damnit. Let's go find this Ben Raines. I'll show you guys how to kick the ass off him."

Several of his people looked dubious at that last remark from Tony. But for the time being they were more afraid of Tony than of Ben Raines.

A condition that would not prevail much longer.

TWENTY-FOUR

Ike worked on the old pickup all morning. Finally he threw the wrench aside in disgust. "No good, Nina. I can't fix it. Been settin' here just too damn long."

"So what do we do, Ike?"

"Shank's Mare," he told her with a quick grin.

"What?"

"We hoof it."

"Oh, goody. Ike? When it warms up some, let's find a stream and take a bath. I feel like I got bugs crawling around on me. I itch."

"After wearin' that damn stinkin' robe, I *know* I got fleas hoppin' around on me. Probably gave 'em to you. You got any soap?"

"Yeah. Found some bars in that old house."

"You ready to go?"

"Too windy to stack BBs," she said with a smile.

"Ain't heard that one in years. Let's go, little one."

TWENTY-FIVE

In his comfortable new quarters in northern California, General Striganov smiled at Colonel Fechnor. "So a cheap hoodlum is going to challenge General Raines, *da*?"

"That is what our intelligence reports, General, And this Captain Willette is somehow involved with some religious group called the Ninth Order. They are rather barbaric, according to the reports we have received."

"Aren't *all* religious orders barbaric to some degree, old friend?" Striganov said with a smile. "Well, I wish Mr. Silver all the luck in the world." He dismissed Tony's chances of doing any real damage to Ben Raines with a curt slash of his hand. "Tell me some good news about our breeding program, Colonel. I need some cheering news."

"Everything is progressing quite well, General. We did lose a number of women due to General Raines' raids on our breeding farms in Iowa. But we picked up more than we lost on the way west. Those women who have birthed, and those mutant females who birthed are doing quite well. And, even more good news, the offspring appear to have much more intelligence than we first hoped."

"Good, good!" General Striganov rubbed his hands together and smiled. "That is good news indeed. We are standing on the brink of a marvelous new day for the world, Fechnor. Our doctors have solved the problem of workers for the menial tasks any civilization faces. Thus freeing the masses for positions befitting their natural abilities. I gather, since nothing to indicate it has passed my desk, your people have not met with much resistance from the minorities?"

"Very little, sir. We crushed the initial thrust upon arrival. It was as you predicted, sir. Many of those with a pure Aryan background stood back and did not interfere."

"But, of course, they did. It's been that way since the beginnings of time. All one has to do is study history. Equality cannot be forced upon a race. It must be earned. Just as respect must be earned, all in accordance with the existing mores of the ruling society. Only stupid people think otherwise." He leaned back in his chair. "So much for that. I have been reluctant to view the . . . newborn for fear I would see monsters. How do the babies look?"

"Some of those crossbred look . . . well, rather hideous, General. But most appear normal, as normal as can be expected, that is, when one takes into consideration each baby has either a father or mother who is a mutant. We've had to destroy several, because of, ah, certain physical abnormalities. But a full ninety percent of the children—and it's incorrect to call them children because of the rapid growth patterns—are coming along splendidly."

"Good, good, Colonel Fechnor. Now, the people in the regions we've claimed as our own—discounting the minorities, of course—how are they responding to our overtures?"

"Very well, sir. We have encountered surprisingly little armed resistance. Many of the people appear to welcome our presence. Most were in rather sad shape."

General Striganov nodded his head. He seemed to be paying only polite attention to his second in command. He seemed preoccupied with another matter. "Smoothly, then," the general said. "Everything is progressing quite smoothly and orderly. Is that how you would sum it up?"

"Yes, sir."

Fechnor had been standing. He was waved to a chair. Tea was brought in by an aide. Both men sipped in silence for a moment, enjoying the fragrance of the tea. Striganov's eyes touched Fechnor.

"You do realize, Colonel Fechnor, that I greatly admire General Ben Raines?"

The colonel shook his head. "No, sir. I did not know that, General."

"Oh, it's true. I won't deny it. What we must use force and lies and half-truths to accomplish, General Raines gains through trust and respect. Not that I have any intention of imitating any of Ben Raines' tactics, mind you," he added quickly. "I still feel our way is the most productive to our system of government. But Ben Raines worries me. He is going to be a constant thorn in our side. I wish the man would listen to reason. I wish he would understand that our respective forms of government could exist side by

135

side." The general shook his handsome head. "Wishful thinking on my part, I suppose."

"Our intelligence reports that Ben Raines is making no moves toward us, General."

"He will," Striganov said softly. "He will, old friend. Bet on it."

TWENTY-SIX

"A large force of heavily armed men moving toward the column, General," the forward Scout radioed to Ben.

"How many?" Ben asked.

"A hundred, at least. Looks like some of those we just kicked out of Dublin." She took a closer look. "Yes, sir. It's part of the same bunch, all right. But beefed up."

"OK, Susie. Lay low until you receive further instructions."

"Ten-four, sir. We'll keep our heads down until I see those ol' boys retreating with their peckers hangin' low."

Gale looked at the radio in the truck. She shook her head. "Jesus. Susie certainly has a way with words, doesn't she?"

Ben grinned. "Susie's a good ol' Southern gal." He keyed his mic. "All right, gang—you all heard her. Set up ambush positions. Let's do it right the first time."

"A good ol' gal?" Gale questioned. "What a dubious compliment."

Ben laughed at her.

The short column pulled off the interstate at the

first exit. It was no trick for them to hide their vehicles in the thick timber and brush that had grown wild and unattended along most of the nation's highways for years. Ben did not worry about airborne spotters. As far as Ben knew, his Rebels and the troops of the IPF* were the only organized forces that still utilized any type of aircraft.

"Here they come," a Rebel said, looking through binoculars. "Cars, not trucks. Long line of them. Three to four men per car. Hard-lookin' crew. Lots of guns."

"OK," Ben said. "Let's make sure we're about to waste the right bunch. Where's the volunteer?"

"Here, sir." A young woman stepped forward. She had changed into jeans and civilian windbreaker. She carried a knapsack.

"Jane?" Ben asked. "You're sure about this, now?"

"Yes, sir."

"OK. Get into position, and be ready to act very quickly. That ditch is deep; it'll give you good protection." He keyed the talk switch on his walkie-talkie. "All right, people. Get ready to blow them to hell if they make any funky moves toward Jane. One mistake on our part means Jane gets shot up. Let's don't let that happen."

Jane took her position on the shoulder of the interstate.

Tony's lead vehicle rounded the curve in the interstate. "Goddamn, Pete," the driver said. "Look at that cunt up there."

"Yeah, I see her. Looks pretty good from here."

*Anarchy in the Ashes

"Pretty good? Man, you need glasses. That's prime gash."

The man on the passenger side radioed Tony, who was in the center of the column.

"Stop here," Tony ordered his driver. "It could be a trap." He radioed to the lead cars. "Rest of you guys go on up there and check it out."

A half dozen cars approached the lone woman standing by the side of the interstate. The lead car stopped, the others grinding to a halt behind him. The driver rolled down the window and stuck his head out. "Hello, sweet thing. You waitin' for a bus, maybe?"

"Could be," Jane replied. She smiled. The windbreaker was draped over her right hand and forearm, hiding the cocked .45 semi-automatic pistol in her hand. Her finger was on the trigger.

"Well, now, ain't you the lucky one, though. No point in you standin' out there, baby. Why don't you just hop your pretty ass in here with us. We'll take you to the nearest bus station. We might decide to have some fun along the way."

"I think I'll just wait for the Trailways, if you don't mind," Jane told him. "One should be along any time."

"Honey, there ain't been no buses on this road for a long time. Now get your ass in here like I tol' you."

Jane offered no reply. She stood alone on the windswept shoulder of the road, matching the man look for look.

The driver's features hardened. "I said, baby, get your ass in here and get ready for a good fuckin'. I'm gettin' a bone just lookin' at you."

"And if I don't?" Jane asked. Her smile had turned grim. Before joining Raines' Rebels, Jane had been taken captive by a group of men and sexually abused. She had been left for dead by the side of the road. She had no patience or mercy for rapists.

The driver could not know it, but he was gazing into the pretty face of death.

The driver laughed and got out of the car. He unzipped his pants and pulled out his thickening penis. "Don't that look good to you, baby? Now why don't you just come to Daddy and grab hold my tool? You can skin it back and get it up real hard for the both of us."

"No thanks," Jane said. "Fucking animals has never been my thing. And you look like a cross between an ape and a pig."

The men still in the cars laughed at that.

The man with his cock hanging out of his jeans flushed with anger. "You gonna know some pain for that smart-mouth crack, girlie." He stepped toward her.

Jane slid back her windbreaker and shot the man in the groin. The heavy .45-caliber slug, from a very close range, separated penis from man. The slug tore through the man's lower belly, slamming him to the ground. Jane lifted the .45 and emptied it into the car, the booming of the pistol not masking the man with the missing pecker's howling as he rolled and began the dying process on the shoulder of the interstate.

Jane leaped for the ditch just as automatic weapons fire cracked and roared and lanced death from both sides of the interstate. The slugs turned the lead vehicles into death traps. Glass splintered and metal howled as slugs whined and sparked and tore through flesh and bone.

A quarter of a mile back, Tony Silver yelled his commands. "Get outta here! It's a fuckin' ambush."

Tony's boast that he'd show his men how to kick the ass off Ben Raines blew into the air like the thin emptiness it was as the cars squalled around and retreated down the interstate. Two miles down the road, they were forced to run the gauntlet of Susie and the other Scouts as they pot-shot from the brush along the roadway.

"Jesus fucking Christ!" Tony yelled. He was crouched on the floorboards, trembling in fear and rage—the rage directed at himself for showing his fear in front of his men. But he did not need to worry about that; his men were more frightened than him. One had shit his pants and one had pissed his pants. Glass showered Tony as slugs slammed the car. Blood splattered him as one of his men took a round through the head and fell forward, his blood and brains and fluid leaking onto the front seat and dripping onto Tony in a red river.

"Floorboard this mother!" Tony squalled. "Get me the hell outta here!"

"Finish it," Ben told his people. "Take a few of the men alive for questioning—if you can find any alive. Get as much information from them as possible then shoot them."

"My pleasure," Jane said.

TWENTY-SEVEN

"I sure would like to find some wheels," Ike said. "I have never been a fan of hikin'. Swimmin', yeah—walkin', no, thank you, ma'am."

"You said you were a Shark?"

Ike laughed. "No, Nina! Not a shark, a SEAL. Navy. Means sea, air and land. Back in my day we were the bad boys of the Navy—so called, that is."

"How come, Ike?"

"Oh," he replied with typical modesty. "I guess 'cause our trainin' was so rough and the dirty jobs that was always handed to us."

"You mean you guys wouldn't run from anything?"

Ike again laughed. "Only a fool won't haul his ass out of some situations, little one. Hell, yes, I ran at times. Run like a thief in the night."

"But I bet you won medals for being brave," she said.

"I won a few. Some I guess maybe I deserved, others I didn't. Ever'body that sees combat oughta win medals." Ike stepped on a rock in the old road. "*Ouch!* Shit! Goddamn walkin'!"

Nina laughed at him. "Getting old, Ike?"

Ike's grin was rueful as it transformed his face, the

years fading away with the smile. "You bet, I am, Nina. I'm pushin' hard at the half century mark."

"No! I don't believe that."

"It's true, kid." Except for the gray in his close-cropped hair, Ike looked about thirty-five. "I don't feel it, but it's true."

They walked down the center of the highway.

"You got any kids, Ike?"

Ike was flung back in time. Back to the original Tri-States, and to Megan, his first wife. "Yeah, but I lost 'em in the battle for Tri-States. Me and Sally adopted a whole brood later on."

"You and Sally been married long?"

"Not long. I lost my first wife, Megan, in the big battle for Tri-States. Me and Sally got hooked up a couple years ago."

"You love her, Ike?"

"I like her," he replied, and Nina knew the subject was closed.

"Was you and General Raines in the SEALs together?"

"No, Ben was a Hell Hound." He saw the confused look on her face. "The Hell Hounds was the closest thing the U.S. ever had to a full-fledged mercenary unit. Mean bunch of cutthroats. I did a year with 'em, but that was long after Ben was wounded and got out. He was probably over in Africa at that time, fightin' with the five or six Commandoes. I don't know. We don't talk much about those days anymore. Brings back too many bad memories; too many good men died over there, Nina. The war got all turned around in the minds of people back home. Hell with it."

And the subject was closed.

The faint sounds of engines reached them. Ike grabbed Nina's arm and jerked her off the road. They climbed up the embankment and hid in the thick timber and brush. The engine noise grew louder.

The first truck came into view. "It's them!" Nina hissed. "The Ninth Order. That's the bunch that's been chasing me ever since I got away from them. I recognize the pickup. That's the one Sister Voleta always rides in."

Ike slipped the M-16 off safety and onto full auto as the drag vehicle came into view. "Two of them," he muttered.

"There will be two men in the back of each truck," Nina said. "Sister Voleta's personal guards. And they know what they're doing."

"That bunch over where they had me captive damn sure didn't know much," Ike countered. "Matter of fact, they were a bunch of amateurs."

Just as Ike was raising the M-16, two more trucks appeared from the opposite direction. A woman got out of the lead pickup to stand in the road.

The other cars and trucks stopped, their passengers getting out. A dozen men and women now lined the road, with guards facing in all directions, armed with M-16s.

"Shit!" Ike whispered. "I could take 'em, but they might take us, too. Can't risk it. They're too spread out."

"I agree," Nina returned the whisper. She clutched at his arm and Ike could feel the fear in the woman transmitting to him at her touch.

"Take it easy, kid," Ike said. "We're gonna make it."

"Promise?"

"You betcha." He looked at the robed woman. "I know that woman."

"That's Sister Voleta. She's head of the Ninth Order. She is evil and perverted and crazy to boot."

"Sounds like ya'll real fond of one another."

"I'd like to jam this .38 up her butt and pull the trigger."

"Listen."

"Captain Willette is not performing up to his capabilities," Sister Voleta said, her voice reaching Ike and Nina. "And those fools at the warehouse deserved what they received for allowing Colonel McGowen to escape. That fat worshipper of a false god is not to leave these mountains."

Ike's face reddened with anger and Nina had to stifle a giggle at his expression.

Sister Voleta said, "We have over five hundred people, with that many more coming in, some with tracking dogs to search for that lard ass."

Ike gripped his M-16 so hard his knuckles turned white from the strain.

Despite the seriousness of the situation—they were only about fifty feet from the roadbed—Nina almost groaned suppressing a giggle at the expression on Ike's face. Sister Voleta, Nina thought, didn't know Ike very well at all. True, the ex-SEAL was built like a fireplug, but he was muscular, not at all fat.

Ike stuck out his tongue at Sister Voleta. He muttered, "I'm gonna shoot your ass off, bitch! And enjoy doing it."

"Tell our people within the ranks of Ben Raines' Rebels to step up their activities," Sister Voleta gave the command. She did not elaborate as to what those "activities" might be. "Already, many of the younger Rebels are swaying toward our side—even if they don't yet realize it. But, for now, recapture McGowen. He is sure to head either south or east. If so, he is ours."

The group split up, returning to their vehicles. The guards were the last to go, backing up all the way, weapons at the ready. Ike agreed with Nina: They knew what they were doing. In a moment, the road was clear, the sounds of engines fading into the distance.

Nina's fingers clutched at Ike's forearm. "What are we going to do, Ike?" There was panic in her voice. "We can't fool *dogs*!"

"Easy, kid. We can fool the dogs if we don't run into them." He smiled at her. "So we're headin' straight north. I'm bettin' they'll expect us to cut 'cross country, but we ain't. We're gonna backtrack on this road 'bout fifteen miles." He dug in his pocket and pulled out an old map of the Chattahoochee National Forest. "See this park road? We cut northeast on it and it'll lead up to Highway 76. Don't you worry, little one. We'll make it. And we might just raise a little hell of our own along the way."

"We're due to raise a little hell of our own," she replied. "Bastards been after me for what seems like forever."

"Can you use a rifle?"

"I damn sure can. You're looking at a girl who can

do most anything."

Ike laughed. "I believe it, Nina. Well, then, we'll just have to find you a rifle."

"One of those flat-shooting .270s, if you can. I like that rifle."

He glanced at her, amusement in his eyes. "Damned if you don't talk a good battle."

"I do more than talk, buddy. Believe it."

"Do we chase them, General?" Ben was asked.

"No. Let them go. No telling how many men he's got as backup. We could be heading into more trouble than we could handle." He looked at his map. The column was just a few miles away from the intersection of Georgia Highway 121. "We'll cut due north here," Ben said, thumping the map. "We want to give this old nuclear plant a wide berth. Here." He pointed out the location. "It experienced a meltdown back in '88. Still might be hot around there. We'll stay with 121 to this point, then cut northwest, come up under Fort Gordon. We'll see if we can salvage something there. Although I imagine it's been picked clean by now."

"What's a meltdown, General?" one of the younger Rebels asked.

Ben smiled sadly. So young, he thought. He was maybe ten years old when the balloon went up back in '88. Since that point in the earth's future, nuclear energy had become a thing of the past.

Ben explained, using layman's language, what a meltdown was.

He looked at the young faces around him. They

147

don't understand, he thought. Even the best educated among them have such a deficiency in the sciences and math.

That simply must not be allowed to continue. For the sake of the future generations, it must not continue.

Yet another problem to face.

Ben sighed. "OK, gang. Finish up with those punks left alive and let's roll it."

TWENTY-EIGHT

They were the younger of the Rebels and the ones with the least education. They had no idea they were being duped and manipulated by Willette and Carter and Bennett. What the three men and those with them said seemed to make sense. If you thought about it. It just wasn't right for the general to go off like he'd done. And yes, even though they didn't like to think about it, they reckoned that gods get old just like everybody else. Kind of. How old was General Raines, anyway?

Nobody seemed to know.

Most just shrugged the question off, saying he was ageless.

Ageless? What did that mean? Most of the younger Rebels had been no more than six or seven years old when the bombs came, back in '88. Most could barely read and write. Some could do neither. And they had no desire to learn. It was just too much of a bother. Too time-consuming. Who needs it?

Ignorance is the father and mother of superstition, the breeder of far-fetched legends, the sperm of ghostly tales, the lover and creator of myth. And these new, young Rebels were prime candidates.

Ageless. Whatever that meant. So . . . it figured

that Ben Raines must be tired.

But they were convinced that all this, all this talking, all this planning, all this was for General Raines' welfare.

But who would be in charge while General Raines was resting? Not Cecil. He was kind of like General Raines . . . in a way. Ike? Naw. Ike was a fighter, not a decision-maker. Then . . . who?

Captain Willette was pretty smart, and an easygoing kind of guy. Up on all sorts of things. Read big books all the time.

Yeah. Captain Willette could handle the job.

"You're in a good mood, Ben," Gale observed. "Cecil must have had some good news."

The column was rolling toward Millen. And Ben always felt good when traveling, seeing new country. He had just spoken with Cecil. "Yes, in a manner of speaking. Gray's Scouts reported a lot of activity in the mountains. Near the area where a big fire and a lot of shooting took place. The searchers are bringing in bloodhounds." He smiled. "Ike got away from them."

Gale shook her head. "Poor Ike. Chased like an animal. I feel so sorry for him. And why did you just grin?"

Ben laughed, and she could not understand the laughter.

"I fail to see the humor in the situation, Ben." There was indignation in her tone.

"You don't understand, Gale. Don't feel sorry for Ike—feel sorry for the people who are chasing him."

"You're right, Ben. I am confused. Ike's being hunted and you sound like you're happy about that."

"Ike is the hunter, Gale. Ike is a master at survival. He knows more dirty tricks than I do. He'll turn those woods into a death trap for those chasing him."

"Jesus, Ben. You act like you'd like to change places with him."

Ben grinned. "Ike's probably found him a woman by now. Might be interesting, all right."

"Very funny. *Would* you like to be up there, Ben?"

"Yes. I think it would be fun."

"*Fun*! Raines, you have the damnedest idea of fun I have ever encountered. Fun?"

"Warriors are seldom understood, Gale. But they are—or were—much maligned. Warriors are not only molded, Gale, they have to be born with that streak within them. Either one has it, or one does not."

"Fun, huh? Well, I hope Ike is having . . . fun."

TWENTY-NINE

Ike and Nina had rummaged through an abandoned old home and found a trunk the rats had not chewed through. The large trunk contained old clothing from members of the whole family. Ike and Nina had found clothing that fit them. They had taken a very quick bath in the icy waters of a rushing mountain stream.

Then they lay wrapped in a quilt from the old home, locked in love-making. Both knew it was a very foolish thing to do, surrounded as they were by danger. But that knowledge only made the love act that much more spicy.

Later they lay by the stream, listening to it gurgle and bubble and race past them, a happy sound to its passage.

"Ike? You really think we're going to get out of this mess with our skins on, don't you?"

"You just watch ol' Ike go into action, Nina. I'm a mean motor scooter when I get my dander up."

She giggled at him. "Well . . . you may get your dander up, Ike, but that's about all you're gonna get up at the moment."

Ike thought about that for a second. He took her tanned hand and placed it on his penis. "Famous last words, darlin'."

She felt him thicken under her fingertips. "Why, you old goat!"

Midmorning of the next day found Ben and his contingent of Rebels prowling through the rubble of what had once been Fort Gordon. The post had been picked clean of anything that might be of use to anyone. Litter covered the broken streets; tin cans rolled unchallenged in the buildings as the breeze, coming through the broken windows, pushed the cans along, bouncing them off walls.

"There's nothing here," Ben said. "Let's roll it. We can be in Lincolnton by early afternoon."

Not wanting to take a chance on the big bridge over the Clark Hill Reservoir being out, the column headed west until reaching Thomson. There they connected with Highway 78 and followed that to the junction of 378 and 47, cutting east to Lincolnton.

Captain Rayle answered Ben's radio call. "Waiting just west of the first town on Highway 43 South, General. Everything is secure. And we have fresh-caught fish for supper."

"Sounds good to me, Roger. OK. Coming in."

An old-time fish fry was underway when the two contingents of Rebels met. Ben was amused at the name of the town.

"Loco, Captain?"

"We thought you'd get a kick out of it, General. Sure isn't much else amusing about the situation back at the base camp, though."

"Give me a thumbnail briefing, Roger. And don't

spare me a thing."

"Yes, sir. Willette and his men have taken in a lot of the young troops, sir. Several hundred of them, at least. Probably more. General, those young troops are not doing it as any act of defiance toward you. Willette has convinced them that you are tired, you need a rest, that you are becoming senile, that that you are so old no one really knows how old you are. The list is staggeringly long." Rayle sighed. "And a lot of people are buying that garbage."

"I know the young Rebs aren't doing this to harm me, Captain. What concerns me is this: What are the odds of us putting this coup attempt down without spilling a lot of blood?"

Rayle shook his head negatively. "Very slim, sir. It's fast becoming a divided camp. And, sir? Colonel Gray is convinced Willette and his crew are somehow tied in with this Ninth Order business."

"I have entertained that thought more than once myself, Roger. And I believe this Tony Silver is somehow tied up in it."

"I read a slim dossier on that one, General. He's pure evil. The dossier stated that Silver is not only into slavery and murder and forced prostitution, but that he is starting up a pornography business down in north Florida. Mostly kiddy porn and snuff films."

"Among other things," Ben added.

"Yes, sir."

"What's a snuff film?" Gale asked, walking up to the men. She had a huge plate of catfish, piled high with french fries.

"Is that for me?" Ben asked.

"Hell, no. It's for me. Get your own. What am I, your servant?"

"Like I said: eats like a horse."

Gale ignored that. She bit into a piece of crisp-fried fish, then fanned her mouth as she made little oohhhing sounds.

"Hot?" Ben asked innocently.

She nodded her head vigorously.

"Watch the bones," Roger cautioned.

"Nothing deters her from food," Ben said, smiling at Gale's antics with a mouthful of steaming hot fish. "She'll kill for a hamburger."

Gale swallowed the fish and took a long drink of water. She sighed and wiped her eyes. "I repeat: What is a snuff film?"

Roger looked at Ben, clearly dubious about telling her. "Tell her," Ben said. "She asked."

"Just at the moment of climax," Roger said, avoiding Gale's eyes. "One of the performers kills the other."

Gale looked at the plate of food, looked at Ben, and grimaced. "You might have had the decency to warn me, Ben."

"You asked."

She handed him her plate of food. "Here, you eat it. Probably did it just to get my food. Be like you." Before she walked away, she grabbed a large piece of catfish from the plate. She walked away, munching and fanning at her mouth.

"They using kids in the snuff films, Roger? And who is buying the goddamn things? And with what?"

"They're not using too many kids, way I hear it.

Mostly women in their mid-twenties to mid-thirties. As far as buying them, sir, it's not so much buying as it is bartering for territory and guns and slaves. Silver is using slave labor on his farms and small factories."

"Blacks?"

"All races, sir. If a woman gives him much trouble in prostitution, Silver whips her into submission. And charges admission for people to see the beating. He sounds like a real nice fellow."

"It's difficult for me to believe this Sister Voleta would be involved with a punk like Tony Silver."

"She's as twisted in her own way as Silver. Sexually bent all out of shape. That young kid, Claudia, told Doctor Chase Sister Voleta gets her jollies from watching people tortured—the torture, more often than not, has sexual overtones. I thought the world was bad, General, but nothing like this."

"Those types have been around for as long as we've stood upright, Roger. They began crawling out of holes in the ground, so to speak, back in the sixties, when the nation's courts became liberal. Liberal means permissive, and that's exactly what happened."

"You wanna know something, General?" Roger asked, an embarrassed look on his face.

Ben smiled. "You weren't even born then, right?"

Roger's smile met Ben's. "Yes, sir."

THIRTY

"Stay in the water, Nina," Ike warned her. "I know it's uncomfortable as hell, but it'll help throw the dogs off our scent."

"It's cold!" Nina responded. "Jesus Christ! My toes are frozen."

"Better numb than having the dogs chew them off," Ike reminded her. "Along with other parts of your anatomy."

"Thanks, Ike," Nina said, slopping along behind him in the center of the stream. "You're a real comfort to me."

Ike grinned. Nina was one hell of a spunky kid. No, he thought, not a kid. A grown woman. And he knew he was getting very much attached to her. He wasn't sure if that was good or bad. But he couldn't help his feelings.

They both heard the baying of the dogs, far in the distance. The baying changed as the animals picked up their scent.

Ike stopped in the center of the stream. He put an arm around Nina's shoulders. "And the chase is on, kid."

"I'm scared, Ike."

"Well, honey, you'd be a prime idiot if you weren't scared."

"You're not scared."

"No," Ike admitted. "Scared isn't the right word. I'm . . . concerned. But you gotta understand something: I went through this many times in 'Nam, workin' behind the lines up in the North. Believe me, I'd rather have those dogs after us than Charlie."

"Charlie? Who the hell is Charlie?" Nina asked, as they began once more wading up the stream.

Ike looked back at her. That war, he thought, isn't even a part of her memory. She wasn't even born when that misfought, misunderstood conflict came to its disgraceful conclusion. So long ago. "The Viet Cong, baby. The bad guys."

"I've heard some about that war. I think."

"Well, now," a man's voice rang out from the bank above them and to their right. "You two just hold it right where you is,"

Ike and Nina stopped, both looking up. They looked into the muzzle of a shotgun, pointed at them. The man stood flanked by other men, all carrying weapons. One of the men looked at Nina and licked his lips. "Ain't that a fine-lookin' piece of ass, boys?"

THIRTY-ONE

"My friends and fellow worshippers of the great god, Blomm, the ever-knowing and all-seeing Blomm. I have spoken with our supreme ruler. Blomm has instructed me to join with another of his disciples to the north, Sister Voleta and the Ninth Order. Now, we will not have to leave our fine and comfortable homes to do this. All I had to do was pledge our allegiance to Sister Voleta." What Emil did not tell his followers was that some brutish types from the Ninth Order paid him a visit late one night. They told him if he didn't cooperate, they would cut his pecker off and stick it in his ear. Emil had almost peed his BVDs at that.

The idea of Blomm had come to Emil one evening while he was blissfully toking and getting off on some really fine weed. The more he toked, the wilder his flights of imagination soared. And Blomm's conception became reality in Emil's drug-soaked brain. He would tell his people that Blomm had just recently left God's side, after growing weary of God's restrictive type of living. Blomm said it was OK to still worship God, but with a few twists added to spice it all up. Kinda like adding three inches to your dick, Emil thought. He giggled at that. Had his way, he'd add six.

It would be OK to fuck and all that good shit, according to Blomm. Do some dope, of course that was OK. As a matter of fact, how about *anything* goes? Yeah. Why not? Blomm was an all right dude. The more Emil toked, the more all right Blomm became. And so, by the time Emil had finished with his King Edward-sized joint, Blomm was no longer a figment of his rather weird and overactive imagination. Blomm was *real*, man! And what a heavy dude, too.

"And so, my friends and followers," Emil said, looking over his ever-growing flock of nuts and bolts, "let us have a love feast in honor of our new friends to the north." Savage motherfuckers, Emil thought. He stepped forward, his foot catching in the hem of his robe, and Emil fell off the raised platform, hitting the dirt, on his face.

"Son of a bitch!" Emil muttered. He was helped to his feet by a throng of concerned worshippers, the dust brushed off his ornate robe. Emil smiled and said, "*Pax vobiscum.* Be bop a lula and shake rattle and roll, too."

His followers smiled and beamed at him. Whatever Emil said was perfectly all right. Etch the words in your heart, man. Gods were supposed to behave a little strangely.

Emil made the sign of the cross. "Bless you all, my children. Joan Baez to you—and Boy George, too."

Emil walked away, toward his beautiful new home, compliments of the Rebels. They moved out, Emil moved in.

"Blomm!" a woman shouted. "All praise the wonderful Blomm!"

"And me!" Emil shouted. "Goddamnit, don't forget me."

"And Father Emil!" the crowd roared.

"Fuckin' bunch of loonies," Emil muttered. But not loud enough for any of his people to overhear. Didn't want to screw up a good scam.

He shuffled toward his fine new home, kept spotless by his followers. Emil never lifted a finger to do anything. Make matters worse, he was getting fat. He tried to be dignified as he shuffled along. Whoever made his robes was going to have to tighten up their act, Emil thought. Goddamn things were too long.

Emil entered the coolness of his home, tripped over the hem of his robe, and fell down on the floor.

"Emil Hite's joining the Ninth Order does not concern me," Ben told Captain Rayle, after being informed of the merger. "Emil just has a non-violent scam going for him. He's laughable in a Jim Jones kind of way. Emil and his cupcakes present no danger. They are more to be pitied than feared. The Ninth Order, on the other hand, is a paramilitary group posing as a serious religious order. They can sucker and con people into the fold, then, I'm sure, use brainwashing tactics to keep them there."

"Yes, sir," Roger said. "We have strong evidence that is how they do it."

"The only thing I am reasonably certain of about this whole confusing business is that General Striganov is not involved with it. Our intelligence reports the Russian is clean on this matter."

"If 'clean' is the right choice of words," James said.

"Yes," Ben replied. He looked toward the north. "Come on, Ike," he muttered. "Hang in there, buddy."

THIRTY-TWO

"Finally caught up with you, eh, pretty pussy?" A man grinned down at Nina. "I seem to recall you got nice, soft titties on you. I'll soon see. We gonna have some fun with you, bitch."

"To claim to be so religious," Nina fired back, "you guys are sure a bunch of scumbags."

"That crack is gonna get you pronged right up the bunghole, baby," he said with a grin. "I can jist hear you hollerin' now."

Any combat-experienced member of any special unit—and all branches of the military had them, when there was a military—knows there is no such thing as a fair fight. Not outside the ring, and even that can be questioned at times. The term "fair fight" is a contradiction in itself. There is a winner and there is a loser. Period. Never give a sucker an even break. One either kills or cripples one's antagonist, or one gets killed or crippled. Was it a fair fight? is a question that surely must have originated from the mouths of lawyers. Shakespeare was right.

While the men's eyes were on Nina, standing proudly and defiantly in the stream, Ike jerked up the muzzle of the M-16 and burned a clip into the three men, standing close together on the bluff of the bank.

Two of them were blown backward. The third one, half his face gone from the so-called "tumbling rounds" of the M-16, fell into the stream, blood and brains coloring the rushing waters.

Changing clips as he ran up the embankment, Ike crested the bluff and inspected the carnage he had wrought. The men were dead or near death.

"Oh. God, help me," one man pushed the words past dying lips.

Ike looked at him. The contempt he felt was evident on his face. "Fuck you, partner."

The man closed his eyes and had the good grace to expire.

Ike called down to Nina. "Help me strip these people down to the hide. We'll put them in the deepest part of the stream and wedge them in tight with rocks. We'll put on their clothing. Shoes, too, if they'll fit. That will further confuse the dogs. Come on, Nina. Let's get crackin'."

Working together and hurriedly, the two of them stripped the clothing from the men before it became too bloodstained. They rolled the bodies off the bank and into the stream, covering them with heavy rocks, wedging them down on the bottom.

The baying of the dogs was getting louder, but Ike knew the bloodhounds—and from their barking, he was afraid they weren't bloodhounds, but Dobermans—were still a couple of miles off.

"Bundle our clothing up and bring it," Ike told her. "We'll sink it in a deep hole further on down. Come on. I'll get the weapons."

Ike tossed one old shotgun into the stream. He kept the second shotgun, a Winchester pump, twelve gauge, chambered for three-inch magnums. He looped the bandoleer of shells around his shoulder and picked up the only rifle among the three men. An old Savage .270. He slung another shell belt over his other shoulder and gave the .270 to Nina.

She inspected the rifle, Ike watching her. She knew what she was doing, Ike concluded.

She checked the four-shot box and grinned. "Full. Other than needing a good cleaning, it's OK, Ike. Now I can do some damage."

"Head out, Nina. Fast a pace as you can maintain comfortably."

"You just watch my stuff."

He grinned.

She caught the double meaning and flipped him the bird.

A mile later, they stopped to catch their breath and Ike wrapped their old clothes around rocks, tied them securely, then sank them up under the lip of the bank, still underwater.

"OK, little one," Ike said. "We stay in the water for another mile or so, then we hit the brush and timber. Once in there, I wanna rig a few surprises for our friends."

"Surprises? What kind of surprises?"

Ike's usually friendly face took on a mean look. "Let's just say they ain't gonna like 'em a whole lot."

Ben and Gale—accompanied by a dozen Rebels laying back a few hundred yards—drove to one of the inlets of Clark Hill Reservoir, on the north side. They walked to the water's edge.

She took his hand. "It's so peaceful here, Ben. So lovely and serene. It's like . . . it's like all the trouble never happened."

"Get careless in this area, Gale, and you'll see trouble quickly."

"Harbinger of doom!" She looked at him. "What do you mean?"

"The peacefulness is nothing but a dangerous illusion."

"Will you cut the suspense, Raines!"

"You notice we haven't seen one human being—other than Rebels—in this area?"

"Yeah. So what?"

"Mutant country, I'm betting. Since I haven't detected any of the foul odor usually associated with them, I'm thinking this may be a group with a higher level of intelligence. That's why they haven't bothered us."

"You mean they're *friendly* mutants. I never heard of such a thing."

"No, not friendly. Cautious. Wary. They've probably seen how heavily armed we all are, and that we never go unarmed. They've had experience with people with guns. They know guns can inflict pain. We're being watched though."

Gale looked around her. "Where? I don't see any mutants."

"They're in the bushes to our left. I saw one just a moment ago, while we were walking down here."

"And you didn't tell me? Thank you so very much, Ben."

"Want to stay for a while and see if you can spot one?"

"Hell, no! Are you nuts? I'll be more than happy to take your word for it. Can we please leave now?"

Ben grinned. "Sure. Come on. We'll head on back."

As they turned to leave, Gale tugging at Ben, a low growl came from the thick timber and brush by the lake.

"Oh, shit!" Gale said.

"Relax. I'm armed, and Roger's got people standing guard right up there by the road. I believe the mutants are telling us to go away, rather than warning of an attack."

"Oh, wonderful. I'm impressed. You speak mutant now, huh?"

Ben playfully ruffled her short dark hair and laughed. "I'm a man of many and varied talents, my dear."

"Great. Ben, I have this fondness for living. So tell me we're not going to spend much time around this place."

"Pulling out in the morning."

"Best news I've heard all day. I wonder if there is any catfish left?" she muttered.

THIRTY-THREE

"We gotta figure a way to get Colonel Gray and his Scouts outta here," Sergeant Bennett said. "I think we got enough Rebels behind us to handle things if Gray and that wild-assed bunch of his can be counted on not to interfere."

"I understand Gray is sending most of his people out into the field," Captain Willette said. "So we don't have to worry about them. But just remember this: When it goes down, it *must* go down nonviolently. At first." He smiled. "At first. That is something Sister Voleta does not understand. Any act of violence on our part—at the outset—would destroy everything we have worked to build. Our new converts would turn on us faster than a striking snake should anyone be hurt—initially. In that, we must all be very careful. We will show weapons, of course, and those opposed to us must be convinced we will use those weapons. But keep violence to a minimum at all times."

"Unless," Lieutenant Carter said, a smile on his lips, "the people could be convinced Ben Raines is their enemy."

"Interesting idea," Willette said, fixing Carter with a steady gaze. "But just how would you go about

168

doing that?"

"Raines pulled out, leaving them leaderless. In the minds of many, even among those loyal to him, he should not have done that. They follow Ben Raines, not Cecil or Ike. I think it's time we got the rumor factory cranked up again. At full steam. Really pour it on hard this time around. A statement from the doctors stating Ben Raines is seriously ill—mentally ill—should start it off very well, I'm thinking. Borderline nuts. Hell, hasn't he done some weird things? Sure he has. Play it up. We can follow that with a rumor that Ben Raines is thinking of breaking up the Rebels; each person will have to go it alone—without Ben Raines. But we'll have to make certain the general doesn't pop back in here unexpectedly and screw it all up."

"I like it," Willette said. "Hell, we have a person with Raines' column. We know where he is. Our people down south—Silver's bunch, along with some of our own—could set up skirmish lines to hold Raines up until we got the job done up here. Yeah. I like it. All right. Let's get to it."

THIRTY-FOUR

"Swing trap," Ike told Nina. She stood quietly, watching the man work. It was obvious Ike had done this many times before. The sharpened stakes he had attached to the limber sapling looked lethal. She said as much.

"You bet they are. It'll catch whoever trips it gut-high. I'll build a half dozen of these. Plus some punji pits. I wish I had some monkey shit for the punji stakes, but they'll do the job without it. Then we'll leave signs we came this way, sucker them in. After they hit two, three of these little darlin's, it'll really slow them down. They'll be afraid to move in the woods." He laughed grimly, a warrior's laugh.

Nina could certainly understand how it would affect their minds. "The dogs worry me, Ike. I'm scared of bad dogs."

Rising to his booted feet, Ike smiled and held out the shotgun. "This is a dog catcher, sweetheart. If they get that close, that is." He secured the piece of rawhide that would trigger the trap. He once more grinned. "Somebody is goin' to be awful unhappy about this. This is one stomach ache there just ain't no cure for."

Ike tore a piece of cloth from his shirt. He jammed

170

the cloth on a dead branch, sticking out chest-high on the old nature trail, actually a centuries-old Indian path. "That ought to do it," he said.

They could hear the dogs far away, circling in confusion, attempting to separate scents. Their baying was frantic and angry, a frustrated yelping. There was a moment of near dead silence, then the baying changed.

"OK, kid," Ike said. "The Baskerville Bastards have picked up the scent. It's time for us to cut out."

"What kind of a dog is a Baskerville?" Nina asked.

Ike shook his head. "Just a joke, kid. Forget it. Let's go. Now the fun begins."

She picked up her rifle and slung the bandoleer of cartridges around one shoulder. "You sure have a funny idea of fun, Ike."

"I've heard that before. OK, baby—wiggle your ass."

She looked at him and grinned. *"Now?"*

THIRTY-FIVE

Tony Silver was wild with rage. His humiliating defeat at the hands of Ben Raines was something he could not get off his mind. And he was taking his rage out on the new young girl, Lilli.

Tony had torn into the young girl savagely, her pitiful screaming only making him that much more angry. She now lay beneath the man, only occasionally moaning, a mewing, pitiful sound as Tony raped her brutally, again and again.

Finally exhausting himself, mentally, physically and sexually, Tony heaved himself off the child. Her blood dotted the white sheet. "You got good gash, baby," he said. "But you need to learn to move your ass. You lay there like a goddamned log."

Tony showered and dressed, stepped outside his room, and walked toward his communications room. "What's the word, baby?" he asked the woman on duty.

"Sister Voleta's people called about ten minutes ago." She grinned nastily. "I told them you were busy."

Tony returned the grin. "Damn right, I was. What's up?"

"They're sending troops down from the north.

You're to mass everybody available and meet them at dawn, day after tomorrow."

"Where?"

"On Highway 24. Louisville. It's something about killing Ben Raines."

Tony flushed for a moment, then regained his composure. "Must be something big in the wind," he muttered.

"That's all they told me, Tony."

Tony met her eyes. He watched as the woman licked her lips. He smiled at her. "Yeah, Patsy, you can play with one of the new girls. Get someone to relieve you and go eat a pussy."

"Thanks, boss."

"Yeah, yeah." Tony dismissed her with a wave of his hand. "Go on now. I'll sit in here until your relief shows up."

She left the cramped and littered radio room and Tony sat down behind the big transmitter. He changed the frequency dial and called his base in north Florida.

"Yeah, boss?"

"Roll two full companies out right now, Johnny," he ordered. "All the ammo they can stagger with. I want 'em up here by noon tomorrow. You got all that?"

"Gotcha, boss. What's up?"

"Killin' Ben Raines."

"Awright!"

Tony cut off the mic and leaned back in the chair. There was a grim smile of satisfaction on his lips. First Ben Raines would be taken care of. After that, Sister Voleta was going to get a bullet up her stupid ass. After Tony shoved a dick up it just to hear her squall. He'd taken just about all the guff he was going to take from that bitch.

At first it had seemed like a good idea, linking up with her. Goddamned ex-whore from Nashville. She'd had some good ideas—at first. Now she was taking all this religious crap too seriously. Christ! The broad actually believed she was some sort of *God*. Perverted bitch. Tony knew all about Sister Voleta. Betty Blackman from northwestern Arkansas. A two-bit hillbilly singer who used her pussy to fuck every record producer and agent in Nashville trying to land a recording contract.

She had never made it. Instead, she turned to running a whorehouse.

Then the bombs came.

No doubt about it, though: Sister Voleta was a persuasive bitch. She began building a following right after the world exploded. Back then she confined her activities to the hills of Tennessee, gradually branching out as word spread. Now she had over two thousand followers. More than Tony, but many of Sister Voleta Betty Blackman's group were yo-yos and fruitcakes.

But still dangerous.

Yeah, she was weird, all right. Tony sent many of the more uncooperative men and women up to Sister Voleta. She got her rocks off torturing them to death. But somehow the positions of the two had changed. Now Voleta thought *she* could give *him* orders. No way Tony was going to put up with that kind of crap for very long. Just no way.

It was too bad in a way, Tony mused, alone in the

silent radio room. The arrangement had been pretty good for several years. Till Voleta started gettin' too big for her panties.

Well . . . all things must come to an end.

First Ben Raines gets his ticket punched. Then Sister Voleta gets sent to that big revival in the sky.

Tony laughed at that. "Pretty good, Tony," he said. "Maybe you should have been a writer."

THIRTY-SIX

"First we take care of Ben Raines," Sister Voleta told her inner circle. "Then Mister Tony Silver gets put out of commission. But I want him taken alive." Her smile was ugly. "I have plans for Tony Silver. He shall amuse us all . . . right to the end."

The robed and hooded inner circle smiled and nodded their approval.

"Get word to our people in the timber. Keep up the harassment of Colonel McGowen and the whore-woman. Leave enough men in the timber to do that. I have given instructions for the bulk of our fighters. Go now. We all have much to do."

"Ike's alive," Cecil's voice crackled through the speakers in the communications vehicle. "Gray's Scouts captured a man from the Ninth Order. They got the information from him. He's in the company of a young woman whose boyfriend was killed by the Ninth Order, at Sister Voleta's orders. He was sexually tortured and then burned alive at the stake. Ike's leading his pursuers on a merry chase, so I'm told."

Ben looked at Gale and smiled hugely. "Told you

Ike would find a woman."

She shook her head. "Man is running for his life and has sex on the brain. I will never, ever understand men."

"Good Lord!" Ben feigned great consternation. "What a sexist remark." He keyed the mic. "I'm about ready to come in, Cec."

There was a short pause on the other end of the transmission. "All right, Ben," Cecil said. "I think maybe you should. I believe it's reached the point where only your presence can defuse the situation up here. But I have to remind you, old friend: You're going to be in a constant state of danger when you return. I can't stress that enough."

"It's that bad, Cec?"

"It could blow at any time, Ben. It's . . . it's just such a helpless feeling up here. We *know* what is going on, but are unable to do a goddamn thing about it."

"I get the feeling maybe I shouldn't have pulled out."

"No." Cecil was adamant on that point. "If you had stayed I think you would have had an accident, Ben. If you know what I mean."

"We covered this before. I know. All right, Cec. See you in two, three days."

THIRTY-SEVEN

They listened to the screaming of the man as he was impaled on the stakes of the swing trap. The hoarse, hideous bellowing echoed through the otherwise silent national park. The man was calling, screaming out for someone, anyone, for God's sake, to help him.

A man ran toward the shrieking and stepped in one of the punji pits concealed along the ancient Indian path. The man's leg snapped at the knee and he fell forward, his scream cut short as waves of pain abruptly plunged him into unconsciousness.

"My, ain't we havin' fun?" Ike said.

"I know I am," Nina said. "Bastards deserve whatever they get."

"You turnin' into a mean bitch, ain't you?" Ike grinned at the young woman.

"I watched some of those same men down there sodomize my boyfriend, Ike. They thought it was very funny. I hope we kill all of them. I really, really do."

"Well, little one, we are damn sure goin' to do our best."

Ike and Nina lay on the bluff of a ridge line, more than a mile from the first line of searchers. The line had stopped. No one wanted to proceed any further. Ike watched them through field glasses.

"Talkin' to somebody on a walkie-talkie," Ike muttered.

"What's up?"

"I wish I knew. Whatever it is, you can bet that bunch is up to no good."

He handed Nina the binoculars. She watched for a moment, then said, "My God, Ike. Those aren't bloodhounds down there."

"No. They're Dobermans. Huntin' dogs, man-killin' sons of bitches. I hate those dogs. Hated them in 'Nam. Unpredictable bastards. I've seen 'em turn on their handlers." He took the field glasses and swept the area below them in a slow circle. "'Bout half of them are pullin' out," Ike said, his tone of voice puzzled. "They may be tryin' to circle us. I don't know. I don't know what's goin' on, but I do know I don't like it. Come on, Nina, let's get the hell outta here."

The men of the Ninth Order who had been in pursuit of Ike and Nina had received hurried instructions from Sister Voleta. Seventy percent of them were to proceed with all haste to eastern Georgia. Tony Silver's paramilitary forces were coming up from the south to join them. Their orders had been quite brief: "Ben Raines has less than a hundred troops with him. Raines and his Rebels must be cut off and held firm. Raines *must not* be allowed to return to his Base Camp. No excuses for failure will be permitted. Just do it."

THIRTY-EIGHT

"It's really true," a young Rebel said. He had tears in his eyes. Many others with him made no effort to hide their concern and tears. "General Raines is suffering from a bad mental disorder." He pointed to the paper he held. "See here. Read it. Says so right on this paper. It was smuggled out of Doctor Chase's office. He and them others have been trying to hide it from us."

Outrage at this blatant deception caused a low rumble from the growing crowd of Rebels. They looked at each other, confusion mixed with anger.

The crowd of mostly young Rebels, male and female, looked at the paper. For all the good it did them. Most could not read further than: See Dick run. See Dick chase Jane. See Jane whomp Dick on head with club.

"This is awful!" a woman said. "Poor General Raines. I feel so sorry for him. But what can we do about it?"

"I guess," the unofficial spokesman said, "whatever Captain Willette tells us to do. We have to see to it that General Raines is helped and protected as best we can."

"But Carter and Bennett both told me—not fifteen

minutes ago—that Colonel Gray and Colonel Jefferys know of General Raines' condition. He said they both refuse to do anything about it."

"That figures," another Rebel said. "Sure. That's 'cause *they* want to run things. They don't wanna see General Raines helped. They *want* him to get worse, maybe even *die*. You all think about it for a minute. Who stands to gain the most from General Raines being out of the picture? If you guess Colonel Ike and Colonels Jefferys and Gray, you damn sure got it right."

The now large group of Rebels, including both young and old, thought it over, talked it over. The group grew to more than five hundred. They came to the conclusion the spokesman was right. It was a damned conspiracy; it was a damned shame and a damned disgrace. And by God they weren't going to sit still for it.

Captain Willette seemingly just "strolled up." Actually he had received a signal from one of his own people within the group of angry Rebels.

"I've taken the situation into my own hands, people," the captain said with a long face. He appeared very concerned. "And I can only hope and pray I have done the right thing. As God Almighty is my witness, I have General Raines' best interest at heart in this."

"We know that, Captain," a World War II vet said. One of the "Grandfathers," as the Russian general, Striganov, had referred to the older men. Just before the "Grandfathers" completely annihilated several companies of Russian troops. "Tell us what we can do to help General Raines."

"Have you all seen the medical report I had stolen out of Chase's HQ?"

They had. It had outraged them all. To think such a thing was being done to Ben Raines. The persons responsible should be shot. They said as much to Willette.

Captain Willette fought to contain his smile of victory. He said, "Doctor Chase is in on this thing, too, people." Willette continued spinning his ever-tangled web of half truths, lies and deceit. "And he'll try to deny it if questioned. So whatever we do must be done quietly and quickly."

All agreed with that.

"What did you mean, Captain: You've taken the situation into your own hands?"

Captain Willette hesitated for a moment. "I'll tell you all in a few hours. For now, the less you know the less the chances of an accidental leak. For now, keep very quiet about what you do know. And be ready to move at a moment's notice. Be careful. Look over there. There's one of Colonel Gray's snoops now. Trying to figure out what we're doing."

"Son of a bitch!" a young woman muttered. "This is like Russia. General Raines would never allow us to be spied on."

"That's right. And that's only one of the reasons we've got to move quickly. We've got to knock those now in power out, and restore Ben Raines' health. And I'll tell you all something else: General Raines' own daughter is one of those plotting against him. And that's disgraceful."

"Tina? No!"

"It's true. She is planning and plotting against her own father."

The Rebels shook their heads. Poor General Raines.

"Stay ready," Willette said. "I'll be in touch. It's going down in a few hours."

THIRTY-NINE

Ben's eyes opened long before the first gray fingers of dawn turned the eastern sky silver. He slipped quietly from the double sleeping bag and dressed in the darkness, his movements as silent as the morning.

He walked through the sleeping camp to the small tent that housed the ever-present urn of coffee and poured a cup of the hot, strong brew. He circled the camp, chatting briefly with each guard, even taking one sentry's place on the line for a moment, allowing the woman to go to the bathroom.

Clearly embarrassed, the woman said, "Sorry about that, General."

Ben laughed softly in the velvet morning and patted her reassuringly on the shoulder.

By nature an early riser, this hour was early even for Ben. He wasn't certain what had jarred him from deep sleep, for he could almost always sleep very soundly. So what had awakened him?

He was aware they were camped in mutant territory, but he didn't believe the mutants would attack a camp this large and well armed. No, the mutants had nothing to do with his awakening.

Then what?

Tony Silver, Captain Willette, Sister Voleta. That's what had pulled him from sleep. Those three were in cahoots, he was certain of it. But what an odd trio. And did he, Ben Raines, represent such a threat to them—*them* being whatever in the hell the three groups personified—they would wage all-out war?

Why?

A supposedly semi-religious order, a hoodlum and a leader of a paramilitary group who had wandered into camp only a few months back.

Odd.

Ben was a hunch player, had been one all his life. Many times his gut reactions and mental warning system had saved his life. And right now, this minute, he had a hunch something was going very badly for someone very close to him.

But who?

Ben walked back to the tent and refilled his coffee mug, his thoughts many and very busy. He was viewing and rejecting ideas every split second, his brain working overtime. He walked to the communications vehicle and started the engine. He turned on the big radio and let it hum for a moment. Base Camp frequency was preset and the scrambler switch was in S position.

Ben called in to home base. No response. He tried again. Nothing. He went to the emergency frequency. Nothing. He tried once more. No reply.

"It's gone down," Ben muttered. "You *bastards!*"

He shook the radio operator awake. She came

awake instantly, eyes wide as she saw who was shaking her. "Move it," Ben said tersely. "Something is very wrong. I've been trying to raise Base Camp. They don't respond. You give it a shot or two."

"Yes, sir."

Dressing hurriedly, she ran to the communications vehicle. She worked frantically for fifteen minutes, meticulously checking out every possible problem. She finally shook her head.

"It's all on the other end, sir. We're OK here."

"You've tried all frequencies?"

"Yes, sir. The last one I tried was the frequency to be used only in any life or death situation. If they didn't respond to that . . ." She hesitated.

"Say it," Ben told her.

"Sir . . . you know how our backup systems work; you designed them. There is *no way* for them to fail. The backups are on separate generators. Should the generators fail, the systems automatically switch to a battery bank. Nothing is fail-safe, sir, but this system comes the closest a human could possibly design."

"Then they've been overrun at home base or the radio shack has been sabotaged. Is that the way you see it?"

"Yes, sir. That's about the only two things that could have happened. I voice activated the alarm up there. No way anyone could have slept through all that. So that means the voice activation didn't get through."

James appeared quietly by the truck, Sergeant Greene and Captain Rayle with him. Ben met the eyes of each man.

"It's begun at Base Camp, people. Roll the troops out. We've got to hunt a hole until we can figure out what's happened and how to deal with it."

"Where are we heading, General?" Rayle asked.

"Sumter National Forest. It's only about twenty miles away. Let's shake it, boys."

BOOK TWO

They were going to look at war, the red animal—war, the blood-swollen god.

Stephen Crane

ONE

"You'll never get away with this, Captain," Colonel Gray warned the younger officer. "This is mutiny. And mutiny is punishable by death from firing squad. Be advised of that, sir."

"You just keep your hands in the air, Colonel," Willette said with a smile. The muzzle of his 9mm pistol did not waver. "And don't get cute."

"Wouldn't dream of it, old man," Dan replied. "But don't strain your resources looking for my Scouts. They're not in camp."

"Does that include the traitor, Tina Raines?" an older man asked.

Unanswered and confusing questions leaped into Dan's eyes. "Traitor? What in the world are you talking about, Walter?"

"Oh, don't deny it, Colonel," the man's tone was filled with disgust. "What you people have done is disgraceful. Knowing General Raines is mentally ill and refusing to help him."

Cecil was pushed into the room, a rifle at his back. He heard the last part of Walter's statement. His eyes touched Dan Gray's steely gaze. "Dan, what in the hell is going on?"

"I haven't the foggiest, Cecil. These bloody fools

wakened me by shoving the muzzle of an M-16 in my face. Now they're ranting and raving about Tina being a traitor and Ben having gone bonkers."

"*What!*" Cecil shouted the words. "I believe you all have taken leave of your senses. Now put down those weapons and get the hell out of here. And that, gentlemen, is an order."

"Shut up, Colonel Jefferys," Willette said. "You people are all under arrest for treason against General Raines."

Cecil frosted the man with an icy look. "That, sir, that last bit, is a fucking lie."

"Watch your mouth, traitor," Captain Willette spat the words at him. "I could have you shot, you know." He would have liked to call Cecil, "nigger" but he needed the support of the young blacks.

Lieutenant Carter shoved Juan Solis and Mark Terry into the room. "Ro and Wade and some of the kids got away," he announced. "Along with that damned old coot, Doctor Chase. But the camp is secure and it is ours."

"Good work, Sergeant," Willette said. "Take these men and lock them up. Don't take any chances with them. If they try to resist or escape, you have my orders to shoot them."

Cecil said, "Willette, when Ben hears of this, your life expectancy will drop to zero."

Willette laughed. "Still denying your part in this treason, Colonel? It won't work. We know all about your part in this. When we locate Ben Raines, he shall be so advised as to your behavior."

A young Rebel, a scared look on his face, blurted, "What in the hell is going on around here?"

"Coup," Cecil said tightly. "Willette and his bunch acted faster than we thought they would."

"Slick," Dan said. "Very well thought out and very slick. But it's going to backfire on you, gentlemen. Believe it."

"Wrong," Lieutenant Carter said. "This coup is on behalf of a very sick General Raines. And don't try denying your part in working against the general." That was directed toward Solis and Terry.

"What?" Mark screamed.

"You're a fucking idiot!" Juan blurted.

"I thought you were my friend," one of Juan's troops said from the open doorway. "But I've seen the medical reports on General Raines—all of us have seen them."

"What fucking medical reports?" Peggy Jones screamed. She was being held by two of Willette's men. "What in the name of God is happening around here?"

"Get them out of here," Willette said.

The room emptied. Cecil, Mark, Dan and Juan were taken to a detention building and locked in separate rooms, with a heavy guard placed around the building. Chances of escape were almost nil.

"You have Raines' position pinpointed?" Willette asked a radioman.

"Yes, sir. They've been trying to reach Base Camp since before dawn. The coordinates place them on the west side of this lake, right here." He pointed.

"Clark Hill," Willette said. "Get all troops up and rolling. They'll meet with Silver's bunch. Blow Ben Raines to hell."

But blowing Ben Raines to hell had been tried

many times in the past. By better people than Willette had under his command.

Ben and his small contingent were moving within the hour. The column turned east on the junction of Highways 378 and 47 and rolled across the bridge into South Carolina a half hour later. At Bakers Creek, Ben halted the column and dismounted his people.

"What's happened, General?" was the question on everyone's mind and asked by a young Rebel.

"I still don't know for certain," Ben told the hundred-odd Rebels gathered around him. "But I would imagine a coup or a coup attempt has gone down. And so far, I have to assume the attempt has been successful. If they—whomever *they* might be—have taken over the entire communications operation, then they've got the camp firm as well." He looked around him. "I want five volunteers to head northwest, find out exactly what has happened."

The entire group raised their hands.

Ben laughed aloud. He felt better for that show of loyalty. He thought: These people are solid, behind me 110 percent. He pointed out five people.

"You five get outfitted as quickly as possible and shove off. For God's sake, though, *be careful.* I'm not sure what we're up against. Someone will be on the radio at all times, monitoring. Remember, I don't want any of you risking your life needlessly. Get in and get out as quickly and as silently as you can. OK. Take off. And good luck."

Standing by the pickup truck, Gale said to Susie,

"And all I wanted was a nice, safe, uneventful life. You believe this?"

The young Rebel, Susie, veteran of a hundred fire-fights and major battles since joining Ben Raines' Rebels at age thirteen, smiled at Gale. "But would you trade what you now have for that?" she asked.

Gale smiled. "Hell, no!" she said quickly. "That is, for as long as I get to keep him."

"You're wisin' up, Gale. No woman keeps General Raines for very long. Not since Salina."*

"He loved her that much?"

"He liked her that much. Rumor is, the general's not capable of loving—not anymore. Maybe he had a bad love affair long time back. I don't know."

"He stayed with her a long time, though, didn't he?"

"Ten years, I think. He's told you about the other women in his life?"

"Bits and pieces. I kid him about repopulating the earth single-handedly. But I don't think Ben is a womanizer in the classic sense of the word. I think he's just got so much on his mind and feels he has so little time in which to do it all, settling down in one spot just never enters his mind."

"That's a pretty good guess, Gale. I think that just about sums it all up." She sighed. "We had the good life back in Tri-States. No crime, no unemployment, good medical programs and fine hospitals, fair and equitable working conditions, without unions. I mean, we had it *all*, Gale. But the central government just couldn't take it. That goddamn no good Presi-

*Out of the Ashes

dent Hilton Logan. He hated General Raines. Despised him. I think part of it was because General Raines used to screw Logan's wife, Fran." She laughed. "I bet that really galled Logan. Well . . . Logan succeeded. He killed a dream come true by destroying Tri-States. Now General Raines is fighting to rebuild at least a part of it. But he's tired. And who the hell can blame him for that?"

TWO

It was a clumsy circling attempt by those left behind. And those men of the Ninth Order left behind were not very good at their jobs. They were not woodsmen. They made too much noise in the brush, they were awkward, and they were amateurs, Ike concluded. And he waited patiently with his knife.

When the first pursuer got close, traveling by himself, Ike quietly took him out by cutting his throat. He left him propped up beside a tree, a large, grotesque, bloody smile under the man's chin. The front of his field jacket was soaked with his own blood.

The man had a canvas pouch hanging by a strap. Ike opened the flap and smiled. Several meals of military rations. And no green eggs.

"Now we go on the offensive, Nina," Ike said, returning to her side. "Now we'll see how good you are with that rifle."

She looked at him, questions in her eyes.

"Start killin' the dogs."

"With pleasure," Nina said with a grin. She dropped to the prone position, thumbed the .270 off safety, and made herself comfortable.

Ike watched her handle the rifle. She handled the

weapon with the ease of an expert. Must be a story behind that, Ike thought. Have to ask her about it when we're in a better position for chit-chat.

After the first man did not return, those of the Ninth Order remaining called in the dogs. Ike watched through binoculars as the men held a hurried conference, with several of the men pointing in Ike and Nina's direction.

They called for the man. Only the silence of the deep woods greeted them.

Scared, Ike thought. Nina read his thoughts.

"They're frightened, aren't they, Ike?" she asked. "All of them frightened of just two people. That doesn't say much for their courage."

"Those types of people aren't courageous, honey. They're little people, mentally. They feel secure in a mob. Yeah, they're scared shitless, I'm betting. I'm also betting they pulled their best people out. Why or for what reason . . . I don't know. But I'm guessing it has something to do with Ben. I wish I knew what in the hell was goin' on. Damn this bein' in the dark."

"Whatever you say, Ike," Nina said. She pulled her attention back to the front. "Well, now, would you look at that."

Ike watched her line up the stalking black form of a Doberman in the open iron sights of the .270. It will be an interesting shot, Ike thought. The slow-stalking Doberman was about 250 yards away.

She lost sight of the animal for a couple of seconds as it slipped behind a tree, then once more got it in gunsights as it reappeared. She took a deep breath and exhaled, slowly squeezing the trigger, allowing the weapon to fire itself. The slug caught the dog perfectly, directly behind the right shoulder. The force of the bullet lifted the Doberman off his paws and dumped it, dead, some five feet away from impact.

"Damn good shootin'," Ike muttered. And it was not a mechanical sentence of praise. It was damn good shooting.

A man appeared beside a thick tree trunk. Nina chambered another round, sighted in, and shot the man in the stomach. He fell to the ground, kicking and howling and clutching at his bloody stomach.

"That's one of the bastards who felt me up," Nina explained. "And he said some pretty disgusting things to me."

"That he was goin' to do to you?"

"Yes." She chambered a fresh round.

"Remind me to always ask permission," Ike said with a boyish grin.

He spun around as a snarling black shape came at the pair from out of the timber behind them. The dog's mouth was open, saliva dripping from the fanged jaws. Nina fought back a scream just as Ike squeezed the trigger of the Remington 870 and the Doberman was dead before it hit the ground, its chest torn open by the rifled slugs from the shotgun.

A third Doberman came at the pair. Its flashing teeth were only inches from Nina's face as she pulled the trigger. The .270 slug hit the Doberman in the left eye, exiting out the back of its slender head, blowing brains and blood with it.

Both heard the whistles and calls as the dogs were yelled back to their handlers.

Nina flipped sweat from her face with her finger-tips. She breathed a sigh of relief. "I have a suggestion, Ike."

"Oh?"

"Let's get the hell out of here."

"I think that's a damn good idea, honey."

Ben motioned for James Riverson to come to his side. "Our back trail covered, old friend?"

"Yes, sir," James assured him. "If they're any good at all, they'll be able to see we camped at Clark Hill, on the Georgia side. But after that, it's clean and cold all the way into South Carolina."

"Very well. Good work, James." He waved to Captain Rayle. "Captain, send a team into McCormick and check it out. Less than two thousand people there before the bombings. It's probably a ghost town, but let's be sure."

"Right away, sir."

Ben looked to James. "Send teams to check out all these other small towns in the forest. So far, we've seen no signs of life, but let's be certain. I don't like surprises. We'll camp here at Bakers Creek for this night. No fires. Cold camp all the way around. Leave no sign of our being here. Guards out and stay alert."

Ben looked to the northwest. Other Rebels followed his gaze.

"I wish I knew what the hell was going on up there," Susie said.

THREE

"From this point on," Willette said, "we must proceed very cautiously. As soon as General Raines is pinpointed, we'll have our people take him. And I don't want him to fall into Sister Voleta's hands, either. That must not happen."

"But Sister Voleta said . . ." a woman spoke, her face alarmed.

"Hell with Sister Voleta!" Willette snapped. "My plan is better, much more realistic. I want Ben Raines taken alive and kept alive. I have in my possession drugs that will destroy his mind. Drugs that will turn him into a babbling idiot." He smiled. "And we can blame it all on McGowen and Jefferys and the others. We can rig evidence that will point directly to them." Again, he smiled. "And to show our 'love' for General Raines, we'll store Raines in a big fine house with some of the older Rebels to look after him. We'll lavish the simple-minded fool with gifts and all kinds of things. Our love and concern for him will be evident. And we'll have evidence that will show McGowen and Jefferys and Gray and even Raines' own daughter, Tina, plotted to destroy him. The people will be so outraged, they'll call for the death penalty for those responsible." He laughed loudly, then looked around him conspiratorially. "The plan is beautiful and perfect, people. You see, with Raines out of the way, we can then knock off Sister Voleta. Most of her followers will move right into line and join up with us."

His people agreed with him, smiling and nodding their heads.

"Sounds good, Tom. But what about this guy Tony Silver?"

Willette shrugged, then spat on the ground contemptuously. "Hell, what about him? We've got him outgunned even now. Shit! Let the hoodlum have south Georgia. We'll take everything to the north and still be sitting in the high catbird seat, and Tony and his soldiers will be a friendly buffer zone to the south. I can't find any flaws in the plan, people."

"How come Sister Voleta hates General Raines so much?"

Willette snarled his reply. "For much the same reason I do. And the son of a bitch doesn't even remember us. Either of us. But he'll remember me just before I destroy him. God, how I hate that bastard."

FOUR

"Oh, you'll pay, Ben Raines," Voleta hissed the words like a snake's warning before striking prey. "You will pay and pay and pay dearly this time, I can promise you that." She laughed, an evil barking of non-humor. "And you don't even know why you're paying."

The woman's hate-filled brain spun its memory banks, flinging her back in time. Back years, backward in time until she stood in a bookstore in Nashville, approaching Ben Raines at an autograph party for his latest book. Back when she was just barely twenty and trying to launch a career as a country singer, back before she learned her cunt was more valuable than her mouth—in some respects. She had flirted with Ben Raines, and he had responded while signing several of his books. They later had dinner together, and bed had followed. Ben had promised to call her before he left town, for another date. But he had never called. Writers being somewhat like wandering musicians in that respect.

Nine months later, a son was born to her. Rather than put the boy up for adoption, which she had considered then rejected, she raised the child. Mother and son had become separated right after the bombings.

during the massive confusion of evacuation. She did not know what happened to the boy, Ben Blackman.

She had tried several times writing to Ben— through his publishing company—but all her letters drew only one response from Ben Raines, and that had come through Ben's attorney in Louisiana.

"If you can prove the boy is mine, I will accept full responsibility for the boy's care."

Her own attorney, whom she was paying with pussy, knowing Betty was sleeping with several other men, told her to forget it.

"But the boy belongs to Ben Raines!" she protested.

"How sure are you, Betty?" her lawyer had asked the woman.

Her hesitation told him the story. "Forget it," he again urged. "Hell, it might even be mine!"

Outraged, Betty added a middle name to her son. Ben Raines Blackman.

She hated Ben Raines.

She loathed Ben Raines.

And she never forgot him, the years only fueling the hate.

She wanted to torture Ben Raines to death.

FIVE

"Ben Raines killed my daddy," Willette said. "Killed him in cold blood. Back in '89, best I can recall. It was down in Georgia. My daddy was with Luther Pitrie's Georgia Militia at the time."*

"I 'member that bunch," an older man said. "They's tryin' to rid the area of niggers, as I recall."

"That's right," Willette said. "And they was doin' a damn good job of it, too. I recall my daddy come home once sayin' they'd hanged more than fifty coons that very day. I slipped out to the hangin' ground that night. That was a sight to see. Them swole-up niggers hangin' like sides of rotten beef from trees. I was . . . oh, 'bout thirteen, fourteen at the time Ben Raines killed my daddy from ambush. Momma was already long dead. That left me alone. Just a tad of a boy. But I swore me an oath I'd some-day kill that nigger-lovin' son of a bitch." He grinned. "But this way is gonna be better. I'm gonna fuck that Jew-bitch right in front of Raines' eyes,

*Out of the Ashes

'fore I mess up his mind, so's he'll know what's happenin'."

"By God, that'll be a sight to see, Tom." One of his men laughed.

"Yeah," Willette said dreamily. "You all can have a whack at her."

SIX

Ben sat up straight and said, "Betty Blackman!" He flung the words from his mouth as recall brought clarity to his mind.

Gale looked at him. They were sitting alone under the shade of a huge tree near Bakers Creek. "I beg your pardon, Ben? What was that you just said?"

He met her dark eyes. "I said, Sister Voleta. That's who she is. My God! I can't believe it. But I'm right."

"No, Ben. You didn't say Voleta. You said something else."

"Betty Blackman and Sister Voleta are one and the same."

"You *know* that fruitcake?"

"I knew her very briefly when she was trying to get started as a country music singer in Nashville, Tennessee. Her name, then, was Betty Blackman. That was about . . . oh, 1981 or '82, I guess. Somewhere around then."

"I see," Gale said. "Tell me, how well did you know her, Ben?"

Ben grinned. "Oh, it was a one-night stand, as best as I can recall."

"Wonderful," Gale's reply was dryly given. "By all means, Raines, do tell me more. I'm on pins and needles."

"There isn't that much more to tell, really. About a year after that, I got a letter in the mail from her. It had been sent to my publishing company. She claimed she had a child and it was mine. I gave the letter to my attorney and told him to follow it up. I said if the child was mine, then I had a legal and moral obligation to help raise it. I never heard another word from her. Good God, I hadn't thought of her in years."

"Marvelous. Raines, just how many damn kids do you have scattered around the world?"

Ben ignored that. "Betty Blackman. She must really hate me."

"Well, Ben, look at it like this: You did try to do what was right. I mean, you offered to help financially. Obviously, she didn't know whether the child was yours or not. And it probably wasn't. Did you receive many of those types of letters as a writer?"

Ben shook his head. "Two or three in a dozen years. I suppose every writer does. Did," he amended that.

She picked up on his tone of voice. "You miss it, don't you, Ben?"

"Writing? You bet, I do. But what I miss more is the stabilizing effects of a working—if not totally acceptable to all people—government. But, yeah, I miss the writing game."

"I want you to go on the road, Ben," she said. "I want you to take as much time as needed to finish your journal. And don't argue with me, Ben. You know as well as I you're never going to be completely satisfied until that work is finished. I'm right, aren't I?"

"Maybe," Ben admitted. "But you're forgetting about this little matter presently confronting us, aren't you, dear? I mean, we are in the middle of a coup attempt back at Base Camp."

"No, I'm not forgetting anything. But all that will be settled shortly."

"Are you psychic?" Ben asked, smiling. "Among your many other talents, that is."

She fixed him with a serious stare. "No, I'm not psychic, Ben. I just happen to be very close to a fellow named Ben Raines, that's all."

"And Ben Raines can do anything, right?" he questioned, a sour note to the query. "Is that it, Gale?"

"I guess that's about the size of it," she said, rising to her feet. She winked at him and walked away.

"Wonderful," Ben muttered. "Now even *she* believes me to be something I am not. Crap!"

He sat alone with his old Thompson SMG and his many thoughts until the scouting parties began drifting back into camp.

"If there are any human beings in the forest, General," the team leader of the first returning scouting party said, "they've become invisible."

Another team leader reported: "The towns are dead, General. We could find no signs of life. Looks to me like there ain't been nobody in these towns for years."

"All right," Ben said. "At first light, we move out." He traced the route on an old, worn map. "We'll cut due east here and head for this point, there are ridges along here. We find the highest one and dig in and sit still for a time, until that first team I sent out reports back with answers to questions. We've got to know where we're going before we can start."

"Very profound, Raines," Gale later told him, a smile on her lips. "Those words will probably go down in the annals of weighty sayings."

"Kinda like, 'The longest journey begins with a single step,' Miss Roth?"

"Oh, at least that."

"I'm going to miss you, Ms. Roth."

"For maybe fifteen minutes, Mr. Raines. When the hell do we eat? I'm hungry!"

SEVEN

"Any of you boys believe the crap this Captain Willette fellow is handin' out?" Abe Lancer asked the gathering of mountain men.

"'Bout as much as I believe in kissin' a rattlesnake," Rance replied. He punctuated that by spitting a long, brown stream of tobacco juice, hitting a hard shell bug dead center, stopping the beetle in its tracks.

"There are some folk in the mountains take offense to that remark," Clement reminded the man. He winked at his buddies.

"Them snake-handlers wanna kiss a rattler," Rance replied, "that's they business. Long as they don't shove that ugly bastard up to me for a smooch. Feel the same way 'bout this Willette person. 'Cept he's worser than a damn rattler."

"I believe that," Willard spoke. "Rattler will give a body some warnin' if he's got time."

"We all agree on that," Abe said, bringing the bantering to a close. "Any of you men, or any of your kin, been approached by Willette or any of his people?"

"Near'bouts all of us," a long, lean man spoke. "And I think we all told 'em the same thing. And that was to get the hell off our property and don't never come back."

All the mountain men shook their heads in agreement.

"They know where General Raines is at?"

"They found out where they *think* he is," Claude said. "I got that from a Reb. And they's 'posed to be an army comin' up from the south part of Georgia to join them troops Willette sent out. They plan is to keep the general away from this area long enough to really convince any holdouts among the Rebs that Willette is really a fine fellow, really doin' all this in the general's behalf." He spat his opinion of that on the ground. "Anybody dumb enough to believe all that bull-dooky would eat shit, run rabbits and howl at the moon."

All the men laughed politely at the old adage.

"What's the chances of us gettin' them held prisoner a-loose?" The question was tossed from the gathering around the porch.

"Slim to none," Andy spoke for the first time. More than five words in a stretch from Andy was considered to be a lengthy speech. "But I'm of a mind that we all oughta give 'er a try. I think, even though ain't none of us ever seen this here General Raines, he come in here not just to help hisself, but to help us too. I think us folk in the mountains, if we try, we could maybe pull this country back together again— or at least give 'er one hell of a run for the money. They's quite a few of us ol' boys left in these parts, and I think we've been sittin' on our backsides long 'nough. Time for us to git our guns and lend a hand in this matter. And that, by God, is all I got to say on the subject."

He stuffed his mouth full of twist chewing tobacco and began chomping.

To a man, the gathering looked in silent shock at Andy. No one among them had ever heard him put so many words together in all their life. Finally Abe spoke.

"Right pretty speech, Andy. You got anything else to add?"

Andy spat. "Nope."

Abe stood up, signaling the meeting was over. "All right, boys. Let's get our guns. Looks like we got us some fightin' to do."

EIGHT

Dan paced the floor of his cell in the Base Camp jail. He had gone over and rejected a dozen escape plans in an hour. He just couldn't see any way out of the jail. The leaders of their respective units had been widely separated. Purposely, Dan thought. And the jail was completely ringed by heavy machine gun emplacements.

Dan sat down on the edge of his narrow cot and quietly fumed.

Cecil stood gazing out the window. He looked directly at a .50-caliber machine gun, the muzzle of the weapon pointing straight at him, not more than seventy feet away. The detention barracks was actually an old jail, unused and unoccupied for many years. It had been condemned by the department of HHS back in '87, a new jail ordered built. The world war had erupted before the new jail even got off the blueprints.

Cecil looked around him and grimaced in disgust. "Pretty goddamn good jail, if you ask me," he muttered.

*　　　*　　　*

away in time. He thought so, since he had not seen Alvaro being jailed at any time since Juan had been incarcerated.

He wondered how many Rebels got away, and how many had been duped by Willette's line of bullshit? And like the others in the long cell block, Juan wondered what would be his ultimate fate?

Mark Terry wondered what was happening to Peggy. He had asked, politely, if they could be housed together.

No.

"Anybody seen Peggy?" Mark called softly.

"Down at the far end, Mark," Cecil's voice reached him. "She's all right. So far, no physical harm has come to any of us. How long that will continue is up for grabs."

"Knock off that goddamn chatter!" a commanding voice shouted. "Talking is not permitted among you traitors."

"That's Jerry Bradford," Cecil said, ignoring the command. "He is one I never would have thought would turn against us."

"Did you hear what I said, Jefferys?" the voice yelled, anger in the tone. "What the hell's the matter with you—are you deaf?"

Joining in the game, Col. Dan Gray called out from the other end of the cell block. "How many got away?"

"Quite a number of our combat troops," Cecil answered the question in a loud voice. "Much more than enough to return and kick the treacherous asses of these malcontents and dirty traitors." He was hoping to get some response from Jerry Bradford.

Bradford ran down the corridor to stand in front of Cecil's cell. He was red-faced and so angry he was trembling from rage. "You're calling *me* a traitor? You? You're nothing but a filthy coward, Jefferys. You took General Raines' friendship and puked it back in his face. I hope you all get put against a wall and shot!"

Cecil stood calmly, listening to the Rebel vent his rage. He met the man's gaze with calm and steady eyes. "Jerry, do you really believe, deep in your heart, that I would do anything to hurt General Raines?"

Jerry didn't back off. "The facts don't lie, Jefferys."

"There are no facts, Jerry," Cecil replied softly. "Listen to me." He wanted to keep the man talking as long as possible. "All that you people have seen and heard was invented." He paused, wanting to choose the next direction very carefully. "I don't know by whom, Jerry. And that is the truth. But I wish you had come to me with the rumors and their source when you first heard them."

Jerry Bradford was a man in his mid-thirties, a college grad. He was a man who held the rank of master sergeant in the Rebel army. A man who was an expert at managing the huge equipment list of the Rebel army. He was a man known for his level-headedness in any type of bad situation. And Cecil played hard on that quality.

Cecil pressed on, knowing the other prisoners were listening. "Jerry, you and the other people don't follow me, or Ike, or Dan, or Juan, or Mark. You follow Ben. We *all* follow Ben. I wouldn't dream of asking any of you to allow me to step into Ben's shoes. Me being black and all."

Jerry's intelligent face became confused. "Black? Hell, Cecil, what has that got to do with anything? None of us care what *color* a person is. You know that."

"I hoped that's the way it still stood, Jerry. All right, now tell me this: Any blacks in Willette's immediate company?"

Jerry was thoughtful for a moment. "You mean those that came in here with him?"

"Right."

Jerry sighed. "Well . . . now that you mention it, no."

"That's right. Any Hispanics, Jews, Orientals, Indians?"

Jerry stared at Cecil for a long moment. Then he abruptly slung his M-16 on his shoulder. "Never thought about it, Colonel Jefferys. But I have to say the answer is no."

Cecil was back to "Colonel Jefferys" with Jerry. He let it slide. "Now see if you can answer this, Jerry: Where did this so-called evidence about me and the others come from?"

"Well . . . hmm." Jerry thought about that. "I don't really know, Colonel. To be honest about it. One of Captain Willette's people always seemed to come up with it. And it seemed like we practically had to drag the information from whoever it was." He met Cecil's eyes. "Pretty slick, huh, Colonel? Yeah. One of Willette's people. And it was always put so we could take it either way. And like I said, they were always reluctant to say anything bad about any of you. At first."

"And then once they had you hooked, they played you all like a big bass?"

Jerry sighed heavily. "Yeah, they sure did, Colonel."

"Beginning to see some light at the end of the tunnel, Jerry?"

"Yes, sir. I sure am. And I don't like what's at the end of that tunnel." He reached for the keys on his belt. Cecil's voice stopped the hand movement.

"No, Jerry."

"Sir?"

"I think this place is not only the best place for us, in terms of you finding out more truth for yourself, but probably the safest place for the time being. Think about it."

After a moment, Jerry nodded his head. "Right, Colonel. I see. Accidents might happen on the outside. Yeah. OK. I'll make sure one of the regular Rebels is on duty at all times. Goddamn it, Colonel, I feel like the world's prize idiot. We . . . none of us had the forethought to question any of what was said. It just . . . it was like a chain reaction, I guess is the best way to put it. Colonel," he said, a worried look on his face, "why did we *want* so badly to believe it about the general and about all of you?"

"Number of reasons, Jerry. We're all very tired. We've just come through one hell of a summer with the Russian and the battles fought.* And I'm just now beginning to realize how smooth-tongued Willette and his people can be. And, don't take this the wrong way, Jerry: We are all just too damned depen-

Anarchy in the Ashes

dent on Ben. And those are his words, Jerry. I've heard him say them many times. And, Jerry, those of us with any type of advanced education are now in the very definite minority. A mob's mentality can be very infectious even to an educated person. There are many more reasons, Jerry. That's just the high points."

Jerry clutched at any straw to help ease his mind. "Was it . . . was it hypnosis, Colonel?"

"No, Jerry. It was mob hysteria and too much love for Ben Raines."

He squared his shoulders. "Yes, sir. You're right. And it was pure stupidity on the part of people who should have known better. And I'm at the top of that list. I'll pick the ones I talk to very carefully, Colonel," he promised. Jerry removed his .45 pistol from leather and handed it and a spare clip through the bars. "You keep this well-hidden, Colonel. When I come back on guard duty, I'll bring a couple more guns until I can get you all armed."

"Jerry?" Dan called.

"Sir?"

"Some C-4 and detonators, too, please."

Jerry laughed. "You betcha, Colonel. Consider it done."

Cecil said, "Be very careful who you discuss this with, Jerry. Very careful."

"Don't you worry about that, Colonel," Jerry assured him. "That sucking sound you heard a few minutes ago was me, pulling my stupid head out of my ass."

Cecil laughed, feeling, for the first time in hours, a slight glimmer of hope. "I have to say this, Jerry.

Brace yourself for Ben's taking off when all this is over."

"We never mentioned it aloud, Colonel, but that was part of it, too—among us older troops. We put too much on the man, didn't we?"

"Yes. Ben is his own man, Jerry. None of us had any right to foist something on him he really didn't want. Took me a long time to reach that decision, but I finally made it."

"Who will lead us, sir?"

"Whoever Ben appoints, Jerry."

"I hope it's you, sir," Jerry said.

"Thank you, Jerry."

"I'll be back in about an hour, Colonel. I'll bring the C-4 and a couple of pistols this next trip."

When Jerry's bootsteps had faded away and the door to the runaround closed behind him, Dan said, "You took an awful chance, Cec. That could have blown up in your face. Awfully cheeky thing you did, but I am so glad you seized the moment and brought it off."

"So am I, Dan. So am I. It was a risk, but I felt it the only chance we had left us."

"I will feel ever so much better when I have my hand wrapped around the butt of a pistol," the Englishman said.

Cecil hefted the .45. "I can tell you, friend. It does feel good."

NINE

She looked at the small contingent of Gray's Scouts that had accompanied her out of the Rebel Base Camp. Roy Jaydot, his Russian wife, Katrina. Tina's fiance, Bob Graham. Mary Macklin. A dozen others.

"We're too small a group to do much damage to Willette's bunch," Tina said. "First we're going to have to link up with the other teams of Scouts that made it out."

They were camped on the northernmost banks of Carters Lake, just off Highway 382. They were well-supplied, for at Colonel Gray's orders, each of his Scouts had slipped out of camp several times, each time carrying a load of food or ammo or mortar rounds, caching them in the deep timber. And in teams of twelve or fourteen, Dan had sent them out of the Base Camp, on some pretext or the other—anything to get as many of his people out before the coup went down.

Most of the highly trained and superbly conditioned men and women known as Gray's Scouts had gotten out, with only a few taken prisoner. Even though the coup had gone down much quicker than anyone had anticipated.

"Have you thought about making an attempt to link up with Dad Raines?" Bob asked her.

"God, yes. Many times during the past few hours. But I don't know exactly where he is. Odds of us finding him are against us. I think we're much better off staying in this area and linking up with the other teams of Scouts."

Tina was team leader, and no one questioned her authority. She was as skilled a guerrilla fighter as anyone in the Rebels, with the possible exception of Ike, Dan or her father.

"Eagle Two to Eagle One," the backpack radio softly crackled. "Lookin' for a home."

Tina moved to the radio operator's side, taking the mic. "This is Eagle One. We're out of the home nest. Come on."

"Jose Ferranza here, Tina. Got my team all with me. Where you wanna link up, Big Momma?"

Tina's team members chuckled at Jose's words. Tina was actually a captain in Gray's Scouts, but like special troops the world over—when there was a functioning world—special troops almost never stood on formality, for theirs was an easy camaraderie that few outside the unit ever understood.

"I'll Big Momma your ass, you wetback." Tina laughed the words, knowing Jose would take it in good humor, as it was meant.

"Your boyfriend is much too large," Jose replied, laughing. "I am a lover, not a fighter."

"Bullshit," Bob muttered. Sergeant Ferranza was one of the most feared guerrilla fighters in Gray's Scouts.

"Give me your coordinates, Eagle Two," Tina radioed.

Tina checked her grid map as Jose gave his position in coded words. "We're close," she said. "We'll find you. Stay put."

"Ten-four."

"Let's go," Tina ordered, picking up her M-16 and automatically checking the weapon. The fire control lever was on auto, the safety on. "We'll find three, four more teams and then we'll be strong enough to do some damage at Base Camp." She glanced toward the southeast. "Sit tight, Dad," she muttered, slipping into her pack. "Don't get it in your head to do something rash. Just sit tight."

The team moved out, as silent as ghosts wearing cammies.

TEN

Dan felt the comforting cool press of the 9mm Browning against the skin of his belly. Bradford had succeeded in arming all the prisoners in the jail, and in bringing in enough plastic explosive to blow up half the building. But Dan knew several hundred more had been rounded up and were being held under heavy guard in an old football stadium nearby. Despite the obvious and, to Dan and those now in jail, quite odious fact that the coup had been successful, Dan could not envision how it had been done so swiftly. Neither could the Englishman fathom the *why* of it all.

He knew more than half of the camp had been subtly swayed by Willette and his people, but that still left more than a thousand Rebels for Willette and his people to contend with. Say, three hundred and fifty had been taken prisoner in the swiftest coup Dan had ever heard of. And most successful, he grudgingly conceded.

But damn it to hell, he thought, that still left over six hundred men and women—all fighters. What had happened to them?

All right, he calmed himself, forcing his anger to

subside and rational thinking to take control. Think about it, he urged his mind. Say, two hundred out of that thousand were setting up homesteads throughout the vast tracts of land newly claimed by the Rebels. They would not have heard anything about the coup. And if they did hear, they would keep their heads low.

That left approximately four to five hundred.

His own Scouts numbered one hundred and fifty. Most of them had gotten free and clear just in the nick of time.

That left, say, three hundred and fifty. Most of them were with Ro and Wade, with some scattered old-timers mixed in, Doctor Chase and his wife included. That bunch had scattered like the wind, heading in all directions.

So, there it was. All neatly added up.

Some of the more level-headed of the bunch, people like Jerry Bradford, older and better educated Rebels, after speaking with Jerry, had seen how they'd been duped and were now back in the fold, so to speak. But they were few, no more than forty, and that might be stretching it.

Time, Dan knew, was the enemy. The real enemy. For with each passing hour, those Rebels with Willette, the younger, more impressionable, poorly educated men and women, would become more firmly convinced Willette was right and Cecil and Dan and the others were the enemy.

Dan ceased his restless pacing and sat down on his bunk. He thought: It's going to be bloody. And there is no way to prevent that from occurring. Lord God on High, but it's going to be a bloody bitch.

As if reading his thoughts, for Cecil had been listening to Dan's restless pacing, he called softly: "I'm not looking forward to pulling the trigger on some of these people, either."

"Nor I, Cec," Dan softly called. "But what I don't understand is the why of it all. It just doesn't make any sense."

"To destroy Ben Raines," Peggy said, joining in the conversation.

"Yes," Dan agreed. "But still that does not answer the why of it all."

"Vendetta," Juan called. "That is the only possible answer. A blood debt, if you will. Probably one so old it is doubtful General Raines himself even remembers it."

"The lengths people will go to settle old scores," Dan muttered. Then, to himself, he said, "It's coming apart. Everything Ben Raines dreamed of is coming apart. Ike is being hunted; Ben is cut off with only a small detachment, while more than a thousand men are hunting him. The camp is divided, with a bloodbath looking us in the face." He sighed. "It's coming apart. Once more, we shall have to pick up the pieces from the ashes of hate and blood and start anew. But what will happen when those of us with age and education and experience are gone?"

The Englishman did not like to dwell long on that last question. For like Ben, he knew only too well what would happen.

"A return to the ashes," he muttered. "Back to barbarism and savagery and paganism. I hope I do not live to see it."

"We shall persevere," Cecil called. "Everything Ben has worked for will, indeed, *must*, endure. It is up to us to see that it does."

"And when we are gone?" Dan called, feeling the weight of his age, even though he was not yet fifty, fall on him with a crushing invisible force.

Cecil did not reply.

ELEVEN

"Take the one on the left," Ike whispered. "Shoot him in the chest. Try to miss that walkie-talkie. I want it. I'll waste the pus-gutted dude on the right."

Two rifles cracked. Two men from the Ninth Order went down in howling heaps. One kicked and squalled in agony, his legs jerking as life slowly left him. Nina's shot had gone high, the bullet striking her man in the throat, almost tearing the head from him with the expanding slug. Blood spurted in two-foot-high arcs until his heart ceased its pumping. The man drummed his booted feet on the earth and died.

"Shit!" Nina said, working a fresh round into the chamber of her .270.

"No point in bitchin' about it," Ike told her. "You got him."

"But I was off the mark by a foot!" she said. "I haven't missed like that in years."

"You were shootin' downhill, little one," Ike said. "Downhill shootin' is always tricky. We'll wait a few minutes, see if any of their buddies come runnin'. Then you cover me while I get the walkie-talkie. Maybe then we'll be able to keep more than one jump ahead of them."

The pair lay in the brush on the crest of the hill. Within seconds after the shooting, the birds once more began their singing and calling. No more men of the Ninth Order appeared. Ike counted off another sixty seconds.

Ike rose to his feet. "You see anything other than me movin' around down there, blow the ass off it."

She leaned over and kissed his cheek, now rough with beard stubble. "Yes, sir."

Ike grinned. "This ain't no time for romance, darlin'."

He made his way cautiously to the site of the dead men. The air was foul with urine from relaxed bladders and excrement from bowel movements. Ike was especially wary of Dobermans, for he was very familiar with those animals who had been silent-trained. They were awesome and deadly. Few people realize just how much damage even an untrained dog can do to a man, and how quickly. Ike was as fully trained in the art of handling an attacking dog as any man who is not an experienced dog handler. But all that was just training, and Ike hoped he would never have to find out how good the training had been.

No dogs were present, much to Ike's relief. And no more live men, either.

He stripped the dead men of their warm, lined field jackets, and took the long-range walkie-talkie. He left their weapons; both carried shotguns. He shoved their bodies over the edge of a deep rocky ravine, thinking perhaps if they were found, the missing walkie-talkie would not be noticed. He hustled back up the hill and flopped down beside Nina, extending the antenna. Chatter came to them immediately.

"They done killed Langford and Benny," the excited voice said. "I heard the shots and then couldn't get neither of them on the radio. You copy all that? Over."

"Stand clear of 'em. Don't get any closer than you have to. Sister Voleta says to keep pushin' 'em north. 'Bout five more miles and we'll have them boxed in the meadow up yonder."

"How 'bout usin' the dogs ag'in?"

"Negative to that. The dogs is being sent south to track General Raines and his bunch."

"That's a relief," Nina said.

"In a way," Ike responded.

The radio crackled once more. "How's things at the Base Camp?"

"Ever'thang is jam up and jelly tight. The Base Camp is ours."

"Oh, god*damn* it!" Ike cussed. "What in the hell is going on?"

"OK. We'll keep pushin' 'em north. Point out."

"Your Base Camp has been overrun, Ike?" Nina asked. "By the Ninth Order? I didn't think they were strong enough to do something like that."

"They aren't. Not by themselves. That goddamn Willette and his pack have to have something to do with this."

"Willette?"

He told her, briefly, all he knew and suspected about Willette and his people.

She was silent for a moment. "Then . . . this Captain Willette must be tied in with the Ninth Order, is that what you think?"

Ike nodded. "I guess so, Nina. Like I said before

230

when we talked about it, this whole business is so screwed up, I really can't tell you what in the hell is going on."

Ike got to his feet and helped Nina up. He looked around him, got his bearings, and started walking—south. There was a determined set to his jaw and a cold look in his eyes.

"Ike!" She tugged at his arm. "We're heading right back toward them."

"That's right, babe. We sure are. We're goin' back to Base Camp. I got the monkey and the skunk syndrome about this mess."

"You mean, you've had all this good stuff you can stand?" she asked with a grin.

"You hit it right, Nina. We don't have to worry about the dogs, and those sorry bastards up ahead don't much worry me. I just hope they get in my way."

"You're cute when you get mad, Ike."

"Aw, shit!" Ike said, blushing.

TWELVE

Tony Silver had every available man he could spare in the long convoy. The group from north Florida had rolled in, and the column had rolled out, heading north. But Tony was having second thoughts about Ben Raines. He had asked one of Voleta's people why she hated Raines so.

The guy had mumbled something about Ben Raines being a false god and a scourge on the face of the earth. Tony thought all that to be a crock of crap. Raines probably screwed Betty one night and short-changed her. Or, he thought with a smile, short-dicked her.

He laughed aloud at that.

His driver met Tony's eyes in the rear-view mirror. "Something, boss?"

"Naw. Just thinking, that's all."

"Boss, what's the deal with this General Raines, anyways? How come it's so important for us to take this dude out?"

"That's kinda what I was laughing about, Bill. 'Cause I don't really know, myself. But we got a deal with this Sister Voleta, and Tony Silver don't never welch out on no deal."

"Right, boss."

Tony leaned back in the comfortable rear seat of the old Cadillac limo. Sister Voleta/Betty Blackman was not leveling with him, and Tony did not like to be in the dark in any deal he was part of. Just too damn many unknowns.

He sighed, thinking: OK. First we kick the ass off Ben Raines, and this time there was no doubt in his mind that would be done. They would have Raines outnumbered ten to one. Then Tony would deal with Voleta. Permanently.

After he screwed her.

The men and women of Ben's contingent dug in deep in the brush and timber on the ridge, digging in carefully, doing so without disturbing the natural look of the terrain. The ridge afforded them the best vantage point they could find, in terms of defense. And to a person, they knew the upcoming battle must be a decisive victory.

In front of them, at the base of the ridge, lay a small creek that would have to be forded by any attackers choosing a frontal assault. That would slow them considerably. To the rear was a long northeastward pointing finger of a lake. Ben doubted any type of amphibious assault would or could be launched against their position. To the east lay a tangle of thorny brush and marshland. The west was thick timber and undergrowth.

Captain Rayle came to Ben's side. Ben liked the young captain, for Rayle would speak his mind . . .

respectfully. "At first I was dubious about your choice of a defendable position, sir," he admitted. "Now I see you have chosen the best possible position in the entire forest."

"Thank you, Captain," Ben replied, hiding his smile. He had not lowered his binoculars. He swept the land once more, in a slow half circle. Lowering the field glasses, he asked, "Everything shaping up, Captain?"

"Yes, sir. We've hidden and camouflaged our vehicles well. Someone would have to literally walk right into them before they were detected. We hid them just off a fire road to our northeast, easily accessible when we decide to leave. We have .50-caliber machine guns facing in all directions, dug in. We've filled every container we could find from the surrounding towns with fresh water. It's been tested and, to be on the safe side, we're in the process of adding purification tablets. We have well-dug mortar pits completely circling the crest of the ridge. M-60s are supplementing the heavy .50s. At your orders, we have no Scouts out forward. All personnel are accounted for and dug in on this ridge, sir."

Ben could ask for no more than that. Captain Rayle's report touched all bases. "Very good, Captain. How's the food situation?"

"More than adequate for a sustained assault, sir. I have people digging a medical bunker in the center of the ridge. Ms. Roth has taken charge of that, sir."

"I just bet she has," Ben muttered.

"Peg pardon, sir?"

"Ah . . . nothing, Roger. Talking to myself, that's all. Instruct your people there will be no firing until

I give the word."

"Yes, sir."

"Very good, Roger. Now comes the most difficult part."

"Sir?"

"The waiting."

THIRTEEN

Tina had linked up with three other teams of Gray's Scouts. They were now less than a mile from the outskirts of the Base Camp, spread out in a thin line to the north of the main complex of buildings. The radiopersons had changed crystals in their walkie-talkies so they could communicate without being detected by Willette's people.

"Big Momma?" the backpack radio crackled. "We have smoke to the west, and . . . I guess some answering smoke from the east. You suppose that would be Wade and Ro talking to each other?"

The two young men, Wade and Ro, and their youthful followers, most between the ages of ten and eighteen, had been, almost to a person, male and female, raised in the savage wilds of the ravaged land once known as America. They had grown thusfar without benefit of mother or father. Most could not read or write. Most did not know the meaning of the word "parent." Love was something that was unknown to them, at least to the point where they could put that emotion into words. Happiness was not being hungry or alone or cold. They grew up eating whenever they could find food; knives and forks and spoons had been replaced by fingers. They carried what they owned on their backs.

These young people had linked up with Ben Raines only a few months back, joining him to fight against the Russian, Striganov. These young people thought Ben Raines to be no less than a god. For all their young lives they had heard of the wonders performed by Gen. Ben Raines, of how the man could not be killed, how he was a nation-builder, how he fought a giant mutant and killed it with only a knife. So much more. They loved Ben Raines, and they were prepared to die for him.

Many were so young in age, mere children, but they were oh-so-wise in the ways of survival. They knew the ways of the woods as well as any living thing, for until recently, that is where they lived, observing and imitating the ways of animals. Ro and his followers in the east, Wade and his followers to the west.

Now they were preparing to make war against those who spoke harshly of General Raines and Colonel Ike and the other older, wiser men of the Rebels.

"I would imagine so, Eagle Five," Tina spoke into the mic. "Those kids are woods-wise and deadly when pushed. They can take care of themselves. I'm just glad they're on our side."

"Eagle One, this is Eagle Six. We've been monitoring your exchanges. We have just moved into position on the south side of the camp. Do you have any firm plans?"

"Affirmative, Eagle Six. We free the birds at 2000 hours tonight."

"Ten-four, Big Momma. We'll begin neutralizing

the guards on the south side beginning at 1958. Good luck. Eagle Six out."

Tina turned to a team member. "Take someone with you and try to make contact with Ro and Wade. Tell them what we're planning and coordinate with them."

Two Scouts slipped silently into the deep timber.

"Woods are too damn quiet," Willette observed. He had been watching the timber through binoculars, attempting to detect some alien movement. He had been unable to spot anything out of the ordinary.

"My guts tell me we're being watched," Carter said. "Small of my back is itchy."

Willette lowered the glasses. "Yeah. Me, too. We're being watched from all sides. Something's in the wind. Inform the people that the traitor, Tina Raines, and those who follow her will probably launch an attack tonight. They'll be trying to free the other traitors. Tell them tonight will be a test of their loyalty. Tell them that while no one among us wants any bloodshed, that may not be possible under the circumstances. And be sure to add that all this is being done for General Raines. Everything we do is for him. Those that choose to fight the traitors will be looked upon favorably in Ben Raines' eyes."

Carter chuckled. "I never thought it would be this easy, Tom. It's slick. Just as slick as owl's shit."

"I only wish we had more people," Willette said. "If we had one more company, victory would be assured. But I think we got it anyway."

"You want me to really fire 'em up, Tom?"

"Yeah. Preach to them." He laughed. "Divide and conquer. It works every time."

"Divide and conquer," Carter repeated the words. "That's good, Tom. Who said that?"

"I think it was Robert E. Lee."

FOURTEEN

Ike listened to more chatter on the walkie-talkie and looked at Nina, lying on her stomach by his side in the brush.

"Blivit," he said.

"Blivit?"

He grinned, the smile wiping years from his face. "Yeah. That's an old military expression. Means ten pounds of shit in a five-pound bag. And that's exactly what's happenin' right now." He shook his head. "My God, how did this thing mushroom so rapidly? A few days ago, it was just rumors floatin' around the camp. Now the new base is overrun, my buddies in lockup, and Ben is on the run. I should have shot that goddamn Willette ten minutes after he joined the convoy."

Nina suddenly tensed. "Ike?" she said, pointing through the thick brush. "Look over there. Almost directly in front of us."

Ike cut his eyes, not moving his head, for movement is picked up faster by experienced woodsmen than sound. A slow smile made its way across his lips. "Well, now," he whispered.

A half dozen men were standing in a knot, about a hundred and fifty yards from Ike and Nina. All the men were heavily armed. A voice, obviously agitated, reached them.

"I tell you all, goddamnit, I heard voices a minute ago."

"Aw, horseshit, Al. Colonel McGowen and his pussy are miles from here. The forward team reported them moving north. If you heard any voices, you was hearin' your own head talkin' from all that moonshine whiskey you drunk last night."

The men laughed roughly.

It was their last dirty bark of humor on this earth.

Ike clicked his M-16 onto full auto, nestled the butt into his shoulder, and burned a full clip into the knot of Ninth Order. The black rifle did its work, the so-called "tumbling" bullets knocking the men off their feet, slamming and jerking them around like so many mindless marionettes, the strings of which were being manipulated by an insane puppeteer. The bullets spun the men into trees and stained the virgin ground beneath them with wet, sticky crimson.

"Come on!" Ike said to Nina.

Together, they finished the job, with a single bullet to the back of the head of any left alive. Working swiftly, they stripped the men of ammo, with Nina discarding her .270 for an M-16. They hung bandoleers of ammo about them like old-time Mexican bandits, the bandoleers crisscrossing their chests. The men all wore canteens full of water, attached to web belts; those went around the waists of Ike and Nina. Ike hooked a half dozen grenades to his new harness and gave several grenades to Nina, showing her how to hook them in place. He showed

241

her how to work the additional walkie-talkie.

"Now you have communications, Nina—in case we get separated. I'll go over the nomenclature of the M-16 once we get some distance between us and them." He pointed to the cooling carnage sprawled unsightly on the forest floor. "Let's split, babe. Now we got some firepower."

"Can we run away now?" Lilli asked.

The three young girls were playing dolls in Tony's motel quarters outside Savannah. Lilli had seen dolls before, lying like shattered little beings amid the rubble of man's hate and destruction, but the child had no earthly idea what one was supposed to do with them. Now it was kind of fun, dressing them up in little doll dresses. Once you knew where to look in the old stores, you could find all sorts of pretty things to dress up all kinds of dolls.

"We're guarded," Ann flatly informed her. "And the windows is barred and the doors got special locks on them. We can't get out. These three rooms," she said, pointing left and right, to the adjoining motel rooms, "is it. You still hurtin'?" she asked Lilli.

"Some. But it's better. It really hurt when Tony done it to me. I'm gonna tell ya'll something: I don't like that Patsy woman none at all. She done things to me made me feel . . . well, kinda dirty. You know what I mean?"

"She done it to me, too," Peg said. "It don't hurt, but I don't like it."

Ann said nothing about the cruel woman called Patsy. Patsy had forced the girl to have sex with her more than once, with Tony watching one time. And she had forced Ann to strap on a huge penis and act like a man. That's when Ann really began scheming and plotting ways to escape. But first she wanted to somehow hurt Tony as badly as he had hurt her. She already thought she knew how she was going to get even with that Patsy woman.

"What's wrong with you, Ann?" Lilli asked. "Your face looked funny for a minute."

"Yeah," Peg said. "You sure are quiet."

"Just thinkin' about ways for us to get out. I can't come up with nothing yet. But I will. I betcha on that."

A key rattled in the lock and the door swung open. A burly man stood in the open doorway, grinning lewdly at the three young girls. "Shuck outta them jeans, babies," he said. "Patsy's on the way up here with another chick. And I'm gonna watch the action. Hell, I might decide to join in. I ain't had me no young gash in a while."

Lilli began weeping, her face pressed into her hands. The man stepped to the bed and slapped the girl, knocking her to the carpet. He jerked up one of her dolls and savagely twisted the head from it. The doll made a momma-momma sound. He dropped the head to the floor, where it bounced into a corner.

"Don't you hurt my dolly!" Lilli screamed.

The man laughed at her, then looked at the other girls. "How'd you like for me to take all your dollies away from you?"

"No!" the girls cried.

"Then git naked, babies. All of you. Show me the bare butts and pussies."

FIFTEEN

The first team of Gray's Scouts ran into a patrol just inside the main compound. A patrol of coup members, leaving for a nighttime search of the immediate woods rounded a corner and came face to face with the Scouts.

Jimmy Paul, leader of the Eagle team, did not have time to raise his M-16.

"Traitors!" the coup member screamed at the Scouts. The leader lifted his sawed-off ten-gauge shotgun and pulled the trigger, blowing Jimmy's belly out his back, part of the stomach lining wrapping around the backbone, ripping and tearing out the stomach along with several yards of intestines.

The patrol and the Scouts blasted away at each other at point-blank range. No one among either side survived the encounter.

The camp erupted in gunfire, the muzzle blasts pocking the night like a Fourth of July celebration planned and executed by a pyromaniac with a full arsenal at his command.

Jumping to his booted feet before the first echoes of gunfire died away, Colonel Gray shouted, "Now!" He hit the detonator, activating the C-4. The cell door lock blew apart. Other explosions rocked the old jail as cell locks were shattered. Gray, Juan, Cecil, Mark and Peggy stepped out into the smoky run-around of the cellblock. Mark was armed with an M-M-10 machine pistol.

"I'll take the point," he yelled, running toward the still-locked door to the cellblock. He held a block of C-4 in one hand.

Before he reached the door, it swung open, two armed coup members stepping into the smoky hall. Firing one-handed, Mark pulled the trigger, fighting the rise of the weapon. The slugs jerked the pair backward in a macabre dance of pain and death. Mark tossed one of their M-16s to Colonel Gray, the other to Cecil. He ripped off their ammo pouches and threw them over his shoulder toward the newly freed prisoners. Dan and Cecil caught the full pouches and slung the straps over their shoulder.

Peggy Jones leveled her pistol and shot a young coup member between the eyes just as he rounded a corner, an AK-47 at the ready. He slumped back against the wall and slid downward, blood and brains leaking from the back of his head, staining the old brick of the jail.

"Take his weapon, Juan!" she yelled, as the hallway filled with coup members.

Gunfire ripped from the coup members' rifles and pistols. Peggy went down, a bullet in her side. Juan jerked up the Kalashnikov assault rifle and swept the hallway clean, using a clip of 7.62 ammo, the slugs slamming young coup members right and left, filling the hall with smoke and pain and the odor of blood and death.

"I'm OK!" Peggy yelled. "The slug just grazed me.

245

It went clear through." She tore off her shirt tail and the belt from a dead man to fix a quick pressure bandage.

"Let's go!" Dan shouted, pushing through the stalled crowd, jumping over the body-littered hallway.

Outside the jail, the situation was chaotic, with no one really knowing who was friend or foe. Coup members were firing wildly in the darkness, many times the bullets hitting their own people.

And Abe Lancer and his men were massing to free those men and women and children held inside the football stadium.

"Anything moving?" Ben asked the young guard.

The young Rebel, attached to Captain Rayle's command, almost jumped out of his boots.

"Jesus Christ!" he said. "No, sir." He calmed himself, taking several deep breaths of the cool night air. "God, sir, you move like a ghost. I didn't even hear you come up behind me. How do you do that, sir?"

Ben laughed softly and patted the young man's shoulder. "Settle down, son," he told him. "They're not here yet. The attack will probably start no sooner than ten o'clock tomorrow."

"How do you know that, sir?"

Other Rebels had gathered around the southeast sentry post. Ben smiled. "Because I changed the crystal in one of our PRC-6s and wired the mic button closed. I strapped the walkie-talkie to a telephone pole in the town of Troy. I've been listening to the forces gather there. Heard some very profane chatter,

246

too. They have no idea where we are. But they did bring dogs, though, and intend to turn them loose with their handlers at first light. Give them two hours, at the most, and they'll pick up our scent. Their main force will probably mount the first assault against our front position about 1000 hours." Ben glanced around him. "Captain Rayle?"

"Sir?" The captain stepped forward.

"Now that we know where our adversaries are, Captain, I want some surprises waiting for them. You send out teams to use what mines we have and lay them there." He pointed out the area. "The terrain all around us is not suitable for vehicular travel, so it will be a foot soldier's nightmare—for them, not us. Have your people, when they have exhausted our mine supply, start constructing swing traps and punji pits. Stagger your teams so none will be working more than a couple of hours. They'll all need rest for the battle tomorrow. It's going to be a bloody one, people. Their blood, not ours."

"Yes, sir." The captain saluted and walked away.

Ben continued his circling of the camp, inspecting each sentry post personally, chatting with the Rebel on duty.

"Can you just imagine that?" a Rebel said, after Ben had walked away. "Strapping a walkie-talkie to a pole and then listening to every word that's said. Now who would have thought of that?"

"Ben Raines," a woman said gently.

SIXTEEN

They set their walkie-talkies on low volume and listened to the speakers whisper the news of what was happening at the Base Camp, far to their south and west. Many of the reports were conflicting in nature. Some were hysterically given. Others were almost incoherent. All were second and third hand given, received and then transmitted from point to point along the network of the Ninth Order outposts, stretching far. One thing was certain: Whatever was happening at the Base Camp . . . it was not going well for Willette and his people.

"You heard it," Ike said, taking the walkie-talkie from his ear.

"Yeah, but most of it was so garbled I don't know what they're talking about."

"Big break out," Ike said. "Some coup members have rolled over and are helping Cec and Dan and the others. That's good news. Tina Raines a traitor?" He shook his head in the darkness of the copse where he and Nina had made their night camp. "It's beyond me how anyone could ever convince anybody of that bullshit. For Christ's sake . . . Tina is Ben's adopted daughter. He's more of a father to her than her real father."

"They have many ways, Ike," Nina said. "They can wear a person down with half truths, twisted versions of what is real and what is not, and just plain outright lies. What did it used to be called? Oh, yeah, brainwashing. That's it. And believe me, Ike, they know all the tricks."

"It's bloody and it's awful," Ike stated the truth quietly. "Friend against friend. Worse than the damned War between the States, I reckon. Or at the very least, a lot like it."

"The War between the States? I ain't never heard of that one, Ike."

"Civil War?" he prompted.

"That one neither."

So very young, Ike thought. But the real sadness lies in the loss of history. She knows *nothing* of history. My God! he mentally raged. It's truly coming apart, just like Ben predicted. If we can't begin some sort of turnaround, with permanent settlements, complete with schools and teachers, any semblance of civilization will be gone in another two decades. All gone. Back to the caves.

Jesus!

"Tell me about that war you just named, Ike," Nina said.

"That was a war that happened a long time ago, Nina. It ended almost one hundred and forty years ago. It was the North against the South. And it was fought for a number of reasons, one of them being slavery."

"Who won?"

"Nobody," Ike said. "The nation did not ever heal properly after that. The slaves were freed, but that would have happened anyway, was happening, all over the south." He started to tell her the story of President Lincoln meeting the author, Harriet Beecher Stowe, and of the president saying: "Mrs. Stowe. The woman who started the Civil War." But Nina would never have heard of Lincoln, much less Stowe.

"Somebody had to win, Ike," Nina prompted him.

"Yeah. The North won."

"I get the feeling you didn't like that."

Ike laughed. "Honey, I'm old, but I'm not *that* old. I was born in the deep south—Mississippi—but I don't hate nobody for the color of their skin. My first wife was black, if you wanna call somebody with skin like burnt honey black. It's just that . . . that ol' war was so *stupid*."

"All wars is stupid," she said flatly.

"Yeah," Ike agreed, then paraphrased a line of George Orwell's. "But some is more stupid than others." He laughed at that.

"What's so funny, Ike?"

"I was thinking of a classic work of literature. A book called *Animal Farm*. I'll find a copy for you to read."

"Will I understand it?"

"I'll help you with it."

The young woman nestled closer to the comforting bulk of Ike. He put an arm around her. She said, "I wish I was smart like you, Ike." Her tone was wistful. "I can read and write pretty good, but I mostly had to teach myself. My formal education ended when I was ten, I think. Maybe eleven. That was . . ." She frowned in recall. "'89, I think. Maybe '90.

Maybe I'm a year older than I think. I just don't know. It's all so confused in my mind."

"Wanna talk about it?"

"I never have before. Maybe it's time." She stirred in his arms and said, "We didn't get hit the way a lot of places did back in '88. We lived in West Virginia. In the mountains. Little bitty place. Yeah, now I remember. It was in the early part of '89. I remember 'cause it was still winter. Mom and Dad went out to look for food. They . . . well, they just never did come back. I had a brother, too. But he went off one day and never come back neither. Then I went to live with an aunt and uncle, but they had a whole passel of younguns and didn't really want another mouth to feed. When I was thirteen, my uncle tried to rape me in the woods. I took off and never once looked back. I been livin' hand to mouth ever since. I like to read though. I sometimes prowl the old stores and find books that the rats and mice ain't chewed up. It's hard readin' at times, 'cause I ain't got a whole lot of knowledge of big words. Them that I ain't real sure of, I skip over. Sometimes I can find a dictionary and look up the meanin'. It helps."

"Don't you ever think about a . . . a permanent place?" Ike asked. "I mean, a home, with a husband and kids and all that?"

"Aw, Ike. In them books I read about them things. Big ships with dancin' and parties and stuff like that. I read about love and romance and pretty dresses and fine ladies and gentlemen. But that ain't never gonna be no more. It's over. I ain't never gonna see New York City or none of them skyscrapers. They're all gone, Ike. I went into a department store one time,

251

think it was in Kentucky, up north. I found me a right pretty dress and high-heeled shoes and all that stuff. Put on some perfume, too. Then I looked in a big long mirror. Good God, Ike! I looked like a plumb idiot. I like to have never got that perfume smell off me.

"No, Ike, them ways is gone forever, and you know it well as me. It ain't never gonna come no more. The people—them that I choose to talk to—don't even talk about them times no more. They're just too busy trying to *survive*, that's all. You know, Ike, I feel kind of . . . cheated, I guess is the right word. I mean, I ain't bitchin' none about it. Don't do no good. It's . . . all them good things . . . it's just *over*. You know what I mean?"

"Yes," Ike replied softly. "Part of what you say is true. But Ben Raines has this dream of putting it all back together. And we did it out in Tri-States."

"Nobody ever put Humpty Dumpty back together again, Ike," she said with childlike honesty.

"And Little Bo Beep and her sheep?" Ike kidded her.

"I know what you mean. Yeah, I heard about Tri-States. Tried to get there a time or two. Got as far as Kansas one time. I think I was sixteen. Near'bout that. Some men caught me and gang-banged me." She said it with no more emotion than discussing a can of green beans. "One of them ol' boys had him a dick looked like a fence post. He really hurt me. I started bleedin' real bad and I guess that scared them. They dumped me and took off. Just left me buck-assed naked in a old house. After I got better, I started practicin' my shootin'. That's when I got me my first

252

.270. I tracked them sorry bastards for two months. Had me a horse back then, too. Good horse. I named him Beauty. I remembered that out of a book I read about a horse and a girl. Me and Beauty followed them men. Took me awhile, but I found 'em and I killed 'em all. Lost Beauty the next year. He just got sick and up and died. I cried."

She said it all so simply, but with such deep feelings in her voice, Ike felt a tenderness touch him in hidden places within his soul.

"You best get some sleep, Nina," he said gently. "And don't worry. I promise you, everything will be all right."

SEVENTEEN

Captain Tom Willette felt his coup attempt coming apart. Gathering up four of his men, they drove to the football stadium amid the wild shooting and shouting. The men stood by the old fence and then, as if on silent signal, they walked to the .50-caliber machine guns placed around the field and without a word opened fire on the weaponless, defenseless prisoners. Willette had a grim smile of satisfaction on his lips as the heavy .50 bucked in his hands, rattling out its death song. The bastards and bitches followed Ben Raines, they were Willette's enemies. That was that. He felt no sympathy for the women and children dying by his hand. Really, he rather enjoyed their screaming and crying.

The belts reached the end of their brass and the .50s fell silent. The Rebels guarding the prisoners looked at the sudden red carnage with horror in their eyes. They knew most of those who now lay dying, chopped to bloody bits on the grass of the old playing field. The screaming was something hideous.

A coup for the sake of General Raines was one thing. But this . . . this monstrous act . . . this was just plain *murder*.

But before they could react, Willette and his men

had vanished.

The young guards threw down their weapons and ran onto the field, calling for the medics to come quick.

Abe Lancer and his men appeared at one end of the old playing field. The scene before their eyes was unreal. That could not have happened. Young children and women lay sprawled in twisted death, the ground beneath them soaked with blood. None of the men had ever witnessed anything to match this awful sight in the blood red night.

"Oh, my God!" Abe said.

"Must be three, four hundred women and kids out there," Andy said. He turned his head to one side and vomited on the grass.

Through the glare of the portable lights that illuminated the field, Abe and his men saw the young guards running toward the fallen victims. Believing them to be the ones responsible for this act of horror, Abe yelled, "Kill them sons of bitches. Kill all them bastards."

Rifles cracked in the smoky, dusty, confused and bloody night.

EIGHTEEN

On the edge of the Talladega National Forest in eastern Alabama, Sam Hartline sat in his communications truck and monitored the radio traffic from Raines' new Base Camp in north Georgia to Ben Raines in South Carolina. The mercenary's smile was huge. He was thinking about a statement made years before, from a Red Chinese leader, speaking of the United States of America. "We won't have to attack that country," the Red leader had stated. "For America will destroy itself from within."

Hartline laughed aloud. He said, "Quite true. And it happened rather along those lines, too. And now—he laughed again—"the same thing is occurring among the troops of President-General Ben Raines." He threw back his handsome head and howled his laughter. "Oh, I love it! I truly love it. Ben Raines, you sanctimonious son of a bitch, you're finally getting your comeuppance at last, and it's long overdue. Oh, I love it!"

Hartline had suffered too many humiliating and disgraceful defeats at the hand of Ben Raines to possess any feelings toward the man other than raw hate. True, that hatred was intermingled with some degree of respect, but the bad blood between the two men far overrode anything else.

"My nemesis," Hartline muttered. "The stinking albatross hanging about my neck. Ben Raines. But this time, Ben, I am gleefully witnessing your little kingdom crashing down around your ears. And I am pleased. Oh, I am so very, very pleased to hear it fall."

Friend shooting friend. Women and babies being slaughtered like dumb animals. This was better than the Civil War.

"I love it!" the mercenary yelled. "Oh, I love it."

He turned up the volume. "And it looks like about two hundred or more people dead or dying," the unknown Rebel from north Georgia said to Ben Raines. "Most of them are women and kids. It's bad, General. The camp is still in a lot of confusion. But we think we've put down the coup attempt. Willette and his immediate group got away."

"But not before they killed the prisoners?" Ben radioed from the depths of the Sumter National Forest.

"Yes, sir. And many of the young Rebels who joined Willette ran off into the deep timber, after grabbing a lot of ammo and other supplies. We have teams out looking for them."

In South Carolina, Ben released the mic button and cussed.

"Probably cussing a blue streak of profanity," Hartline said with a mocking, knowing smile. The mercenary was as freelance now as when he was working for the CIA in Laos in the early seventies, for the Mozambique-based units of SWAPO in the late seventies, for Qaddafi out of Libya in the early eighties, and for the Russian IPF forces only recently.

Sam Hartline answered, totally, to no master. His services, his army, was for hire to the highest bidder; and unlike most mercs, Hartline would switch sides as quickly as a snake strikes—money was the only master.

Of late, though, money was no good. It was power and women Hartline sought. And now he had broken, temporarily and very amicably, with the Russian general, Striganov, and his IPF forces. Hartline pulled his army out with him. His army was a short combat battalion of thugs and perverts and malcontents. Hartline was looking for Tony Silver. Tony was a man Hartline could understand, for although Hartline would not admit it—indeed, he did not know it—he was as mentally twisted as Silver. Hartline enjoyed torturing people. He enjoyed listening to women scream in pain and sexual humiliation. He enjoyed breaking people, mentally and physically, reducing them to slaves, eager to do his bidding, however perverted and cruel it might be—and usually was.

His men were as twisted as Hartline, most of them—but just like Hartline, they were excellent soldiers, understanding tactics and logistics and weapons and discipline.

And that was something Tony's men were not: good soldiers. But once Hartline got them under his command, he would whip them into shape, both mentally and physically.

Sam Hartline and Ben Raines had one thing in common: They were both fine soldiers. Any similarity ended there.

Hartline turned cold eyes to his radioman. "You

have them located yet?"

"Yes, sir. They're in the Sumter National Forest in South Carolina."

"Very well. We'll let those foolish people who call themselves the Ninth Order suffer some losses trying to take Ben Raines. They'll fail. I don't care how they have him outnumbered, they won't take him. His troops are too good. With any kind of luck, Raines will suffer some casualties. We'll take him on his way out."

He turned to a man standing quietly in the darkness, just outside the open door at the rear of the truck. "How are the men, Captain?"

"Well rested and spoiling for a good fight, sir. They're getting fat and lazy with nothing to do."

"Well, if we tangle with Raines' people, they'll damn sure have a good fight on their hands," Hartline assured the man.

"Looking forward to it, sir."

"Yes. So am I."

"Transmissions from the Ninth Order commanders to the men planning to attack Raines, sir," the radio operator said. "They just received the go-ahead."

"Good," Hartline said with a smile, rubbing his hands together. He turned once more to the captain. "Get the men up and moving. Warm up the trucks. I want us to be east of the ruins of Atlanta by dawn."

"Yes, sir."

Hartline said, "You've got a hundred tired troops, Raines. I've got five hundred fresh ones. This time, you bastard, I'm going to kill you."

NINETEEN

"I hear them," Ben said, appearing by the sentry's side on the bluff of the crest. "Head's up now. Be ready for anything."

Dawn was three hours old, the air clear and cold on the ridge. Dogs bayed in the distance. The wind was blowing west to east, a point in the Rebels' favor.

"You sure can move quiet, General," the young Rebel said. "'Bout as quiet as anyone I ever heard walk."

"Some people think I'm a ghost," Ben kidded the Rebel.

And knew immediately it had been the wrong thing to say.

The Rebel looked at Ben strangely, an odd glint in his eyes.

"Don't take that seriously, son. I was only kidding you."

"Yes, sir." But the young Rebel wasn't so certain about that. He'd heard, many times, all the stories told about General Raines. All the amazing things. General Raines just had to be a little bit more than mere human. Or, the thought touched him with a light chilling effect, a little bit less.

Ben looked at his watch. 1000 hours. The troops of

Tony Silver and the Ninth Order were right on time.

The Rebel Ben had spoken to the previous night was also checking his watch. "The general said they'd be here at ten o'clock," he said to a group of Rebels. "And here they are. Right on the money."

The Rebels shook their heads. No one ever questioned Ben Raines.

One more rung on the ladder of legend.

The distant baying of the dogs changed. "All right," Ben said. "Get ready. The dogs have picked up scent."

The thin line of defenders waited for several moments. The dogs drew closer, their barking more excited.

"I can't spot the dogs, sir," a lookout called.

"They'll be along," Ben said. "Mortar crews facing southeast, stand ready with twelve pounders. You have coordinates, observers?"

"Yes, sir! Still too far away for effect, but they're closing fast."

"Sing out when they reach range."

"Yes, sir. The dogs are visible, sir."

"The first wave will be right behind them."

Several hard explosions reached the Rebels dug in on the hill, faint screaming following the explosions.

"Claymores got a few of them," Ben said with a faint smile. He knew first-hand how deadly the feared Claymores could be.

Mines buried in the ground began crashing, flinging bits of bodies into the air. The painful howling of dogs could be heard.

"I hope it killed all them damn dogs," the young

sentry said. "'Fore I joined up with you, General, I was travelin' with this girl. Beth was her name. I was seventeen, she was fifteen, she thought, wasn't really sure how old she was. We was over in central Texas, between Austin and Abilene. Come up on these men. They turned dogs loose on us. No reason for it. They just done it to see what we'd do, I guess. I guess they thought it was sport. The dogs got us separated. I will never forget it. There wasn't nothing I could do. Them dogs tore her to pieces. Them men just laughed like it was the funniest thing they'd ever seen. I got back to our truck and got my gun. Killed two of 'em. Or at least hit them. The others run off. I hate dogs. I know it ain't right for me to hate all dogs for what just a few done, but I can't help it. Can't seem to ever get that sight out of my mind."

Psychiatrists could have a field day with me and my bunch, Ben thought. The shrinks would be leaping for joy. I wonder how many shrinks are still alive? Ben silently pondered. Not many. Those liberal bastards probably couldn't survive in the real world.

Ben, like so many men who were a part of military's special, highly elite troops, had a dim opinion of most psychiatrists.

"No one in their right mind could blame you for feeling the way you do," Ben told him. "Not after seeing what you saw."

The observer halted any further conversation. "The first wave has halted at twenty-five hundred meters, sir," he called, his voice crackling out of Ben's speakers. He had them hanging loosely around his neck.

Ben put on the headset and asked, "You have them locked in?"

"Yes, sir," the mortar crew chief replied calmly. "I can put them right up their noses."

"All right, Sergeant. Then go ahead and clear up their sinuses."

Ben heard the sounds of tubes being loaded, the *thonk* and the following flutter as the rockets flew toward target.

A few silent seconds lapsed between firing and impact. Then the ground below the men and women on the ridge erupted in sound and fury. The mixed mortar rounds, HE and WP, turned the area into an inferno, the white phosphorus rounds igniting the dry brush and timber. Burning shards of WP slammed into human bodies and began burning their way into flesh. Men ran screaming in agony; some flopped on the ground and rolled about, trying to ease the burning.

Nothing they did would stop the horrible pain as the phosphorus burned through flesh and bone.

"Gonna be forest fires come out of this," the young Rebel standing beside Ben observed.

"It will be raining by two o'clock this afternoon," Ben told him, not taking the binoculars from his eyes. He viewed the wreckage below with a soldier's satisfaction.

The young Rebel looked toward the skies. The sky was clear and cloudless. But if General Raines said it was going to rain . . . get your poncho out.

"Continue lobbing them in," Ben spoke into his headset. "Drive them back. Let's clear their ranks out as heavily as possible during the first wave."

The mortar crews continued working steadily for two more minutes before Ben called for them to cease firing. Lifting his field glasses to his eyes, he viewed the ripped low ground before him. He smiled as he looked at the smoking battleground.

Broken, shattered and bleeding bodies littered the scarred landscape of the earth. Arms and legs and heads had been torn from torsos and flung yards from the mangled trunks. Small fires were burning on the south side of the creek. A burning pine tree suddenly exploded like a bomb going off as the sap ignited.

"I count almost a hundred dead, General," Captain Rayle said, appearing at Ben's side. "They've probably dragged forty or fifty wounded out of our line of sight, back into the deep timber. We hurt them, all right."

"They'll leave us alone from that direction for a while," Ben said. "You lookouts on the flanks and to the rear, heads up, now. They'll be sending out sniping teams." Ben walked to the hastily dug communications bunker. "What's the word from the Base Camp?"

"Nothing since last night, sir."

"Mopping up," Ben told her. "The worst job of them all."

TWENTY

"How many did we lose?" Tina asked Colonel Gray.

"Too bloody many," the Englishman replied. "Counting the wounded, the dead, the desertions, we have had our strength cut by about forty percent. Old General Walker was killed, along with about half of his old soldiers who joined us. Walker died with a rifle in his hands, though. Reports say the old boy killed several of Willette's men before they gunned him down."

"Eagle Three is reporting some pockets of resistance still to the east of us. The Scouts say they'll have it contained in a few hours. I'm sorry about General Walker. I liked that old man. Did he really fight in World War II?"

"He sure did," Dan replied, just a touch of awe in his voice. "With Merrill's Marauders in Burma. He was a hero again in Korea, and was a general during the early days of Vietnam."

Cecil strolled up, his face grim. "I have ordered our people in the field to offer surrender terms only once. After that, if our teams are met with armed force, the coup members are to be destroyed. I want this put down hard!"

"That's all we can do, Cec," Mark Terry said, joining the group. There was a bloody bandage tied around his head and he had taken a nick on his left arm. He was grim-faced. "About twenty percent of my people were involved in the takeover attempt. I'm having those who survived shot at this moment. I warned them after that fiasco with Hartline and the IPF forces that any breech of orders would result in a firing squad."*

The group was silent for a moment, listening to the punishing shots roll from just north of the camp. Mark's eyes were tortured as he listened, knowing those were his people he had ordered put against the wall.

"How is Peggy?" Dan asked gently.

Mark sighed. With a visible effort he pulled his attention away from the shots of the firing squads. "She's OK. Her wounds were not serious. Doctor Chase and his medical people just returned to camp. That old man is *randy*, folks. He was leading a team of guerrillas in the woods. His people killed two teams of Willette's people." Mark kicked at a pebble with the toe of a jump boot. His eyes were downcast, as if something heavy was weighing on his mind.

"Something on your mind, old man?" Dan asked.

Mark blurted, "Sally McGowen was among those killed at the football field."

"Oh . . . *balls!*" Dan said.

"How about the children?" Tina asked.

Mark shook his head. "Dead. Sally tried to protect them with her body, shielding them. It was a brave

*Anarchy in the Ashes

but futile gesture. The .50-caliber slugs went right through her. The kids bought it."

"That's not going to set well with Ike," Dan said. "He and Sally have been experiencing some troubles in their relationship, but he adored those children."

Juan Solis and his brother, Alvaro, walked up. Both were bloodstained and dusty. "Willette and what was left of his bunch are gone. Disappeared into the timber, witnesses say. And it was Willette and some of his men who killed those people at the football field. Shot them in cold blood. Laughing as they murdered them. Witnesses who survived say Willette treated the entire matter as one big joke. Some of the Rebels guarding them, when they saw what was happening, dropped their weapons and ran to aid the wounded. Abe Lancer and his men were attacking the stadium, got there just in time to see the guards running. They thought the guards were a part of the murderers and opened fire on them. It was a night of confusion all the way around."

"That couldn't be helped," Cecil said. "I'll speak to Abe and his people. We're at the point where a traitor is a traitor is a traitor—to paraphrase Gertrude Stein."

"What outfit was she in?" a young Rebel sergeant asked the ex-college professor turned guerrilla fighter.

TWENTY-ONE

"They're pulling out of the timber," Ike said, after listening for a moment to his walkie-talkie. "But before we make any hasty moves, let's lay low for a few hours. It could be a trap."

"You mean, they may know we have communications, now?"

"Yeah. But from what we just heard, the coup attempt at the Base Camp failed. But we took a lot of casualties puttin' it down. Lots of folks got killed."

"Your wife?"

"I don't know," Ike replied. "I'm worried about the kids." He looked at Nina. "Don't read that as hard as it sounded. Kids and olds folks always take it on the chin in any war. I've seen too much of it not to know that's the way it goes down."

"I don't wanna grow old," Nina said flatly. "I feel sorry for old people. I seen it time after time, old people just pushed aside. Bad people abusin' them. It ain't right."

"That's the way it was when the government of the United States was operatin' at full tilt, too, Nina. Don't get me started on that subject. I always did feel there should have been special laws for the punks and crud who attack and abuse old people."

"What law would that have been, Ike?"

"Put the punk sons of bitches against a wall and shoot them."

Together they lay in a thicket and listened to their walkie-talkies. Within moments of the initial pull-back order, the radios fell silent as the searchers pulled out of range. Ike and Nina waited for an hour. The surrounding timber was silent except for the singing of the birds and the barking of squirrels as they went about their yearly tasks of gathering nuts for the fast-approaching winter months.

"Pretty and peaceful," Nina said. "I wish the whole world was peaceful."

"Maybe it will be someday," Ike replied.

"Don't put no money on it," her reply was pessimistic.

The pair ate a cold lunch, washing it down with fresh water from a rushing mountain stream. At Ike's orders, they gathered up their weapons and other gear and moved out, heading south.

This time they moved slowly and as silently as possible, stopping every hundred or so yards to check for sound or movement in the deep timber.

But only the natural sounds of forest inhabitants greeted them. They neither saw nor heard any of the men who had been chasing them.

Nina touched Ike's arm. "I think they're really gone."

"Yeah, I agree, little one." He looked at an old road map and then glanced around him, getting his bearings from deep in the timber. He pointed to a spot on the map. "We'll head out for this little town. This state road right here shouldn't be too far off.

269

We'll find it, and take it into town. If we have any luck at all, we'll find some wheels and barrel-ass back to Base Camp. I wanna find out what's happened to Ben."

"You're really worried about Mr. Raines, aren't you, Ike?"

"Worried maybe ain't the right word. Ben is tough as wang-leather. It's just . . . well, we've been together for a long time."

"Kinda like the way brothers is supposed to feel?" Nina questioned.

"Yeah," Ike said with a smile. "Brothers."

"OK. So lead on, Mr. Shark."

Ike wore a pained expression. "I keep tellin' you, damnit. It's SEAL, not shark. SEAL!"

TWENTY-TWO

"Here they come," Ben's headset whispered the lookout's words. "They're gonna try to make the creek and that little stand of timber this side of it. They reach that timber, we're in trouble."

"Settle down," Ben said. "They won't make it. Mortar crews! Commence firing. Snipers, in position, ready when and if they get into range. Hold your fire, all others. They're too far off. We don't want to waste ammo."

Ben was thoughtful for a moment as the first rockets left the tubes. He turned around and looked the area of the Rebels over. "Flanks and rear!" he yelled. "Stand ready. I think this is a diversion tactic. Keep your eyes glued to your perimeters."

Captain Rayle came to Ben's side. "Too few of them for a major assault, sir. I've ordered snipers to the flanks and rear."

"Concentrate your people to the east and west, Captain. Leave a few at the rear. It's much too wet and marshy back there. The terrain would slow them up too much and there isn't enough natural cover."

Ben adjusted his headset and pressed the talk button. "Mortar crews, slack off firing. Just let them know we're here. Chiefs, readjust every other tube to

271

the coordinates at the timber and brush lines east and west. Pronto."

"Yes, sir," came the immediate reply. "Readjusting."

Removing the headset, Ben walked to the crest of the ridge, stopping behind old fallen trees and newer felled trees the Rebels had chain-sawed down and then covered with natural brush and other foliage. He lifted his binoculars and caught the rustle of leaves at the timberline a few hundred meters from the base of the hill. He turned to a machine gunner, sitting patiently behind a big .50. Another Rebel squatted beside the heavy man-killer, ready to assist-feed the belt into the weapon.

"Adjust down a few degrees, son," Ben told the machine gunner. "I want the fire from this weapon directed left and right of that old lightning-blazed tree. See it? Good." Ben patted him on the shoulder. "You three with .60s—over here." Ben pointed silently and those Rebels manning the lighter .60-caliber machine guns nodded and slipped into position.

"Let them think we're not aware of their plans," Ben said. "Let them get clear of any cover before opening fire. When you do commence firing, I don't want any left alive. All right? Good. Hang in there, people."

Ben walked across the wide tabletop of the hill, now cluttered with instruments of war and hastily dug bunkers, housing mortar teams and communications equipment. He studied the base of the hill and its westward lie of underbrush and stunted timber. The mortar teams were laying down a slow but steady fire. Those men who had attempted the push from the front were retreating, leaving behind them their dead and wounded.

Ben studied the land below through his binoculars, James Riverson standing patiently by his side, the big senior sergeant towering over Ben's own six-feet-plus height.

"There," Ben muttered, catching a slight wave of tall grass, brittle-appearing now in late fall. He looked at Riverson. "You catch that, James?"

"Yes, sir. They're amateurs."

"Direct the operation from this flank, will you, James?"

"Yes, sir." Riverson began calling softly for machine gunners and mortar crews to readjust degrees.

The men below the ridges were not amateurs, but they were not much better, certainly not professionals. All the men and women with Ben were trained to the cutting edge. They were as professional a group of soldiers as any left anywhere in the nuclear and germ-torn world. And they were far superior to most. Every man and woman in the Rebels was cross-trained in at least three specialties. A machine gunner might be a qualified medic and a demolition expert. A medic might be a sniper and a tank driver. That type of training was a holdover from Ben's days in the U.S. Army's elite Hell Hounds, a spin-off of the Ranger/Special Forces units. The old Hell Hounds had been such an ultra-secret group that even among top ranking officers of the military, many did not know of their existence.

Ben and his people waited motionless, deliberately

allowing the men on the ground below them to get into position. They waited until the flanking attack began, and still waited, waited until the men were clear of any near cover. Then the Rebels opened up with everything they had at their disposal.

The Rebels caught the troops of Tony Silver and the Ninth Order in the open. The screaming of the wounded and the dying on the slopes of the flanks filled the air as heavy machine gunfire literally sliced the foot soldiers to bloody rags and bare bone and steaming, ripped-open bellies. Mortars pounded the earth and grenade launchers lobbed their payloads into the smoky air.

The firefight lasted no more than two minutes. Two minutes that to those receiving the lead and shrapnel and feeling the pain seemed more like two years.

"Cease fire," Ben spoke into his mic.

Just as the last echo was fading into memory, the radio operator called out. "General? I've got the fix on their radio frequency. You want to listen, sir?"

Ben held one headphone to his ear and listened, a smile playing across his lips.

"Pull back!" the voice shouted hysterically. "God-damnit, pull back."

"Give us some covering fire!"

"Shit! They ain't shootin' no more."

"I don't give a fuck! I ain't moving 'til I git some coverin' fire."

"Goddamnit, they're creamin' us. They's too god-damn many of 'em and they got better firepower than us."

A firm voice overrode the frenzied, frightened voice.

"Platoon leaders—report!"

"First platoon here. And I'm *it*! I got no more men left. Every fuckin' one of them is dead. I'm gettin' the hell outta here."

"You men stand firm!" the hard voice of command ripped the order.

"Oh, yeah? Well, *fuck* you! And fuck Ben Raines, too."

"Yeah," another man's voice took the air. "And fuck the horse he rode in on, too. I'm takin' my boys and gittin' the hell away from this death trap."

"This is Tony Silver," a calmer voice took over. "All my men fall back. We'll regroup over at a town called McCormick. Move out now and gather at the trucks."

"Ten-four, Tony," a man said. "We're pulling out now."

"Silver! You have your orders from Sister Voleta. If you disobey them, I'll—"

"Stick it up your ass, Wally," Silver cut him off. "I'm not sayin' we run away. Just usin' common sense and orderin' a regroupin'. Think about it, man. Look at them dead bodies down there. Hell, they didn't even get *close* to Raines' position. The god-damn creek is runnin' red with blood. Everything is all fucked up at Base Camp; Willette's people blew it, man. Use your head. We got no mortars, no artillery. No way we'll ever get to Raines. He'll sit up there on that stinkin' hill and kill us all, one at a time. And you can bet on this, too: Anytime he wants to leave, him and them people with him can punch a hole in our lines bigger than a whore's cunt. OK. So we lost a battle. One battle, man. That don't mean we lost the whole war. Some famous dude said that, long time back. There is always another time, man. Think about it.''

Silence for several heartbeats. "All right, Tony. You're right. Sister Voleta will just have to accept the loss and draw up another plan. All troops around the hill withdraw and backtrack to McCormick. We'll regroup and map out plans there.''

"What about the wounded, Wally?'' another voice was added to the confusion.

"You wanna go out there after them?'' the challenge was laid down.

No one picked it up. The airwaves remained silent.

"That's what I thought,'' Wally spoke.

The wounded lay beneath the guns of those on the hill. They lay screaming as life ebbed from them, staining the ground under their broken and torn bodies.

"Fuck Ben Raines,'' someone finally spoke. "And fuck them people with him. Jesus. Them people fight like crazy folks.''

"Pull out,'' Wally said.

Ben laid the earphones on top of the radio. He winked at the radio operator and she smiled at him. Ben said, "It is the spirit which we bring to the fight that decides the issue.''

"That's pretty, General,'' she replied, the admiration she felt for the man shining in her eyes. "Did you just make that up?''

Ben laughed. "No, dear. A man by the name of Douglas MacArthur said that, a long time ago.''

"Oh. What was he, sir, a poet or something?''

TWENTY-THREE

"How far are we from the South Carolina border?" Sam Hartline asked his driver.

"'Bout three hours, sir. We've really been pushing it."

"We have made good time. OK. Let's take a break and get some rest. Our forward patrol reported the interstate out up the road a few miles. They're scouting an alternate route now. We'll angle up toward Clark Hill Lake when we get cranked up again. Our last frequency scan showed Raines and his people to be around the town of McCormick. I want us to hit them just at dawn. This time I'm going to wipe the pavement with Ben Raines' ass."

The driver chuckled. "Won't Raines be surprised? Hell, he thinks we're still in California."

"He won't be surprised long," Hartline said. "Just long enough for me to shoot that bastard right between the eyes. McCormick. That's where you die, Raines."

"Scouts out, now!" Ben ordered. "Just as soon as you see their bugout is real, let us know. We're pulling out right behind them. I've got a hunch about this place. I think we've overstayed our welcome."

The Scouts slipped down the brush-covered sides of the ridge and vanished into the timber.

Ben took Captain Rayle and James Riverson aside. Opening a map, he said, "We're going to take this old road over to Highway 28, head north all the way up to Anderson, then on to where we pick up Highway 76. We'll follow that across the top of Georgia and swing down, come into the Base Camp from the north. No one will be expecting us from that direction. Instruct the radio personnel to use only short-range radios. I don't want *anyone* to be able to track our movement and pinpoint our location by radio frequency. I want to know exactly what has happened at Base Camp before we go blundering in there."

"Yes, sir."

Within the half hour, the Scouts reported the enemy's bugout was for real. The men of Tony Silver's army and the men of the Ninth Order had tucked their tails between their legs and ran like frightened rabbits.

Ben looked at the dead men on the ground below the ridge. "Take what equipment we can use and get all their ammo. Start tearing down here and loading the trucks and Jeeps. I want us on the road by two o'clock."

He went to Gale's side. Throughout the battle, she had sat with and comforted the wounded in the center of the camp, in a shallow, hastily dug bunker.

Ben stood for a moment, watching her calmly change the bandage on a young man's arm. The Rebels had taken no casualties during this fight, but still had some seriously wounded from the previous firefights of this trip.

"How's it going, old girl?" Ben asked.

She lifted her eyes to his. *"Old girl!"* She shook her head. "Why I'm just fine, Ben. All my teenage years were spent longing to meet a man who would keep me constantly sitting in the middle of a war."

Ben laughed at her.

She smiled at him and said, "Come on, Raines, tell the truth, now. You enjoyed every second of the battle, didn't you? Come on, admit it. You live for the thrill of combat, don't you?"

"Me, darling?" Ben rolled his eyes in protest. "Why . . . I'm a peace-loving man, full of love for my fellow man."

She made a disbelieving, choking sound. "What you are, Raines, is so full of bullshit I don't see how you can walk."

He laughed and stepped down into the shallow bunker. Leaning down, he kissed her. The wounded in the bunker applauded them both. Gale blushed and Ben bowed courteously. All the Rebels loved to hear Gale and Ben have at each other. And most were amazed the relationship had lasted this long, for General Raines was not known for staying with one woman very long. Not since Salina.

"We'll be pulling out soon, Gale. I'll send someone over to help you with the wounded."

"We heading home?" she asked.

"In a roundabout way, yes."

"But first you have to see if we can get in another fight along the way, right?" she asked dryly.

Ben smiled. There was truth in what she said.

"We'll get back to Base Camp in one piece," he assured her. "Sure you won't change your mind and come with me when I go traveling?"

"Not on your life, Buster. I want to have my babies in Chase's clinic."

"*Our* babies," Ben corrected.

"I can see it all now," Gale said. "Years from now, telling the twins about where their father was while they were being born. 'Oh, he was out toodling about the country, starting wars and rescuing people and probably chasing after every woman he could find. For he has it in his head to single-handedly repopulate the earth.'"

The wounded Rebels cheered and applauded.

"Darling," Ben said, "you know I'll be true blue to you while I'm gone."

Gale fumbled in her duffle bag and pulled out a roll of toilet paper, handing it to Ben. "Like I said, Raines: full of it."

TWENTY-FOUR

When the engine in the old GMC pickup coughed and sputtered and finally roared into life, Nina clapped her hands and squealed in delight. She had never learned to drive. The one time she tried, she drove slap into a huge oak tree and cut a gash in her forehead. After that, she either walked or rode horses. Hell with cars and trucks.

But this time was different: Ike could drive.

The GMC had been found inside a locked garage behind a barn. The owner had put the GMC short wheelbase pickup on blocks, and then removed the rubber. Using a hand pump, Ike inflated the tires and lugged them down tight.

A battery had been located, still in its factory box, and acid was added to the cells. The transmission was stiff from lack of use. Ike changed the fluid, changed the oil, checked the brakes, and he and Nina were on their way.

They found an old gas station just down the road, and using a long hose, Ike hand-pumped gasoline into containers, storing those in the rear, then he filled the tank.

Mice had found their way inside the cab of the GMC, and the seat was badly chewed, with several springs sticking out. Nina covered the seat with a comforter from a house.

"How far is it to your place, Ike?" Nina asked.

"Pretty good jump, kid. And we're not going to be able to push this old baby too hard." He patted the fender of the GMC. "We got some pretty rugged country to travel over." He unfolded an old road map and laid it on the hood, tracing their proposed route with a blunt finger. "We'll take this road to Dahlonega, and then cut due west. We'll be home this time tomorrow, I'm betting."

"Providin' we don't run into more trouble, that is," she cautioned him.

"Yeah," Ike agreed. "There is that to consider." He smiled and patted her shapely butt. "You ready, kid?"

"That depends on what you got in mind."

Ike laughed. "Travel, baby. Get in the truck."

"I'm so disappointed."

"Well . . ." Ike hesitated.

"We got time," she said.

"Yeah," he said, his voice husky. "I reckon we do, at that."

Ben and his Rebels pulled onto Highway 28 just as the sky darkened ominously and the black clouds began dumping silver sheets of rain on the small convoy. The young Rebel Ben had spoken to earlier about rain glanced at his wrist watch. It was two o'clock.

He told the Rebel sitting next to him about the general's statement concerning forest fires and when it would rain.

His companion, a Rebel buck sergeant who had been part of Raines' Rebels for years, merely shrugged. "The general knows things we don't know and never will. I learned a long time back not to wonder about it too much. Just accept it."

"I guess that's the thing to do."

The rain made Gale nervous. The heavy down-pouring on the roof of the pickup sounded like bullets. "This is not just a rain, Ben. This is a damned storm."

"Yeah. Next month it'll be sleet and freezing rain. We've got a lot of work to do back at Base Camp before hard winter locks us in, and not much time to get it done. I've noticed that since the bombings, back in '88, the winters all over the country are getting more severe each year, and the summers more savage."

"My friends at the university, scientists, said the bombings changed many of the weather patterns. I remember them saying that countries that had never experienced snow and ice before were now having hard winters."

"That's true, so I hear. I suspect future generations will have a great deal more to contend with, weatherwise."

She picked up a sour note in his tone. She had heard it before. "You really don't hold much promise for the future, do you, Ben?"

Ben waited until a particularly hard drumming of rain on the cab of the truck abated before replying. "Not unless what is left of the population does a drastic turnaround, Gale. Oh, *we'll* make it all right. The Rebels, I mean. I suspect this recent coup attempt will be the first and the last among our ranks. We'll just be much more selective from now on as to whom we allow to join us. And *we'll* set up shops and small factories and businesses and schools, give our people some degree of formal education. And I suspect there are other *older* people around the world doing much the same—right this moment. But *older* is the key word, Gale. As we—you and I, and others within our age spectrum—grow older and die, the burning desire for knowledge, book knowledge, will fade and die with us. Not all at once, certainly, but more like a gradual diminishing.

"Now, that does not mean civilization is going to abruptly roll over and die. What it does mean is that most will return to the land, a nation of small farmers and craftsmen." He smiled. "Excuse me, crafts-*persons.*"

"Very funny, Raines. Ha-ha. Please continue. Try to keep me awake."

"I'll do my best, dear. It has been a rather boring day, thus far, right?"

"Raines . . ."

"OK. OK. I can foretell it with as much accuracy as Nostradamus—unless this nation picks itself up and turns it around, and does it quickly. After we're gone, the younger ones will keep the old cars and trucks running until they fall apart. But in a hundred years, Gale, few will possess the knowledge to *build* a car or truck. Airplanes will be something for people to sit and look at, wondering what in the hell they can do with them. I don't want to lecture, Gale, for you know what I'm driving toward."

"Education," she said quietly.

"That's right. And Gale, we now have in this country, one *entire* generation—those who were, say, eight to ten when the bombs fell—who can't read or write. It scares me, Gale. It really frightens me.

"Look at the area we've traveled through these past months, Gale. Look at what is occurring in this nation. Only very small pockets of men and women—for the most part, *older* men and women—are attempting to set up schools and organization and have some semblance of law and order and rules of conduct. The thugs and punks and assorted criminals that seem to crawl out of the gutters in times like these are at their glory. And it's going to get much worse as time marches on. Tony Silver, for example, is nothing more than a modern-day warlord. Sister Voleta/Betty Blackman is, well, nuts, I think."

Gale went on the defensive. "But the young can't be blamed for their attitudes, Ben. They've had no examples to look up to."

Ben surprised her by agreeing. "That's right, Gale."

She narrowed her eyes. "Drop the other shoe, Raines."

Ben grinned. "One cannot blame the young for their lack of judgment because they never knew, really, any type of civilized society. And those now in their late twenties and early thirties, like you, Gale," he said blandly, "knew only a very permissive, liberal type of government as teenagers, before the bombings. Blaming them is just as pointless. Blame the mothers and the fathers and lawmakers and judges and record producers and TV programmers, beginning in the mid-sixties and continuing right up to the bombings for the lack of understanding of discipline and work ethics and moral codes and rules of order—if one just has to point a finger of blame. I did enough of that back in the late seventies and all through the eighties, as a writer. A lot of us did. Those of us with any foresight at all. The majority chose not to listen. Fine. Now I can sit back and take a grim satisfaction in the outcome of it all.''

Gale did not vocally counter-punch with Ben on that, for in her time with the man, she had learned Ben was almost totally unyielding in his philosophy as to what had contributed to the breakdown of the United States of America. As a teenager in St. Louis, after the war of '88, Gale was one of those who had taken part in human rights marches against Ben Raines and the nation he and his Rebels had carved out west: the Tri-States.*

Ben's philosophy was that there had been too much government intervention into the operation of privately owned businesses, too much interference in the personal lives of citizens from big government, too many lawyers and too many judges and too many lawsuits. Ben felt that when there was a United States of America, it was probably the most sue-happy nation on the face of the earth.

"Don't forget a common sense return to government," Ben broke into her thoughts. "Something Americans refused to demand from their lawmakers and assorted great nannies in Washington."

"Raines, I wish you would stop getting into my head like that. All right. What are you going to bitch

*Out of the Ashes

about now? You going to jump all over the ACLU again?''

"Nope," Ben said, surprising her again. "I am certain that group did a lot of good work defending the poor and indigent and the elderly. And a lot more. But most of their good work never reached the ears of the majority. All we heard about was their screaming about those poor misunderstood folks being put to death for brutally murdering an entire family, or for raping, torturing and killing some five-year-old girl. We heard they defended those slobbering punks, trying to get them off with every cheap legal trick they could think of. I think the ACLU must have had a lousy PR department.''

Gale bristled, as Ben knew she would. That was why he'd said it.

"You consider human life very cheaply, don't you, Ben?''

"Cheap human life, yes. But I've put my ass on the line far more times than I can remember for decent, law-abiding folks, Gale.''

"Stop twisting my words, Ben Raines. You know what I mean. Maybe that group of lawyers you're so down on simply placed a great deal more value on human life than you?''

"But on *whose* human life is what always baffled me, Gale,'' Ben countered. "The victim's or the criminal's?''

She opened her mouth to retort and caught Ben's smile. She knew he was deliberately goading her, for he loved to make her angry.

"Way to go, Raines. You did it again. How come you like to get me all upset, huh?'' She stuck out her chin defiantly.

"Back in the 'good ol' days,' dear, one of my greatest delights was in putting the so-called needle to liberals."

"You would. Well, you're not going to get another rise out of me. I just won't play your game anymore." She turned her face and gazed out the window at the stormy afternoon.

"OK," Ben said lightly. "Isn't this a pleasant day for a drive in the country?"

She narrowed her eyes and glared at him. "All right, Buster—I know you're up to something. So give."

Ben's face was a picture of innocence. "Darling, I'm not up to anything. I'm just adhering to your recent request."

"Uh-huh. Sure you are. When pigs fly, baby."

"Well, since you insist, I was thinking about an old buddy of mine who lived in New York City. We were in the service together." He stopped speaking and looked straight ahead, concentrating on the rain-swept old highway, twisting the wheel to avoid the debris that littered the highway.

"Well?" she asked.

"Well, what?"

"Your *buddy*! What the hell else?"

"Oh. Well . . . what is it you want to know about him?"

"Raines, you are the most exasperating man I have ever known." She shook a small fist under his chin. "How'd you like to have a fat lip?"

"I thought you didn't believe in violence?"

"You . . . you . . ." she sputtered.

"All right, all right. Mike was coming home from work one evening and a couple of New York City's more baser types tried to mug him. He quite literally beat the shit out of both of them. Broke the neck of one. Almost tore the arm off the other. He did break it in about six places. Mike must have really been pissed off. The punks went to that . . . ah, particular organization of lawyers we were speaking of a few miles back—that one you no longer wish to discuss—and with their help, the bastards sued my buddy. The *criminals* sued the *victim* for damages. Did you hear me, Gale?"

"Yes, Raines!"

"I just wanted to be sure. Anyway, since mugging obviously isn't, or wasn't, a particularly odious offense in the Big Apple, and the punks knew their chances of going to prison for what they'd done was slim to none, they admitted what they'd done, sued my buddy—and *won*. Now, would you care to ask me why I don't—or didn't—particularly care for that organization? And for asshole judges with shit for brains; let us not forget those pricks."

"Raines, I realize any further debate with you on this subject is pointless, since you have a head as hard as a billy goat, but have you ever even vaguely considered the thought about the punishment fitting the crime?"

"I believe that is the longest question I ever heard in my life. But in reply: no. Not since I grew up and realized it was a pile of garbage."

Gale almost choked on the apple she was munching on. "A pile of garbage! Ben, that is the most insensitive thing I have ever heard you say."

"Why?" Ben asked, a puzzled look on his tanned face. As usual, a liberal question or statement confused him, had all his life. "The one thing the government never did try in their so-called war on crime is to completely eradicate it. To me, it's very simple: If a country has no criminals, that country will have no crime. I proved that in Tri-States. It isn't a theory, Gale. It worked."

She shook her head and stubbornly held on. "That philosophy would never work in a nation as large as the United States."

"That's what I advocated some years back. Now I'm not so certain. It's a moot point, anyway." He fell silent, lost in his thoughts.

Gale dropped the apple core into a paper bag and glared at Ben. "Oh, hell, Raines. Go on, get it said."

"You sure?"

She laughed at the dubious expression on his face. "I'm sure, Bem. I told you I'd be the first to let you know if I ever got tired of you and your soapbox."

"Very well. You're too young to remember much before the bombings. You were just a kid, and since both your parents were liberal, it's doubtful you got the entire picture, free of whitewash."

"Oh, *way* to go, Raines." She sighed and shrugged her shoulders. "But you're probably right. Just get on with it, huh?"

"It'll take more than a few words, Gale." He spun the steering wheel to avoid colliding with a downed tree that was blocking half the road. "Because it takes several things to make a crime-free environment. And not necessarily in this order. It takes full employment. Two or three or six percent unemployment won't do it. Full employment is the only way. Why do you want to hear this, Gale?'' Ben looked exasperated. "What are you, a masochist?"

"Beats looking at the weather," she replied. "Just get on with it."

Her flip reply gave her inner feelings away, at least to Ben. Liberalism had failed miserably. If there was to be, ever again, a workable society built out of the ashes, it had to be something other than the unworkable flights of fancy the liberals had forced upon the taxpayers of America. She wanted to explore all avenues.

"We had full employment in Tri-States, Gale. We had it because healthy, able-bodied people were required to work." He cut his eyes at her and smiled. "You may interrupt at any time, dear."

"You *forced* people to work, Ben?"

"I certainly did, darling. But not at a job they were physically unable to handle. I wouldn't put a person with a bad heart out digging ditches or a mental defective working at a computer."

"Very commendable of you, I'm sure," she said dryly. "Please, do continue. It's fascinating." She found another apple and chomped away.

"Back before the bombings, certain organized labor unions advocated a thirty-five hour work week, in order to put more people to work. Very nice of them. But they wanted no cut in pay; they wanted business to absorb the cost. And that leads me right into a restoration of the work ethic. A day's work for a day's pay. Pride in one's work and a cessation of living solely for the weekend and never mind that the product the assembly-line workers were building was shoddy. And many of them were just that.

"In Tri-States, we took a hard look at the way factories and businesses were run, and we changed the structure of it all. Employee ownership is one way we found that really works. And we did it without the threat of unions hanging over our heads.

"We completely reworked the income tax system. We found that a rigidly enforced graduated scale worked best for us. It was difficult for one to become a millionaire in Tri-States, but certainly not impossible. *Everyone* paid their share of income tax—everyone. There were no exceptions. We closed virtually all loopholes and made the filing form so simple a sixth grader could fill it out. You see, Gale, we were able to do that because we did not allow lawyers to have a goddamn thing to do with it. There weren't many lawyers in Tri-States. There were no fancy lunches or dinners to be written off the income tax as 'business related.' We stopped virtually all that nonsense, because we all knew it had been so badly abused in the past.

"We started by attacking and challenging many of the so-called 'little items.' Company cars, for example, incorporating for another. In Tri-States, one could incorporate all day if one wished. But it wouldn't help a bit when it came to taxes. No tax breaks there. One could write off a company car, but only for the time one actually used that in the operation of the business. And God help the person who tried to cheat, for the system came down hard."

"How in the world did you people make it work, Ben? I . . . it boggles my mind. It just seems so . . . unworkable."

"Because we did a one hundred and eighty degree turn, honey. We returned to the values this nation was supposedly built upon. Oh, we had people who cheated. Sure we did. But over the years we found them. The system was such that it was almost impossible to get away with crime. I guess it all came back to our type of government. It was a common sense type of government."

She held up a slim hand. "Whoa, Ben. Kindly explain that, please. Every Rebel I talk with says the same thing. What in the hell is a common sense type of government?"

"Gale, before the bombings, the government of the United States was so top-heavy with bureaucrats it was sinking under its own weight. The government had laws on top of laws, not just the federal government, but local and county and state. The individual citizen had practically no control over his or her life. Day to day living had turned into a stroll through a minefield of legal entanglements. Criminals had more rights than victims. The average citizen really did not know if he could legally protect his life or property or family with deadly force or not. Much of government, while not corrupt—although a lot of that was going on—was confused. Much like the left hand not knowing what the right hand is doing. I became very apolitical. That's not a strong enough word. I, along with millions of others, became discouraged with government. Depressed with the entire system. Our national debt was staggeringly high, with no end in sight. Something had to give. And it did. The whole damned world exploded in war."

Ben paused, looking around him through the gloom of the raging afternoon's storm. Common sense form of government, he thought. God, how to tell this gentle lady who still could not hit the side of a barn at point-blank range with *any* type of weapon—how to tell her? How does one who wholeheartedly adopts the fact—and Ben knew it was fact, not theory—that society does not reject those who choose a life of crime, the criminal rejects society, how does one explain that to a person who throughout her formative years had been not-so-subtly brainwashed by a liberal doctrine? Ben had tried a few times before . . . failing each time.

He took a deep breath—sighed heavily. "Gale, if a person puts a No Trespassing sign up in the front yard, it does not mean the back yard can be explored at will by anyone who so desires. That sign means, quite literally: Keep your ass off this property. All this property. Anyone who possesses even a modicum of common sense wouldn't set one foot on that posted property. Now I'm not saying the person who put the sign there has the right to kill a trespasser by ambush, without any warning. But I do maintain that if the property owner steps out with a shotgun in his hands and ordered the trespasser off, and the trespasser refuses to leave, what happens after that lies solely on the head of the person who violated the property owner's rights. Do you follow me?"

"Reluctantly, Ben. Of *course*, I follow you. I'm not stupid."

"Perhaps we're getting somewhere at last," Ben said with a chuckle. "But, Gale, a liberal doctrine, which is by no means based on any semblance of common sense, theorizes that no one has the right to use deadly force in the protection of property rights or private possessions. And that is precisely why the nation endured a crime wave unparalleled in its history, beginning when the Supreme Court and federal judges began sticking their goddamn noses into the lives of private, law-abiding, American citizens. States' rights became a thing of the past. Not that the states didn't abuse some of those rights, because they did, in many ways. But if a state chooses to put a criminal to death, after going through proper procedures and reviews, then that should be the individual state's prerogative, and the federal government should keep the hell out of it.''

Ben laughed aloud, laughing at himself. "Sorry, Gale. Government interference was always a sore point with me."

"I never would have guessed, Ben," she said, smiling. "Was it really that bad, Ben?"

"Yes. And getting worse with each year. Along about . . . oh, the early eighties, I guess it was, we finally put a man in the White House with courage enough to try to get Big Brother off the backs of the citizens. And oh, Lord, did the sobbing sisters and weak-kneed brothers howl. And, to their credit, the Supreme Court, I think, finally woke up and began to see the writing on the wall. The death penalty was restored—over the howlings and moanings and weeping of many liberal groups—and the states began the slow process of barbecuing and gassing and shooting murderers."

"Ben, that's awful!"

"I don't see it that way and never will. Gale, in Tri-

States, our kids were taught from a very early age to respect the rights of others. That it is against the law to kill, to steal, to cheat, to trespass, to practice blind prejudice, and that they could get seriously hurt, or killed, if they violated the law. And, Gale—it worked. We proved all the so-called experts wrong. Flat wrong. We of Tri-States *proved* that crime does not have to be tolerated. We proved it can be eradicated. I really hope I am not the only person planning to chronicle the last days of this nation's—indeed, the *world's*—history, for I want somebody else, with a fair and reasonable nature to point out to the future generations, that Tri-States worked. That crime and greed and laziness and stupidity do *not* have to be accepted. That they can be wiped from the face of any society if that society will work together, be of like mind, but not a nation of clones. That is my wish.''

Gale put a hand on Ben's arm. "You're a hard man, Ben Raines, but you're a pretty good man, too. Would you pull over right there?" She pointed to a cut-off gravel road.

"You have to go to the bathroom in *this* weather?"

"No. I wanna get that sack of canned fruit out of the back. I'm hungry!"

TWENTY-FIVE

The rain was not confined to the South Carolina area; it was pouring down all over the southeastern United States. A sudden and very violent storm was sweeping the already ravaged land. It was as if the hand of God was punishing the battered earth.

The storm forced Ike and Nina to seek shelter in an old barn. They holed up there for the night, Nina clinging to Ike.

The remaining troops of Silver and the Ninth Order, now a beaten and bedraggled and sodden and sullen bunch, elected to spend the night at McCormick. They made plans to pull out in the morning. Nothing would be moving this night. So they thought. But Hartline and his men would be on the move. Toward McCormick.

But something began gnawing at Tony's guts. He had a bad feeling about McCormick. Some intangible sense of warning tugged at his streetwise hoodlum's brain. He gathered up fifty of his men and pulled out quietly just as darkness wrapped her evening arms around the rain-soaked, lightning-and-thunder-pounded area. Tony and his party headed south on Highway 221, spending the night just outside Augusta.

It was a move that saved his life. For a while longer, that is.

At the Base Camp in northern Georgia, Tina Raines ran through the heavy downpouring to the communications shack. Slipping off her poncho and hanging it on a peg by the door of the old home, she turned to Cecil.

"Any word from Dad?" she asked.

Cecil shook his head. "Nothing, Tina. But that doesn't mean anything has happened to Ben. Your father is the toughest man I've ever seen. Ben is very hard to kill."

She nodded her head. Most of what was said about Ben was no myth. "How about Ike?"

"Intercepted messages from the Ninth Order tend to substantiate initial reports that Ike played hell with those chasing him. Them, I should say. But nothing from Ike himself. Ike is as tough as an alligator, Tina. And when he gets stirred up, as mean as a cobra. Ike's all right."

"The base is secure," Tina reported. "We didn't lose as many people as first thought. Thirty-five percent max. Many of our people headed for the deep timber when the coup attempt went down. They're straggling back in now, in small groups."

"That is good news," Cecil said with a smile. "What do Gray's Scouts report about the strength of the Ninth Order?"

"A Mister Waldo—he's some relation to Abe Lancer—who lives up near a town called Tellico Plains says the Ninth Order is still strong. Strong enough to do us some damage. That crazy woman who heads up the Order is said to have really pitched a fit when her people failed to kill Dad. She has—again, this is according to Mister Waldo—some sort of long-standing grudge against Dad. Goes back years and years, so the report went."

Cecil frowned and shook his head. "It's so odd, Tina. I don't recall Ben ever mentioning anything about her."

"Neither does anyone else. I've spoken with Jane, Jerre, Rosita, Dawn. . . ." She paused and then began laughing. The laughter proved highly infectious. Within seconds, the room of people were all laughing, the pent-up tension within them all flying out the open window into the stormy night.

After a moment, Cecil wiped his eyes with a large bandana and said, "All of Ben's women, you mean? Those you know about, at least—right?"

Tina nodded, still chuckling. "Yeah. My old man is something of a Romeo, isn't he? Anyway, none of those I spoke with know anything about any woman named Voleta."

"Probably changed her name," Mark said. "Lots of people did after the first bombings wiped out so many records. Juan was correct when he pegged this whole thing as a blood debt. God, she must really hate General Raines."

They all nodded their agreement. Each with their own thoughts as to what they would like to do to the woman called Voleta. None of the individual thoughts contained anything pleasant.

Tina looked at Cecil. "We have volunteers tagging and body-bagging the victims of the coup. This storm is supposed to blow out of here before dawn—that's according to the mountain people. I'm opting

299

for a mass grave, Cecil. How about you?''

"Yes,'' Ben's second-in-command and close friend replied. "Easiest and most sensible way. But we'll do it with as much dignity as we can muster. I spoke with a stone mason who lives near here. One of Abe Lancer's men. He said he'd start work as soon as we furnished him with a complete list of the names of those who died.''

"We'll do that first thing in the morning. The volunteers have said they'll be working right through the night.''

"Yes,'' Cecil said. "All of us want this hideous chapter of our lives over and done with as quickly as possible.'' He met Tina's eyes. "Has your father said anything to you about wanting to leave here—alone, I mean?''

"He's mentioned that he wants to get away for a time, return to his chronicling of the events leading up to and just after the bombings of '88. Yes, I imagine Dad will do just that.''

"And . . . Gale?'' Cecil asked softly.

Tina smiled. "She wants him to go—alone. She is fully aware of the fact that no woman holds Ben Raines' attention for very long. Not since Salina. Dad is going to fall really in love one of these days. And when he does, it'll be a sight to see. But for now, he wants us settled in tight, Gale to have a home, and then he'll wander.''

"He's not going to want any bodyguards,'' Mark said.

"No,'' Tina agreed. "And if anyone tries to burden him with them, he'll find a way to shake them.''

Cecil sighed. "Let's face that when the time comes

around, people. Right now, though, let's all get some much-needed rest for a few hours. We've still got a lot to do.''

Ben halted his convoy at a motel complex just off Interstate 85 and ordered then to eat and rest. Everyone was beat, some near exhaustion. Ben looked as refreshed as if he'd just risen from an uninterrupted eight hours' sleep.

After a cold meal, most of the Rebels unrolled their sleeping bags and bedrolls and crashed on the floor. They were asleep in five minutes, oblivious to the storm that raged outside the motel complex.

Ben and Gale, after tossing everything in the motel room outside, and checking the carpet for fleas and other vermin, inflated the air mattress and laid a double sleeping bag over the gentle firmness. Gale was sleeping in two minutes.

Ben stood just outside the closed motel room door, watching the lightning lick across the night sky, the wicked needles lancing furiously, bouncing and lashing through the low heavens.

Ben looked at the firmament. "Where is it all ·leading?'' he questioned the night. "Are you going to give us one more chance, or is this your way of saying the human race has had it, all because we failed you?''

Thunder crashed and scolded the sodden ground; another burst of lightning flickered acidly, illuminating the lone man standing by the railing of the second floor. More thunder rolled, punishing the air with waves of fury.

"Sorry," Ben said, "but this display further con-

vinces me that you had a hand in all that happened.''
Ben's words were not audible over the howling fury.
A line from a long-ago Tennessee Williams play
came to him: Hypocrisy and mendacity. "That's the
way the world was leaning, right? Sure. Get drunk on
Saturday night and dress up in finery on Sunday and
go to church and pray for forgiveness at best, go to
church for the show of it at worst. Cheat your friend,
your neighbor, the customer, and fuck your best
buddy's wife. Right? Yeah. Buy expensive grown-up
toys while half the world's children starved to death
and this nation's elderly had to grub around in garbage cans just to survive. That is, if the summer's
heat or the winter's cold or the damned street punks
didn't kill them—right?''

The worst and harshest slash of lightning Ben had
ever seen lit up the entire sky. The sulfuric display
was followed by a deafening crash of thunder. More
lightning danced from cloud to cloud and from
cloud to earth.

Ben stood undaunted and unafraid and alone on
the balcony. "What are You attempting to tell us, or
me?" Ben questioned the almost mindless fury of the
storm. "Or are You trying to say anything at all? Do
You even exist? Or were You just a figment of someone's vivid imagination thousands of years ago?''

The earth trembled under the barrage of God's
wrath.

Ben stood with his face to the heavens—and
toward Him. "All right, all right," he said. "What's
the matter; can't You take a joke?''

The lightning and thunder ceased abruptly, the
rain picking up in volume.

"That won't do it," Ben said. "I don't believe in miracles, and the rain alone won't wash it clean. Hundreds of years must pass before portions of this earth—Your earth—will once more be inhabitable. I believe You allowed the disaster to happen. Now what are You trying to do, ease your conscience?"

The lightning and thunder began anew.

Ben laughed. "I'm not afraid of You. I respect You. But I'm not afraid of You. I'll tell You what: I think You've given up on this planet. That is my belief. I have always believed this planet earth was only one of many You populated with beings. And now You have turned Your attention to others. Fine. I don't blame You a bit. Now I don't know about this fellow called the Prophet who is wandering about, following me. I don't know what he's trying to tell me. But I do know this: I am *not* the man to restore Your earth. A little part of it, maybe. But the rest is up to You. So get off my back. I'm tired. I'm going to wander for a year. Maybe longer. Alone. Leave the machinery of government and building nations in someone else's hands. Cecil Jefferys. He's a good man. One of the best I've ever seen."

The lightning and thunder and driving rain eased off a bit.

"Interesting," Ben noted aloud. "I've had some strange conversations in my time, but this takes the cake."

A lone spear of lightning touched down.

"All right," Ben said. "It's pure survival from this point on, isn't it? Sure. Little pockets of determined people will set up fortresslike villages and try to pull something constructive from the ashes. Maybe they'll—*we'll* succeed. I've got something like that in the back of my mind. After I return from my wanderings. I think we've got maybe a seventy/thirty chance of success. With us on the low end of the odds scale."

The rain had dwindled down to a sprinkle; the lightning had completely stopped.

"All right," Ben spoke to that which only he could hear at that moment. "Fine."

He walked back into the motel room, undressed, and lay down beside Gale. She turned to face him in the darkness.

"I thought I heard you talking to someone, Ben."

"You did. I was carrying on a sort of conversation with God."

Several moments of silence passed. "Really?" she finally said. "Did He reply to your mutterings?"

"Well, yes. In a manner of speaking."

"Sometimes I worry about you, Raines. I really, really do."

She rose from the pallet and wandered around the barren room.

"What in the hell are you looking for?" Ben asked. He was thoughtful for a moment. "Don't tell me; let me guess: You're hungry."

In reply, she bit deeply into the crisp tartness of an apple.

TWENTY-SIX

The savage torrents of rain and storm blew past the town of McCormick, South Carolina, in the early morning hours. But the raging passage had also concealed the movements of Sam Hartline's men as they slipped silently into position in the town. With practiced ease, the mercenaries planted explosives around the town, enough explosives to flatten three towns the size of McCormick.

Easy, Hartline thought, smiling in the night. Raines has become so confident he's let his guard down.

The top mercenary knew that happened to the best of people at times. He remembered the time when he'd had one of Raines' women, Jerre, the blond beauty. He, too, had become overconfident and let his guard down. That moment of carelessness had almost cost Hartline his life.*

He remembered it with bitterness and hate on his tongue.

Smiling, he lifted his walkie-talkie. "Now!" Hartline whispered hoarsely into the speaker cup.

The small town of McCormick blew apart from the

*Fire in the Ashes

massive charges of explosives planted in key locations. The gasoline in the cars and vans and trucks of Tony Silver and the men of the Ninth Order ignited and blew, sending flames leaping into the air and illuminating the now clear and starry night.

Bits and pieces of bodies were hurled through broken windows to land in a sprawl on the littered street. Great bloody chunks of once human beings were flung about like damp bits of papier-mâché. Ropelike strands of intestines coiled and steamed in the fall coolness. Screaming, mortally wounded men crawled about on the street, yelling for help, watching their life's blood pour from them. Heads without bodies bounced and rolled on the concrete.

As the men being attacked fought their way out of sleep and fear and confusion, reaching for their weapons and their pants, running out into the streets, they were chopped to bloody shards of flesh by heavy machine gunfire. AKs and M-16s and M-60s and heavy .50-caliber slugs ripped and tore and spun the men around to fall in dead heaps on the concrete.

"No prisoners!" Hartline yelled over his walkie-talkie. "Kill them all except Ben Raines. I want to shoot that son of a bitch personally."

"Ben Raines!" One of Silver's men lifted his head to look at Hartline through the blood dripping from a massive head wound. "But Ben Raines ain't—"

He never got to finish his sentence. A .45 slug from one of Hartline's men put the final period to the man's life.

The firefight was short and bloody and savage. And totally without mercy. Sam Hartline's men took no prisoners. They hunted down the wounded and those few who had escaped the initial carnage and shot them.

Just as dawn was pushing silver gray into the eastern skies, Sam Hartline, cigar clamped between strong, even white teeth, walked the streets, inspecting the bloody havoc he had ordered. Hartline snorted his disgust as he walked up and down each stinking, bloody street that had housed what he had assumed to be Raines' Rebels.

"I should have known better," he muttered. "Goddamnit, I should have known better."

Hartline's final smile before he reluctantly accepted what had happened was anything but pleasant.

"The lucky son of a bitch did it to me again," Hartline said.

"What do you mean, Sam?" his second-in-command asked.

"It was too easy. Just too easy. I should have spotted it. But I didn't. Who in the fuck are these people?" He threw the question at anyone who might know the answer.

His men stood around him, bewildered expressions on their faces.

"Look at the condition of these weapons," Hartline said, pointing to an M-16. "You think Ben Raines would allow a weapon that filthy? Hell, no, he wouldn't. Look at the clothing. Raines' Rebels wear tiger stripe, black, or leaf cammies. These yo-yos are dressed in anything they can find. Shit! In short, people, we hit the wrong bunch."

Captain Jennings, his second-in-command, was incredulous. "Well, who in the hell are these people, then?"

Hartline shrugged. "Damned if I know. I'd guess the bunch Raines was fighting when we intercepted the radio messages. No telling where Raines got off to."

"Well," Captain Jennings struggled to find something bright out of the butcher job. "At least this gives us fewer people to have to worry about fighting at some later date. Right, Sam?"

Hartline laughed and punched the man lightly on the upper arm. "Right, Jennings. I knew I could count on you to find something of value out of this mistaken identity."

"So what now, Sam? Do we chase Raines?"

Hartline thought about that for a few seconds. He shook his head. "No. If I know Ben Raines, and believe me, I do, he won't be using any long-range radio transmissions. So we'd be chasing the wind just trying to determine where he is or where he's going. Let's head south. We'll break the good news to Mr. Tony Silver about the misfortune that befell his little army. Without his strong-arm boys to back him up, I think Mr. Silver should be quite easily persuaded to join our ranks."

"I'm told he's got the market cornered on young chicks," Jennings said with an ugly, anticipatory smile.

Sam felt a warmth spread throughout his groin. The images of moaning young girls and firm flesh and tight pussies filled his head. Just the thought of inflicting pain excited him. "Yes," he said, returning the smile. "So I understand."

TWENTY-SEVEN

Ben's convoy reached Highway 76 and edged west by northwest, traveling slowly, with heavily armed Scouts spearheading the way. They saw a few signs of life passing through Seneca, in western South Carolina, but the smoke from cooking fires coming from chimneys was all they saw. Ben made no attempt to contact any of those inside the closed and shuttered homes.

At Westminster the convoy swung still further north and moved into the mountains, again entering another part of the Sumter National Forest, edging toward the Chattahoochee National Forest, an immense tract of mountainous terrain that stretched for almost a hundred miles across the top of Georgia. The Rebels crossed the Chattoga River and Ben ordered the column halted for the noon meal and some rest at a town called Clayton.

"A hundred and fifteen miles to go, people," Ben told his contingent. "Approximately. But we're going to take our time getting there. We're going to keep our heads up and stay alert. This is Ninth Order territory, so be alert for ambushes. When we get up to Lake Chatuge, up near the North Carolina border, we'll contact Base Camp. See what's shaking down there. If they can tell us we're close to the headquarters of the Ninth Order, we may just wait there for more troops and just go on and wipe that bunch of nuts from the face of the earth. We'll just have to wait and see. For now, you people get some food in you and take a rest."

"Like I said, Raines," Gale told him. "You get off on combat. When did you get your first gun as a child?"

"When I was about six months old," Ben said with a straight face.

"Come on, Raines! Will you get serious?"

"I am serious. I literally cut my teeth chewing on the barrel of my great grandfather's old Civil War .44. It was a Remington, I think."

"I believe it, Raines. I really believe it." She walked away, muttering, toward the chow line.

TWENTY-EIGHT

Ike failed to see the huge hole in the old highway and the right front wheel dropped off into the weather-rutted pothole, slamming both him and Nina around in the cab. Both of them heard metal popping and both began cussing.

Then they saw the entire wheel, with tire intact, go rolling down the old highway.

Nina said some very unladylike words, ending with, "Well, Ike, I guess it's back to walking."

Ike looked at the right front of the pickup. There was no repairing this damage. Ike said a few choice words and pulled the pickup out of the road, parking it on the shoulder.

Both of them looked at the highway marker on the right side of the road. BLAIRSVILLE. The mileage was unreadable, but it had been a single number.

"At best it's one mile," Ike said. "The worst it can be is nine miles."

Ike was thoughtful for a moment, then checked the old map. "I got a hunch, Nina. Let's forget about Blairsville and head for this lake up near the North Carolina border."

"Why there?" she questioned. "Won't we be going

away from Base Camp?"

"Yeah. But like I said: I got a hunch. You game?"

"I'm with you, Ike."

The pair gathered up what they could carry and began trudging up the center of the road, Ike bitching with each step.

TWENTY-NINE

A huge hole had been scraped out of the damp earth and the bagged bodies of the men, women and children killed in the coup attempt were carefully laid in the excavation. The earth began claiming them as the bulldozers covered the silent shapes of friends, wives and husbands, lovers, mothers and fathers, sons and daughters.

Those men and women who had sided with Captain Willette in the coup attempt were placed in another pit far away and covered with earth. Their final resting place would go unnoticed and unmarked.

Cecil read several passages from the Bible as he stood over the raw earth. The names of those killed had been given to the stone mason and he was working at his laborious task. It would be weeks, perhaps months, before all the names were cut into several large stones.

Cecil closed his Bible, shook his head at the tragedy of it all, and walked away from the grave site. A runner from the communications shack found him and handed him a message.

"It's from that fellow that General Raines told us about," the runner said. "That Harner fellow down in Macon."

Cecil looked at the handwritten message. "Have word that a large force of mercenaries destroyed Tony Silver's army along with most of the troops of the Ninth Order who had been in combat with General Raines' Rebels in South Carolina. Have word that slave revolts occurring on many of Silver's work farms in both north Florida and south Georgia. Still about five hundred of Silver's army left and about that many men of the Ninth Order. A full platoon of Silver's men camped just east of the ruins of Atlanta, around Stone Mountain. We skirted them this morning and are proceeding toward your Base Camp. Will arrive camp area noon tomorrow. Harner."

"Slave revolt!" Cecil said, folding the paper and tucking it in his pocket. "Dear God. *Slaves!* I thought all that ended about 1865."

"It's a big land, Cec," Dan Gray told him. "We really don't know what is happening out there." He waved a hand.

"Yes," Cecil replied. He looked south. His eyes were bleak. "I can but wish the slaves the best of luck."

"I wish we had the personnel to help," Dan said.

"So do I, friend. So do I."

THIRTY

"No reply from any of our people up north," Tony was informed. "And I've been trying to contact them all day. What do you think it means, Tony?"

"I think it means they've bought it," Tony said.

"Yeah."

Tony slumped back in his chair. That feeling of impending doom he'd been experiencing all day once more settled around him like a damp, stinking shroud. And he couldn't seem to shake it. Not even liquor would dull the sensation.

"Any further word from north Florida?" Tony asked.

"Yeah. All bad. The big plantation down at Live Oak was completely overrun by the slaves. I don't know how they got them guns. The last report we received, the guards had barricaded themselves in the radio building. You could hear all sorts of shootin'. Then the radio went dead. So I guess them guys bought it, too."

"How bad's our strength been cut?"

The man shook his head. "Well, if our guys up in South Carolina bought it, that means we lost sixty, seventy percent, Tony. But a full company got out of Perry. They're headin' up this way."

"Ben Raines and his Rebs musta circled around," Tony said.

"Yeah, boss. He's a sneaky bastard, that one is."

But Tony didn't believe it was Raines who had wiped out his people and the troops of the Ninth Order. Tony did not possess second sight, but he could tell when things were going sour.

"It wasn't Raines," Tony said. "I been kiddin' myself about that."

"What do you mean, boss? If it wasn't Raines, then who in the hell was it? You don't think maybe it was them Russians, do you? Last word we got all them folks was out west."

"No, I don't think it was the Russians. We've had no reports of them being anywhere near here. But I sure would like to know who the son of a bitch was that zapped my men."

"Why, my good fellow," a voice came from the open doorway. "Regrettably, I did."

THIRTY-ONE

Ike lifted the walkie-talkie and listened. From the strength of the transmission, he figured he and Nina must be practically sitting on top of the Ninth Order's headquarters.

Together, they listened in silence. When the transmissions had concluded, Ike summed it up, speaking more to himself than to her. "So the soldiers sent down south were wiped out, to a man, along with several hundred troops of this guy Silver." He looked at Nina. "You know anything about this guy named Silver?"

"He's a whore-master. He is just as evil as Sister Voleta, in his own way. I've never seen him, but I've heard stories about him. He keeps slaves to work his farms. He has—" she pursed her lips—"oh, I heard about a half dozen farms and ranches down south, in Florida. And he likes young girls. I mean, real young girls. Eleven and twelve, that young. He likes to hurt them during the . . . sex. He has several hundred women of all ages in whorehouses around the country. Young boys, too. And he supplies women and girls and boys to warlords around the country, too."

Ike looked at her, a dozen questions on his lips.

"Warlords, Nina? Tell me more. Where have I been to have missed all this?"

"You really don't know about the warlords, Ike? You're not just funnin' me?"

"No, I'm not funnin' you, honey. You see, we were kinda isolated—the Rebels—for almost a decade."

"What's that mean?"

"Isolated?"

"No. Decade."

"About ten years."

"Oh. Well, warlords is kinda like in some of them books I read. Back in the olden times, I mean. This one man, he gets hisself a bunch of other men together, and they stake out a certain parcel of land. So many miles thisaway, and so many miles thataway. Him and the men control all that by force. All the land is hisn."

"His, baby. His. Not hisn."

"His," she corrected herself. "Anyways, all the people within the land claimed by the guy pay him for protection. Whether they wants to or not. They ain't got no choice in the matter. If they don't pay, the warlord kills them. They's all kinds of them people spread out acrost the land. You really didn't know, did you, Ike?"

"No," Ike said softly. "No, I didn't. But it doesn't surprise me. I . . ." he sighed. "I guess I should have expected something like it. You've traveled around the country quite a bit, haven't you, Nina?"

Her face brightened in recall. "Oh, yeah! I sure have, Ike. I been all over. I been all the way up to the big water the Indians call . . . what was it them

Indians called it? Oh, yeah, I remember now. Gitche Gumee. I been—"

"The what?" Ike looked at her, a very startled expression on his face. "What did you just say? Gitche Gumee?"

"Yeah. Ain't you never heard of that before, Ike?"

"Why . . . sure I have! It's from Longfellow's 'Song of Hiawatha.' Oh. OK. You must be talking about Lake Superior?"

She cocked her head and looked strangely at him. "I don't know nothing about that, Ike. You see, there ain't no white folks up where I went. It's all Indians. That land belongs to them, so they said. And I sure as hell wasn't gonna argue with 'em none. They didn't hurt me a bit. They was real friendly and kind. Give me a bed to sleep in and warm food. And then the next morning, they showed me around the lake and their camp. Tepees and all that. Just like the old times in the books I read. But they called the big water Gitche Gumee. I don't know and never heard of nobody named Hiawatha. Why don't you tell me about him?"

"Well." Ike opened his mouth, then promptly shut it. No point in confusing her, and that would be just about all he would accomplish. Longfellow cast Hiawatha as an Ojibway. But in truth, he was based on the exploits of the Iroquois tribe. That in itself would probably boggle the girl's mind. Ike sighed heavily. Shit! he thought. Hiawatha, you are just going to have to wait a spell.

Nina looked at the expression on Ike's face. "You're sad with me, aren't you, Ike? I done something wrong.''

"No, no!" Ike looked at her and smiled. "No, I'm not sad or mad with you, Nina. Not at all. I'll tell you the story of Hiawatha someday. I promise. Right now, though, I'd like for you to tell me about these warlords. How many have you seen or heard of?''

"Oh, golly, Ike.'' She shrugged. "Bunches and bunches of them. That's what this here Sister Voleta is, kind of. But she's really weird. Up north of here, right on the edge of the big mountains, is a guy name of Joe Blue. He's a mean bastard, but he ain't evil like Sister Voleta. Blue'll just shoot you if he takes it in his head. But he'll do it clean. Blue claims . . . oh, four, five counties. All the way from Johnson City clear up into Virginia. There's another feller named Henshaw over to Boone in North Carolina claims a lot of land, too. I mean, a right smart piece of ground. Up in Kentucky now, over to the Daniel Boone Forest, all that is claimed by a man and woman named Red and Nola. They're crazy, I think. To the east, now, I traveled as far as the big water would let me. I got captured by these men call themselves the Brunswick Vigilantes. They claim all the land for miles up and down the big water. That's the . . .'' She was thoughtful. "Yeah! The Atlantic. Them men didn't hurt me none, but they sure made it plain they wasn't happy to see me. They gimmie some food and told me to leave and don't come back. And to warn others not to venture—that's the word they used— over in that part of the country. Oh, Ike, I seen warlords near'bouts ever'where I been the past two, three years.''

Ike sat silent for a few moments, deep in thought. So Ben was right, he reflected. As usual. Ben said it would come to this. The survivors are spinning backward in time much faster than our ancestors progressed. Somehow, someway, we—and it's going to be up to men and women my age—must put the brakes on this backward slide.

But how?

"Education," he said aloud.

"What'd you say, Ike?"

"Education, honey. That's the key. Education. Unlike what was advocated back in the sixties and seventies and eighties, there must be *one* type of education for everybody, regardless of race or religion or whatever. It's that kind of shittiest-assed thinking that helped get us in the shape we're in now. But if you said anything back then, you were immediately branded a racist,"

"Ike, what in the hell are you talkin' about? I don't understand nothin' you just said."

"Let me put it this way, Nina. You know anything about mules?"

"Hell, yes. Horses, too."

"Well, then, if you was to put two males in harness, and one wanted to go gee and the other wanted to go haw, you wouldn't get a whole hell of a lot of plowin' done, would you?"

"Any fool knows the answer to that. You sure as hell wouldn't."

"That's the way it was with education when the country went liberal on us."

"What's liberal mean?"

Ike sighed and then laughed. "Honey, don't get me started on that. Let's just say that instead of trying to get a curriculum . . ."

She looked strangely at him.

"That means a course of study."

"Oh."

"A curriculum that would best educate all, regardless of color, some folks said that was unfair. Some among them—not all, certainly, but some—wanted to bastardize education. Instead of saying we are all Americans, we are going to live and work and speak in English, as set forth by men and women much more intelligent than me, we are going to call an object by its proper name, some wanted to twist and change all that. Some, again, not many, but some, wanted to bring the level of education down to their level, instead of really making an effort to climb upward. It didn't work, Nina. One cannot regress, one cannot stand still. There is only one direction, and that is forward."

"You sure do talk pretty when you want to, Ike. You know that?"

Ike laughed. "That's the trick, honey. I can butcher the King's English, but I have a solid base in good education. Some folks didn't want that solid base."

"I sure would like to have it. Anybody that wouldn't must be next to a fool in their thinking."

"That's my opinion on the matter. And I'll see that you get an education, Nina. I promise."

"How much further to the lake?"

"We won't make it today. We're gonna have to take it slow and easy from now on. We're right in the middle of Ninth Order territory." He got to his feet and slipped on his pack, picking up his M-16 and slinging the shotgun. "Let's head out, Nina. And remember this: Before we stick our heads around a curve in the road, we quietlike check what's around the bend first. We've come too far to get caught now."

THIRTY-TWO

The man lifted his eyes and surveyed the smoky scene that lay before him. Lines of fatigue creased his face. His upper body was burned to a shade of mahogany from years of working shirtless under the harsh sun. He held a bloody knife in his left hand, a .38 revolver in his right hand. Bodies littered the yard of the old plantation home in Live Oak, Florida, that Tony Silver had called headquarters before pulling out for south Georgia.

It had been a terrible, bloody fight between the guards and the slaves, and the slaves had spared no one in their fight for freedom. Many of the guards had women with them, and the women had fought alongside their men—and died along with them.

Those women who had been especially cruel to the slaves, some of whom had performed acts of perversion that would have at least paralleled the atrocities committed by the legendary Bitch of Buchenwald, were dying especially hard. Their screaming echoed faintly over the dusty, bloody grounds.

The freed slave looked toward the big house as a harsh scream ripped the air. Some of the guards' women had enjoyed acts of sexual perversion—performed upon the men slaves. Now they were getting a taste of their own evil corruption. And they did not seem to be enjoying it.

A freed slave came out of the great, old plantation house, zipping up his trousers and fastening his belt. He turned to a friend, "Damned bitch liked to see men being sodomized, thought I'd see how she liked it."

"And?" the man asked.

"You heard her yellin'."

A single gunshot blasted the still air. The woman's screaming ceased abruptly.

The man with the gun in one hand and the bloody knife in the other turned his face from the plantation house. He didn't blame the men for seeking vengeance, but he wanted no part of it.

From the women's slave quarters a hideous yowling seemed to float forever on the warm air. The male guards who had forced the women slaves into acts of perversion with both men and women—and sometimes animals—were dying hard at the hands of the freed women slaves.

He could not and would not blame the women for seeking revenge.

He turned at the sound of footsteps.

"Soon all will be dead, George," the woman said, coming to his side. "We're free."

George Berger looked at the woman dressed in tattered, faded blue jean shorts and ragged T-shirt. She wore no bra, and her breasts were full and firm, the nipples jabbing at the thin fabric of the T-shirt. That she was part Indian was obvious: The thick, black hair and high cheekbones and wide, sensual mouth marked that heritage. But her eyes were an Irish green and her body was slender and stately proud. Her name was Joni. She had been captured by Silver's men in the south of Florida and held in slavery for more than a year. She had been beaten and chained and raped and brutally sodomized, but her proud spirit had never been broken. She had been stripped naked and chained under the hot sun; she had been put in harness and forced to pull a plow like an animal; she had been humiliated in every conceivable manner, but her captors could not break her. Joni was the leader of the slave rebellion.

"Free from the bonds of slavery, yes," George replied. "But where the hell do we go and what the hell do we do when we get there?"

Joni laughed, her laughter not quite covering the screaming from the men in the women's quarters. She narrowed her eyes and glanced toward the low building. She shook her head and looked at the man. "You don't like that, do you, George?"

"Do you, Joni?"

"No," she said softly. "But nothing the women could do would compensate for what was done to them over the years."

"I suppose so, Joni. I repeat: What are we going to do?"

"I keep forgetting, George, that you have been a slave for a long time. Have you ever heard of Ben Raines?"

George smiled. Despite the years of backbreaking work and physical and mental abuse, he still wore laugh lines at the corners of his eyes and mouth. "Joni, I haven't been a slave *that* long. Sure. Ben Raines. That's the man who formed his own nation out west—back in '89, I think it was. What about General Raines?"

"I think we should take the people and head north. There, we can join Ben Raines and his army of Rebels. The word I get is that he's moved his people into north Georgia and is forming another nation up there. As far as I know, General Raines is the only person attempting to bring back civilization, with schools and businesses and law and order. I think we should do that."

George sighed as he nodded his head in agreement. "You suppose the general would have room for an unemployed accountant?"

Joni touched his arm, hard and muscled after more than three years of backbreaking field work. The touch was surprisingly gentle in the midst of the bloody carnage surrounding the man and woman. "If he doesn't, George, then you and I will just have to move on. We've come through too much together to be separated now."

The man and woman standing in the middle of grotesque death, embraced and kissed.

The screaming from the women's slave quarters and the howling of the women from the plantation house ceased. The immediate area was strangely silent. Other men and women, all wearing tattered rags of clothing, with many still bearing the savage marks of the blacksnake whip, joined George and Joni. They were armed with everything from kitchen knives to AK-47s and M-16s.

"It's over, Joni," a woman announced. "The bastards are all dead or dying."

"And the bitches," a man added.

Joni stepped from George's embrace and faced the men and women gathered around the pair. She counted the heads. Just over sixty. They had taken fearful losses in their fight for freedom. Almost a forty percent loss.

"All right, people," Joni said, her voice firm and strong with the conviction of one who is right. "There are other slave farms. And there are schools—so-called—where young girls are taught the art of prostitution. There are many elderly people who are forced to cook and clean and perform household chores for Silver's people. The old are beaten and humiliated and sometimes put to death because they are old. All those people must be freed, all of them, before we can even begin to think of our own well-being. I don't know how many farms Silver has, or where they are all located, but we'll find out. And we'll help free those imprisoned there. With each success, we'll grow stronger in number. For right now, let's bury *our* dead, gather up all the weapons and bullets, and get organized. We've got a lot to do."

THIRTY-THREE

"Great jumping balls of fire!" Emil yelled. "What in the hell was that?"

Gunfire was ripping the mid-morning quiet of the cult. Emil ran to the picture window in the den, tripping on the hem of his robe only twice, and jerked open the drapes. He looked out at a motley crew of men, all heavily armed, and at his flock of followers, running in panic in all directions. Some of his people were lying on the ground, and they were not moving. Dark crimson stains were appearing on their robes, the blood leaking onto the ground.

"Worst than fucking Vietnam," Emil muttered. "Oh, shit! What am I gonna do?"

An automatic rifle cracked, from the sound of it, Emil guessed it to be an M-16, and the window to his right erupted in a shower of broken glass and splintered wooden frames. Emil ran shrieking from the den into his bedroom. He jerked open the closet door, grabbing up his AK-47. Chambering a round, he slipped the weapon onto full automatic and ran back into the den.

Only Emil's guards knew anything at all about guns of any type. For Emil's was a peaceful cult. Rather perverted in many ways, but all that was about to change. His followers smoked bunches of dope and fucked a lot, but when it came to guns, they were a bunch of schmucks. Emil remembered that word from a Jewish chick he used to ball when he sold used cars up in Chattanooga. For a few seconds, Emil wondered what had ever happened to that chick.

Emil stuck the muzzle of the AK out the broken window and pulled the trigger. Luckily for Emil, a dozen armed men were at the front of the house just as he pulled the trigger. He emptied the clip into the knot of men, knocking most of them to the ground. Emil quickly changed clips and ran out the back door of the house. He ran out into the yard, tripped over the hem of his robe, and fell on his face. It was a very good move on his part, for a hard burst of gunfire blasted over Emil's head.

Emil jumped to his feet, leveled the AK, and chopped three more of the attackers to bloody bits. It was an awful sight.

"Yuk!" Emil said.

The sounds of hard gunfire reached Emil's ears. That and the sounds of surrender.

"Don't shoot no more!" a man's voice reached Emil. "We give up."

"Why, you son of a bitch!" Emil muttered.

Emil felt the muzzle of a weapon press coldly against the flesh of his neck. He peed on himself.

And he knew his little scam was over. No more tight, young pussies for Emil. No more young boys to entertain him. No more being waited on and pampered by his flock.

All gone.

"Git on your feet, funny man," a hard voice told him.

Emil stood up.

"What the fuck is you people, monks?" the man asked.

A light bulb lit up in Emil's brain. "Why, ah, yes, sir. That is exactly right. We are the, ah, Light of Life order of monks."

The unshaven, smelly brute knocked Emil sprawling on his butt. "What you is, little man, is a liar. And what else you is," he said with a grin, "is our prisoners."

"Right nice spread they got here," another man said, walking up. "Be a good place to hole up for the winter."

"Oh, shit!" Emil muttered, from his position on the ground.

"Yeah," another man said. He held one of Emil's followers in his arms. The young woman could do nothing as his hands crawled over her body. "Lots of grub and lots of pussy. Some of these . . . whatever in the hell they is, got away, but we captured a bunch of them." He lifted the woman's robes, exposing her naked belly. "Jist look at the bush on this one, will ya? 'Nough fuckin' material 'round this place to last us all winter."

"Father Emil!" the woman cried. "Do something. Evoke the powers of the great god, Blomm."

"Yes!" some of the other captives cried. "Bring down curses on these barbarian's heads. Use your mighty powers to call down the wrath of Blomm."

Emil struggled to his hands and knees. He had a frightful headache where that brute had popped him

with the butt of his rifle. "Oh, blow it out your ear,"
Emil muttered. "The game is over; the scam is
through."

"Game?" a man questioned. "Scam? Why . . .
whatever in the world do you mean, Father Emil?"

"Father Emil!" one of the attackers said with a
laugh. "Father Emil!"

Emil was jerked to his feet and held there by two
brutish looking men. God! it was so embarrassing.

"Point your finger at these horrible men and slay
them!" a young woman cried. "Evoke the powers of
the mighty Blomm, Father Emil."

Emil looked at her, disgust in his eyes. "Oh . . .
fuck you, you ding-a-ling!"

THIRTY-FOUR

The morning dawned clear and cold, with patches of frost where the sunlight had not warmed and the winds of the night had not touched. Lake Chatuge, which lay in parts of what had once been known as North Carolina and Georgia, shimmered under the first rays of sunlight.

Ike and Nina stood on the crest of a hill overlooking the silver-blue waters of the lake. Using his binoculars, Ike scanned the trucks parked neatly on the west side of the lake, just off Highway 76.

"Well now," Ike said. "Would you just take a look at that. Makes a body feel right at home."

Nina watched as a huge smile began working its way across his face.

"You see something down there that makes you happy, Ike?"

"I sure do, honey." He cased the binoculars and took Nina's hand in his. "Come on. Let's meet the gang. That's Ben and his people down there."

But Nina pulled back.

"What's wrong?" Ike asked, not understanding any of this.

"I'm afraid of going down there."

"Afraid? Afraid of what, Nina? Those are my

friends down there."

"Is Mister Raines among them?"

"I sure hope so. Is it Ben? You're afraid of Ben?"

"Yes. For the past few years I have heard many people talk of Ben Raines. About how he is God. I have seen monuments built in his honor. I have heard talk of how he is immortal. I have heard about all the times he has been shot and blown up and stabbed and all sorts of things. Yet, the person called Ben Raines will not die. He has built nations, and mortal men do not do that. I have heard whispered talk of a man called the Prophet, and what that ageless one has said of Ben Raines. Yes, Ike. I am afraid of Ben Raines."

Ike squeezed her hand. "Don't be, Nina. Ben doesn't want that. You'll see, Nina. You're wrong about Ben."

She shook her head. "I am *right* about Mister Raines."

Reluctantly, she walked alongside Ike, toward the silent camp.

THIRTY-FIVE

Ike and Nina walked to within three hundred yards of the camp before a sentry spotted them coming down the center of the road.

"Halt!" he shouted, bringing his M-16 around to cover the pair.

"Hold it!" Ike shouted, stopping Nina with a quickly outflung arm. "Don't anybody get trigger-happy down there. This is Colonel Ike McGowen and friend. We're comin' in."

The camp suddenly poured forth all its occupants, all runnig toward Ike and Nina. Ben's harsh voice stopped them, roaring over their heads.

"Halt, goddamnit!"

The crowd of men and women stopped still as if controlled by one central mind. No one among them moved.

"You all know better than that!" Ben yelled. "What in the hell is the matter with you people? It could be a trap. Guards, get back to your assigned posts and by God—stay put!"

The sentries raced back to their posts and, once there, did not turn around. The others looked at the sky, the earth, the lake, their boots—anywhere but in the direction of Ben Raines.

Ben walked out of the camp area and up the center of the old highway, striding toward Ike and Nina.

"The black gun!" Nina whispered. "I really see it. The enchanted weapon."

Ike could detect real fear in her voice, and he could feel her trembling as she pressed against him.

Ben was still several hundred yards away from the pair.

"What are you talking about, Nina?" Ike asked. "What enchanted weapon?"

"From the big waters to the north, to the big waters to the south, and everywhere in between, monuments are built not only to Ben Raines, but to the black gun he carries. I told you, Ike, I am afraid of him."

"But Ben's not a god," Ike protested. "I told you, he's just a man."

"You say. But many more say he is a god. I'm sorry, Ike."

Then Ben stood before them, a smile on his face. "I knew no one could ever force you into setting me up, Ike. But a little reminder of discipline is good for the soul."

"I heard that, Ben."

Ben held out his hand and Ike shook it. It was much more than a gesture of deep friendship; it was more an act between two brothers.

Nina could not take her eyes from the old Thompson SMG Ben carried. The weapon was a newer model of the old Chicago Piano of gangster days. A .45-caliber spitter. Ben had taped two thirty-round clips together for faster reloading.

He had carried the weapon, or one like it, since the world blew up in nuclear and germ warfare back in 1988.*

Ben looked at Nina. "And this is?"

"Nina," Ike said.

Ben extended his hand toward the lovely young lady and she shyly and very hesitantly took it. She seemed surprised the hand did not burn her or strike her dead with some magical powers. Such were the ever-growing myths concerning Ben Raines and his supposed immortality. Ben smiled at Nina and she relaxed just a bit.

Ben released her hand and looked at Ike, his expression hardening. "I just came from the communications truck, Ike. We've been in scrambler contact with Base Camp. I'll . . . give it to you straight. Sally's dead."

Ike flinched as if hit by an invisible blow. He paled and then cleared his throat. "How 'bout the kids?"

"They were killed with her. I'm sorry. Ike. Sally was trying to protect them with her own body."

"I see," Ike replied. When he again spoke, his voice was harsh. "Who did it, Ben?"

"Captain Willette and his bunch."

"He's mine, Ben. All mine. I want your word on that, ol' buddy."

"Ike . . ."

"No! Give me your word, Ben."

"You've got it."

Ike nodded his head. He touched Nina's shoulder. "She's had a rough time of it, Ben, and not a whole lot of formal education. I said we'd see to that. But she's one hundred percent Rebel material. She'll do

*Out of the Ashes

337

to ride the river with."

And that was the highest compliment Ike could give a person.

"You look like you could use a hot meal and about twelve hours sleep," Ben said to Nina. "We'll talk more later." He smiled at her and this time she responded with a shy smile.

At a nod from Ben, one of the Rebel women stepped from the crowd and walked up to the trio. "Come on," she said to Nina. "How about a hot bath and hot food and clean clothes?"

"That'd be great," Nina said. She walked off with the woman.

"Let's talk some now, Ben," Ike said, when Nina was out of earshot. "What're your plans? And why have you stopped here?"

"We're right in the middle of Ninth Order territory," Ben said. His eyes found Ike's walkie-talkie. "But I suspect you already know that."

"Yeah. The first transmission I heard like to have blown my ear off. So?"

"I've sent a coded message to Base Camp. Colonel Gray is sending out teams of his Scouts. I want the positions of all Ninth Order troops pinpointed. While that is being done, this afternoon, we'll head for the deep timber, up in North Carolina, near Murphy. It's not that far a jump—about twenty, twenty-five miles, and out of their territory. I'm hoping the Ninth Order will think we're pulling out and away. When we get there, we'll pull in deep and lay low, send out Scouts of our own. When we get it mapped out and coordinated, we'll attack from the north, let the others come in from all other directions." He removed a map from his field jacket pocket and spread it out on the hood of a truck. "See this highway here, Highway 11, with Lake Nottely to its west?"

"Yeah."

"I've ordered Juan and Mark's people to seal this road. When that is done, we'll have the Ninth Order in a box. I think we can then wipe them out and forget them."

"I want to pick my own teams, Ben," Ike said. "Experienced guerrilla fighters."

"All right." Ben smiled, knowing what was coming. "I suppose you want to spearhead the attack, too?"

"You got that right, Ben."

"Done."

Ike relaxed. "We ran out of grub this morning. I'm hungry. Think I'll wander down to the mess truck and rummage around some."

Ben grinned.

"What's so funny?" Ike asked.

"We have a lot of C-rations left."

Ike narrowed his eyes. "What . . . kind . . . of . . . C-rations?" he asked slowly, bracing himself for Ben's reply.

"Canned bacon and eggs."

Ike shuddered. "Then I reckon I'll just get me a cane pole and go catch some fish for breakfast. I just can't eat that crap."

"Ike? First come along with me. I've got something to tend to."

The men walked to the center of the encampment. There, Ben nodded to James Riverson. "Bring him to

339

me, James."

James nodded silent understanding.

"Trouble?" Ike asked.

"A traitor," Ben replied.

James and Captain Rayle walked toward Ben and Ike, a young Rebel between them. The man had been disarmed. His face was pale and he was scared as he faced Ben.

"You remember Larry Armstrong, Ike?"

"Yeah. I've seen him around."

Ben fixed the young Rebel with a cold stare. "Some Indian tribes have a saying, Larry. That it's a good day to die. You ever heard that?"

"Can't say that I have, General," Larry replied. He was sweating and his skin appeared clammy. His eyes were constantly moving from left to right, flitting like a snake's tongue.

"You didn't do much accurate shooting from the ridge, Larry," Ben said. "Matter of fact, you didn't hit anything except air and trees and grass. Care to explain that?"

"I reckon you already know the answer, General. Else you wouldn't have brought me here unarmed."

The camp had gathered around the men, standing silently. The staring eyes were cold and menacing.

Larry looked at the circle of men and women. He blurted, "Ya'll are following a false god! You got no business comin' in here, pushin' people around and tryin' to make others bend to your will. It ain't right."

"Who have we pushed around, Larry?" Ben asked. "And what 'will' are you talking about?"

"We got a right to live the way we want to live," the

340

young man said, his face sullen with anger and fear.

"Yes," Ben told him. "As long as you don't violate the basic rights of innocent people. But you Ninth Order folks don't seem to want that."

Gale almost dropped her sandwich. Almost. "Ninth Order!" she gasped. "You mean . . . Ben, you mean you've known he was part of them all along?"

"Since before we pulled away from the main column," Ben said, not taking his eyes from the young Rebel. "Or at least I suspected. I wanted to see just how deeply Voleta had penetrated our ranks. How long have you been part of her group, Larry?"

The young man sensed the longer he talked, the longer he would live, for he had no illusions as to his ultimate fate. "Since last summer. I was on patrol when I ran into some of the Ninth Order people up in north Mississippi. Got to talkin' with them. What they had to say sounded pretty good to me. Love and peace and all that. Sure beats fightin' all the time, like it is with you, Raines." Sure death had restored bravado.

Ben shifted his bleak eyes to a young woman. "Mary, take this traitor and shoot him."

The young woman hesitated briefly. That was all that was needed for two Rebels to move close to her, effectively blocking any lethal moves on her part.

"Let her live," Larry begged.

Mary spat at Ben, the spittle landing on the toe of one boot.

"Why?" Ben swung his eyes back to Larry.

"God, I hate you!" Larry hissed the words. "I hate everything you stand for."

Again, Ben had to ask, "Why?"

341

But Larry would only shake his head. He refused to answer any further questions, from any of the Rebels.

Ben looked at Mary. "Why did you switch sides, Mary? That bothers me. What is it that we—the Rebels—are doing that is so . . . so repugnant, so evil, that would change you into a traitor? Why would you turn your back on your friends?"

But she would only shake her head.

Ben looked at James Riverson. "Dispose of them, James."

"With pleasure, sir," James said.

A minute later, two shots rang out from the edge of the camp.

THIRTY-SIX

Tony Silver had jumped to his feet, his hands balled into fists, his face flushed with rage. "What in the hell do you mean, you killed my boys? And who in the hell are you?"

Captain Jennings lifted the muzzle of his AK-47, the gesture stopping Tony cold.

"Steady now," Sam Hartline said with a smile on his lips. "That's a good fellow. You have my deepest apologies, Mister Silver. I assure you, it was an accident. I was operating under the assumption those were the troops of Ben Raines. We all make mistakes. Oh, excuse me. I'm Sam Hartline and this is my CO, Captain Jennings."

Under the circumstances, there was little Tony could do except stand easy and back off. He calmed himself and looked at the big mercenary standing just inside the open doorway of the old motel. Tony sighed and shook his head. "Well, what's done is done, I suppose." Then he smiled, the smile very sarcastic. "So you and your boys blew it with General Raines, too, huh?"

Hartline caught the sarcasm. He shrugged his heavy shoulders. "That is . . . one way of putting it, yes, Mister Silver. However, I can assure you, there will be a day of reckoning."

I hope so, Tony thought. He waved the men to chairs. "Coffee?" he asked. "Or maybe something a bit stronger?"

"I never drink during the day," Hartline said, as primly as a nun confronted with a stiff cock. "But some coffee would be very nice. I take mine black, with one sugar."

"Hot and black," Jennings said.

Tony smiled. "I like 'em like that myself ever' now and then."

Both Hartline and Jennings smiled at that. They sat down in chairs around a coffee table.

Steaming mugs of real coffee in front of the mercenaries, Tony sat opposite them across the low table. Tony looked at the men through slitted eyes for a moment, then dismissed his own men with a wave of his hand.

Hartline smiled. "Trust is so important between prospective allies, is it not, Mister Silver?"

Tony merely grunted his reply, not sure exactly what the mercenary meant. "Whatever," he said. "All right, world conditions being what they are, I don't think you boys came down here just to offer your heartfelt condolences for wasting my people. So let's cut out all the bullshit and get down to brass tacks, huh?"

Hartline never took his cold eyes from Tony. "A man of most direct action," he said. "I like that. Very well. How many men do you have left, Tony? Excuse me. May I call you Tony? Thank you. I'm Sam."

Tony's years as a streetwise punk in New York City loomed up strong within him. Something about this mercenary fairly oozed confidence. And Tony fought down the bitter taste of fear that welled up within him. "You hit me pretty hard," he admitted. "Pretty hard."

"Yes, I suspected that," Hartline said, after taking a sip of coffee. He smiled. "Just right. I do love good coffee. It's becoming so difficult to get. You must have a good stockpile."

It was not a question and Tony did not reply to it.

Hartline's smile was knowing. "Tell me, Tony. What are your feelings toward black people?"

"Niggers? Shit, I don't like 'em. Don't trust 'em. What is there to trust about a junglebunny? Sometimes you can find a high-yellow gal to fuck, but that's about all they're good for. Other than to do work that's beneath a white man. I have—had," he corrected with a grimace of distaste, "a bunch of 'em workin' my farms down south. We've, ah, had some trouble down there."

"Yes," Hartline said, leaning forward. "We intercepted several radio messages—some of them quite frantic—indicating you had, ah, something of a problem on your hands. Something about a slave revolt, I believe it was."

And Tony knew then his organization was laid wide open to the scrutiny of this hard-eyed mercenary. Hartline had missed nothing. And would miss nothing.

Tony reluctantly nodded his head in agreement, waiting for the other shoe to fall. "That's right, Sam."

"Very well, Tony," Hartline said. "Let us strike a bargain. You see, I believe that together, you and I, why, we could build an empire. You seem to be quite good at organization, while I am quite good at my profession. You are a businessman, I am a soldier. You take care of the business end, and I shall, ah, take care of the more, shall we say, physical problems that might arise. What do you think about that, Tony?"

Tony stared at Hartline for a short moment and then rose from his chair. He walked to the motel window and looked down at Hartline's men. Hundreds of them, They looked like Tony imagined professional soldiers might look: lean and mean and menacing, capable of handling any situation that might confront them. He slowly turned to face Hartline.

"What choice do I have, Sam?"

Hartline smiled that totally disarming smile of his. "Well," he laughed. "Actually, none. But consider this: Why should we fight each other? All that would accomplish is both of us taking physical losses. However, my way would guarantee us both enormous profit."

Tony was anything but a fool. His mind was now racing hard. Hartline was right, of course. With the mercenary backing him, Tony could expand his operations tremendously. But could he trust the mercenary? His smile was hidden at that. Trust? Between two crooks?

Hartline seemed to pick up on the thought. "Trust is something one has to consider, isn't it, Tony?"

"Yeah."

"I am not really a trusting man," Hartline admitted with a smile. "Except where women and power are the ultimate goal. Then one must trust. On the other side of the coin, Tony, there is this: Can I trust you?"

"Just as long as you play it straight with me, yeah," Tony said. "You do that, and I'll play it straight with you."

"That seems reasonable to me."

"All right," Tony said. "We have the cards on the table, face up. We have a deal."

Hartline rose to his booted feet with the fluid movements of a man in the peak of physical condition. "Very good, Tony! A decision I am sure you will not regret. Now then, let's discuss this slave revolt down south, and then I'll take my men and settle matters on your—" he smiled—"*our* farms."

THIRTY-SEVEN

When the code word came down the line and out of the speaker, Ben keyed his mic and said, "Confirmed. Report."

The voice of Col. Dan Gray popped from the speaker. "Juan and Mark are moving into position, General. From the north. They left under darkness last night. It will be go at 0600 tomorrow."

"We'll be in position," Ben said.

"Ten-four to that, sir. I have Rebels moving to beef up your contingent. They should rendezvous with you late this afternoon. The code word is Tiger."

"I copy that. Luck to you, Dan."

"And to you, sir. Base out."

Nina and Ike stood just outside the door of the communications vehicle. Nina tugged at Ike's sleeve. "What is to prevent the people of the Ninth Order from listening to that conversation?"

"The message is scrambled, Nina," Ike told her.

She cocked her head and looked at him, confusion in her eyes.

"Both Colonel Gray's and Ben's words, while they are going through the air, are unintelligible until they come out of the speaker. There is a little—" he paused, choosing his words carefully—"box inside the transmitter that puts the words all in the right order and then, a split second later, spits them out so the person on the receiving end can understand them.''

Nina's mouth formed an O. "Like magic?" she asked, her eyes wide.

Ike's eyes held a touch of sadness. He thought: She is so very much like a child. "Kinda like that, Nina. But it's . . . well, I will explain it to you, I promise.''

"OK," she said brightly. "But you sure have got a lot of explainin' to do, Ike.''

Ben looked at Ike and he smiled. Turning to Nina, he said, "Feel free to ask any questions you like, Nina. For that is the only way anybody ever learns anything.''

"Yes, sir," she said, standing very close to Ike, for she was still very much afraid of Ben.

Gale, sensing the young woman was fearful of Ben, put an arm around her shoulder. "He doesn't bite, Nina. But he sure can snore.''

Nina looked horrified.

"I do not snore!" Ben said.

"Like an elephant trumpeting," Gale countered.

"There are people in this world who would kill you for saying things like that, Miss Roth," Nina told her.

That stopped Gale for a few seconds. She blinked and said, "You're serious, aren't you?''

"Yes, ma'am. There are places of worship all over the nation, built to honor General Raines.''

Ben smiled. "Now, then, woman. Show a bit more respect for me, will you?''

She looked at him. "I wonder if those people ever

read any of those cheap sex books of yours?"

"I did not write sex books! Well . . ." Ben was thoughtful for a moment. "Maybe one or two."

"Uh-huh," Gale said dryly. "And the truth shall set ye free."

"You wrote *books*, too?" Nina blurted. "I love to read books. But I have a lot of trouble with real big words."

"We'll take care of that, Nina," Ben assured her. "We'll have schools operating in just a few weeks where you can learn all sorts of things."

Ike and Nina walked away, holding hands. Gale watched them and said, "I think Ike is in love, Ben."

"That and a guilty conscience, Gale. Sally's death hit him a lot harder than he let on. He told me several months ago that it wasn't working between them, but he didn't know what to do about it."

"I still say he's in love."

"Or in heat."

"Raines . . ." She looked up at him. "I give up." She walked off, Ben's voice halting her. She turned around. "Raines, what do you want?"

"I said you're going in the wrong direction," Ben called with a smile. "The food truck is that way." He pointed, then smiled at the gesture she flipped him.

"The one universal sign that will never die," Ben said with a laugh.

THIRTY-EIGHT

The guard, Lennie, unlocked the door to the girls' bedrooms and stood for a moment, looking at them, an evil grin on his unshaven face. "Well, babies, I got news. Yes, indeed, this is gonna be a real kick. Tony just linked up with Sam Hartline, and I hear Hartline's got him a dick like a horse. And he likes his chickie-babies young and tender. I sure would like to be around when he tries to get that salami of hisn up one of you babies' pussy."

Lilli began crying.

"Shut up, Lilli," Ann told the young girl. "That won't help none." She looked at Lennie. He was the one who had made her perform oral sex on him the other night. "Fuck you!" Ann told the man.

Lennie laughed. "That's the spirit, kid. Hey, what's the matter, anyways? I thought you liked lickin' my pole the other night?"

Ann stuck out her tongue at him and hissed her revulsion.

Lennie grinned. "I'm gonna be sure to suggest you to Sam Hartline, baby. Then I can listen to you scream."

Ann spat at him.

Lennie laughed and closed the door, locking it

from the outside. His footsteps faded down the balcony floor.

"Please don't let 'em hurt me no more, Ann," Lilli begged, tears running down her cheeks. "I can't stand no more. One of them the other night tried to get his thing up my behind. I thought I was gonna die it hurt so bad."

Ann sighed, wondering how all of a sudden she had been elected leader of the young group. Both Peg and Lilli looked to her for advice and leadership. It was a job she did not want.

"Look, kid," she said to Lilli. "This is get tough or die time, now. I mean it. You heard what Lennie said about this guy Hartlink, or whatever the hell his name is. He likes his girls young. And the bastard probably likes to hurt women, too. The more the women fight him, the more he likes it, 'cause that means he can hurt them that much more." Unknowingly, the young girl had pegged Hartline as accurately as anyone ever had. "You follow all that, Lilli?"

Lilli nodded her head glumly. But still the tears fell.

Ann said, "Now I still ain't got no plans for gettin' us out of here, but I'm thinkin' hard on it. But I got to have both of you helpin' me. I can't do it by myself."

"You got something on your mind, though," Peg said.

"Yeah, for a fact. Listen. Lennie likes you, Peg. So I want you to try to get him in that bedroom in yonder and give him some."

"No!" Peg hissed.

Ann slapped her, the force of the blow leaving fingermarks on the girl's face. "Listen to me, damn

352

you. I got to get that knife outta his pants pocket. And I can't get to it with him in them britches. So that means his pants has got to come *off*. You follow me?"

"Y-yes," the girl stuttered.

"Look, Peg," Ann softened her words. "I ain't sayin' you gotta like it when he puts it in, but you gotta do it. And all of it's gotta be done before Tony gets back. *I'm* the one's gonna get picked by Hartline, girls; *I'm* the one's gonna get hurt no tellin' how bad outta this deal. You heard what Lennie said. So's the least you two can do is help me out just a little bit. OK?"

Peg and Lilli nodded their agreement.

"OK," Ann said. "Now then. All of us get naked. Then you, Peg, go tap on that door and get Lennie's attention." She turned to Lilli. "You go wash your face and get them tears outta your eyes. 'Cause if this don't work, girls, I don't know what in the hell we're gonna do. Ya'll heard them guys talkin' the other night. Pussy's gettin' old. They gonna roll us over next; and you all know what that means, don't you?"

The fear of being sodomized wiped out all other fears. The girls moved quickly. They washed their face and combed their hair and stripped. Peg tapped softly on the motel room door.

"Lennie?" she called. "You still out there, Lennie?"

A moment's silence, then footsteps moving closer to the locked door. "Yeah, pretty, I'm here. What'd you want?"

"I . . . we've got a surprise for you, Lennie. Come on, open the door."

Another pause. The silence deepened. "What kind of surprise you talkin' about?" There was open suspicion in his voice.

Ann thought very quickly. She leaned close to Peg and whispered, "Tell him we're sorry for being so mean and want to make it up to him."

Peg relayed the message.

"Stand away from the door," Lennie growled.

The girls stepped back into the center of the motel room. Ann called, "OK, Lennie, we're away from the door."

A key ground into the lock. The door swung open, and Lennie stood grinning at them. He licked his lips at the sight of the young, just-budding, naked bodies.

"Well, now," Lennie said, his voice no more than a whisper. "Well now. Just what do we have here, pray tell?"

"We decided to give you a present," Ann said, her eyes flirting with him. "You know, for bein' so mean to you and all. I mean, if you want it, that is, Mr. Lennie."

"You birds are finally gettin' some smarts, ain't you?" Lennie asked. His eyes touched them all, but as Ann had guessed, they settled on the slimness of Peg. Her little breasts were just beginning to bud. Lennie scratched his crotch and carefully closed the door, after taking a quick look up and down the deserted corridor. He walked to Peg and ran his hands over her slim body. "You and me, little bird. You and me."

Peg shyly touched his swelling crotch and Lennie groaned. "Yeah. That's the ticket, kid." He took her slim arm and led her into a bedroom, his other hand working at the buttons of his dirty shirt. Muted, murmuring sounds drifted out the bedroom door. The sounds of boots dropping onto the old carpet, followed by the soft jangle of belt buckle hitting the floor.

"Gimmie some head first, baby," Lennie said, his voice more a pant.

A few moments of silence, then Lennie said, "That's good, baby. Come on up here and spread them pretty legs."

Peg groaned as the man's weight covered her young body.

"Goddamn, baby," Lennie said. "You so tight I can't hardly get it in. Come on, baby, help me. *Ah!* That's it. Goddamn, that feels good."

Peg cried out softly as Lennie penetrated her.

"Ain't that good to you, baby? Sure it is. Come on, kid, move your ass."

Then there came the sounds of hard breathing, and the slap of naked flesh onto naked flesh. Lennie muttered filth into the girl's ear, and Peg cried out as he fully penetrated her.

Lennie began making animal, grunting sounds as he rutted on the young girl.

Ann slipped into the semi-darkened bedroom on her hands and knees, crawling low. But there was no need for that much caution. Peg had positioned herself on the bed so the man's back would be toward the door. Lennie's naked, hairy, pumping buttocks faced Ann as she crawled into the room.

Quickly, Ann felt for Lennie's dirty, stinking jeans. Her fingers found the heavy clasp knife in one pocket. She removed it and edged her way back toward the door.

"Oh, baby," Lennie groaned. "That's the tightest little box I ever had. Ain't that good to you, baby? Sure it is."

Ann showed Lilli the knife and together they grinned.

Step one toward freedom was complete.

THIRTY-NINE

Sister Voleta knew she should pull what remained of her forces out. Just get out and regroup and then, when she had rebuilt to full strength, when she had once again inflamed her people with her twisted interpretation of the gospel, then attack Ben Raines and wipe the bastard from the face of the earth.

But her hatred for Ben Raines was so intense, so mottled and hairy and scaly from years of smoldering within her, she could not do that. Never. She was prepared to risk all in one final attempt to see Ben Raines dead.

She thought of her son and wondered if he was still alive. She felt certain he was—somewhere. She hoped he was well and happy. He had been such a beautiful child. So full of life. She pushed those thoughts from her. It was unhealthy to dwell too much in and on the past.

She thought of the warlords around her area, and of her pleas for them to join forces with her. It had been a good plan, but they were so shortsighted, men of such little minds, they had, to a person, rejected her plans.

Fools!

And then she allowed her hatred of Ben Raines to wash over her in waves of furious and dark acrimony. She allowed this even though she knew in her heart the man was not really to blame. Even though the boy had looked something like Raines. Still she wondered about it.

Calming herself with a visible effort, Sister Voleta began to think in a more rational manner. All that day she had attempted to make contact with Tony Silver. No reply from his base down south. She wondered if he was dead, or had turned traitorous?

Probably the latter.

She walked out of her house and motioned for her commanders to come to her. They had been squatting in the street in front of her home, smoking and talking in low tones.

She faced the men. "You are certain—all of you— that Ben Raines has only a hundred or so troops with him at Lake Chatuge?"

"Positive, Sister. And our scouts report there has been no unusual movement from the camp of the Rebels down in Georgia."

Ben's Rebels had all moved out the night before, silently, rolling without lights on their vehicles. Juan and Mark were almost in position, as were Colonel Gray's people. Cecil was personally leading the assault from the west.

Sister Voleta gave the order she was certain would bring victory to her and ensure the death of the man she hated and blamed for all her misfortune. She was certain that Ben Raines had somehow managed to kill her chances of becoming a singing star. Although she wasn't real certain how he could have managed that.

"Move our people out," she ordered. "Death to Ben Raines."

FORTY

"We intercepted these messages, Joni," George said, looking at a notepad. "Somebody named Sam Hartline is moving this way, with a lot of armed men. Who in the hell is Sam Hartline?"

Joni felt a chill crawl up and down her spine. She once had a friend who had been taken by Sam Hartline. Back when the United States was struggling to pull itself out of the horrors of germ and nuclear warfare. Back when VP Lowry was running the country. She had seen what Hartline had done to her friend. Hartline and his men had broken the man. They had sexually abused him and tortured him and broken not only his body but his mind.

Joni shook off the hideous memories. "You must have been captured just as Hartline came to power," she said. "He's a mercenary. He was one of Al Cody and VP Lowry's bully-boys. He's worse than Tony Silver ever thought about being. If Hartline is heading this way, that probably means he's linked up with Tony Silver. We've got to get our people together and move out. We've got to get over to Perry and assist those slaves in the fighting. Let's move, George. We don't have much time."

Some of the slaves were still wearing the remnants

of leg irons when George began shouting out the orders to work faster. The banging of hammers intensified, and finally the last ankle-shackle was broken free. Every man and woman there wore the scars of the leg irons.

The former slaves of Tony Silver left the bodies of the captors and guards where they had fallen in the battle for freedom. Left them to stiffen and stink and bloat under the Florida sun.

The work camp and plantation house and guards' quarters had been thoroughly searched for more weapons and ammunition. The trucks and cars and vans were gassed up and containers filled with fuel for their journey. Food and water were stored in the vehicles. Now they were ready to move out.

When the last vehicle had rattled over the cattle guards at Tony Silver's old HQ, the small convoy of armed ex-slaves heading for another slave plantation just outside of what used to be known as Perry, Florida, they were only three hours ahead of Sam Hartline and his mercenaries. Sixty-odd men and women, armed with a mishmash of weapons, against the hundreds of trained, combat-seasoned, and well-armed troops of Hartline.

But the slaves possessed something not even Sam Hartline had ever known: a burning desire for freedom and an equally fierce inner flame for revenge and justice. And that is an awesome combination for any army to fight.

The vultures had been slowly circling, high in the blue skies of Florida, watching and smelling the food that lay sprawled on the ground. Now, as the men and women pulled out, the carrion birds began their slow drift downward, their huge wing span carrying them ever closer to food.

On the ground, the grotesque birds began feasting, their sharp, fierce beaks ripping and tearing at dead human flesh. They worked at the small of the back first, tearing at the choicest and tastiest food: the kidneys.

The carrion-eaters feasted throughout the day, until they were so bloated with dead meat they could not fly. They waddled off and allowed the wild dogs and wolves and coyotes to snarl and tear at what remained.

Then the dusty grounds became as silent as the scattered skeletons that lay in the torn dirt, small bits of red meat still hanging from bones that would soon be picked clean.

FORTY-ONE

The morning of the day that would forever wipe from the face of the earth the troops of the perverted rule of the Nine Order dawned misty and cold in the mountains. Fall was ebbing in its season in this section of the battered and war-torn earth, the chilly winds of winter blowing close on the waning season's heels. Breath became white steam in the pre-dawn hours.

Ike and his hand-picked teams had pulled out in the early hours of the morning. By now, they would be moving silently and deadly, deep inside the territory of the Ninth Order, killing quietly and swiftly as they went.

Ike had kissed Nina's sleeping lips, and with the image of Sally and the kids, broken and torn by gunfire, etched in his brain, the ex-SEAL had dressed silently and linked up with his waiting teams.

Ike had noticed Ben standing tall and silent in the gloom of pre-dawn. Ben had walked over to his long-time friend.

"What happened to Sally was not your fault," Ben had spoken softly, so only Ike could hear. "You do not have to go off on what might be a suicide mission simply because you met and made love to another woman—while the both of you were running for your lives. You know that, Ike."

"That's not it, Ben. It really isn't. Me and Sally had already made up our minds to split the blanket. It's . . . hell, I don't know. It's the *way* Sally and the kids bought it that I can't seem to shake. I talked with Lieutenant Bolden last night. I practically had to drag the story out of him, but I got it all. Damnit, Ben. Killing unarmed women and kids is just too much for me to take."

"And there is this: Nina told me about meeting warlords wherever she traveled. *Warlords,* Ben. The country is spinning backward fifty years with every passing month. This has to be reversed, somehow, or we're going to be in ever-deepening trouble. Willette and Hartline and Silver and this fruitcake Voleta . . . hell, they're all one and the same. Put 'em in a big sack and shake 'em up and you couldn't tell 'em apart." Ike caught his breath and his temper and gripped Ben's arm. "I gotta go, buddy. Luck to you."

"The same to you, Ike. Let's put an end to the terror in these mountains today, friend."

"I heard that, buddy." Ike turned and walked toward his waiting teams. They vanished silently into the deep timber.

Now, as the first silver fingers of light fought to open against the misty horizon, painting the east a deep gray, Ben stood alone in the center of the encampment, listening. The sergeants had rolled their people out an hour before. The men and women of Raines' Rebels had awakened and become active with the same noises troops had made for thousands of years. Coughing, clearing their throats, hacking and spitting, grumbling and bitching. Caesar's Legions probably sounded much the same as they rolled out of their blankets and reached for swords and shields and spears.

Ben looked around him. No light betrayed their position. "I want a cold camp," he had ordered. "No lights."

Two full combat companies had quietly joined Ben's ranks as his people had moved into position just south of Murphy, North Carolina the afternoon past. Two more full combat companies were waiting at Murphy for the general. It brought his strength up to a short battalion.

Cecil and his command were spread out north to south, from Ducktown in North Carolina, to just west of Higdon in Georgia. Mark and Juan had their people covering north to southeast along Highway 11, from the junction of 19 and 129, down to Blairsville in Georgia. The remainder of the Rebels, under the command of a Major Woodward, which included Abe Lancer and his people and the older of Wade and Ro's young people, were covering the area running west to east in Georgia, from Higdon all the way over to Blairsville.

Colonel Gray and his Scouts, and Colonel McGowen and his teams would engage the enemy in a guerrilla type action, while acting as spearheaders for the main forces, moving in from three directions, slowly pushing the troops of the Ninth Order toward Juan and Mark, who by now had their troops dug in deep and heavily fortified with .50-caliber machine guns, M-60s and mortars.

The Ninth Order, without realizing, had stepped

into a box, and the doors were closing around them.

Ben's troops were mounted, in full battle gear, ready to roll, when Ben's radio crackled. Cecil's voice was firm and strong. "We have the enemy in sight and are engaging them."

"Luck to you," Ben said.

Ben's radio crackled again. "Have found the enemy and driving them northward," Major Woodward reported.

"Good luck," Ben said.

"In position and dug in," Juan's radio operator said. "Waiting for the enemy to show."

"Good luck," Ben told him. "Move out," he told his troops.

Cecil's troops slammed through the line of Ninth Order defenders. They took no prisoners. His troops, with Cecil leading them, moved through Higdon, Copper Hill, and McCaysville simultaneously: one long, hard, coordinated, violent punch. They struck the enemy and hit them totally without mercy.

After the Ninth Order had fled eastward in panic, and Cecil's troops rolled in with APCs and light battle tanks and Jeeps and trucks filled with troops, many civilians slowly came out of their homes, relief and welcome in their eyes.

"Are you people the army of the United States?" a woman asked. "God, I hope so. Who is president? Will there be help in here soon?"

"There is no government of the United States," Cecil said. "It collapsed two years ago and has never been reformed. I'm doubtful it ever will. We are from the army of Ben Raines. I'm Colonel Cecil Jefferys."

"That's even better, Colonel," a man said. "At least Ben Raines had more than his share of common sense in running a nation. I'll be more than happy to follow his rule. Those people from the Ninth Order been holding us virtual slaves in here for near'bouts two years. Them and their damned off-the-wall religion. If that's what you want to call that mess."

"Which way did the bulk of the Ninth Order troops go?" Cecil asked.

"They split up. 'Bout half of them went thataway, to the east. The other half went thataway." He pointed north. "Toward the gap and the Fields of the Woods."

"Which group was Sister Voleta with?"

"The one headin' due north. Toward the Fields of the Woods."

Cecil's smile was grim. "Straight into Ben." He turned around, held his arm straight up, and began pumping it up and down. He ended in a pointing motion, due east.

The column lunged forward.

"Luck to you boys!" a man shouted. He took a closer look at the Rebel troops. "And, uh, you girls, too."

About three hundred men and women of the Ninth Order decided to cross Highway 11 at a small, deserted town just north of Lake Nottely. They made it as far as the old city limits sign. There they died in the single street leading into the town. They were not expecting an ambush; indeed, their scanty intelligence reported no Rebels from Ben Raines' army this far east.

About eighty of their members made it out alive and set up positions just west and north of Ivy Log. They dug in and sent word they were prepared to fight to the death.

"How noble of them," Juan's brother, Alvaro said. "I see no point in losing anymore troops to this nonsense, Juan."

Juan and Mark looked at the tough little ex-street fighter from Tucson turned Rebel.

"Yes," Alvaro said. "You see, the troops of the Ninth Order have further placed themselves in a most unenviable position. They are—" he smiled— "dug in in deep timber. In approximately one hundred acres of timber. The wind is quite brisk today, blowing from south to north. Why not just set it on fire and let nature take care of the rest?"

Mark smiled, teeth flashing very white against his dark face. "You have a cruel streak in you, my friend."

Alvaro shrugged and smiled. "No doubt my Aztec heritage coming to the front."

"We don't want a raging forest fire on our hands," his brother cautioned. "It could burn unchecked for weeks."

"Of course not, hermano," Alvaro replied indignantly. "I plan to set backfires to contain the main blaze. I have nothing against nature. Only the troops of the Ninth Order."

"A splendid idea, Alvaro," Mark said. "Why don't we do just that?"

Raines' Rebels shot the troops from the Ninth

Order as they ran screaming from the man-made inferno. General Raines had said no prisoners, and that was the order of the day.

When the killing was over, and the fires had been contained, Juan turned to Mark.

"I cannot understand why we have to fight. Why can't we all just live in peace? What is it within the beast called man that prevents that?"

"When that question is solved, my friend," Mark replied, "we will be entering the gates of heaven."

"Here they come," Colonel Gray said, removing his headset. "It's Captain Willette and his bunch."

Ike and his teams had linked up with Dan Gray and a small contingent of Scouts at the ruined and deserted town of Mineral Bluff. Tina Raines was among Gray's Scouts.

Gray said, "They're about three miles outside of town, traveling south on Highway 245. A full company of the bastards."

"Haulin' their asses, huh?" Ike said with the contempt of the professional soldier. Or, as in his case, the professional sailor.

"That would appear to be the case," the Englishman replied calmly. "And heading south intrigues me. Preparing to link up with Silver, perhaps?"

"We're gonna have to deal with that scumbag someday," Ike said.

"Quite," Dan said.

Ike turned to a young Rebel. "I want Captain Willette alive, son. Pass the word down the line."

"Yes, sir," the Rebel replied, lifting his walkie-talkie. He spoke softly, then looked at Ike. "Done, sir."

Gray clicked his weapon off safety and onto full auto. He glanced at Ike. "What do you propose doing with Willette, Ike?"

Ike's eyes were cold. "I propose to hang the son of a bitch—slowly,"

"Rather a nasty business, what?" Gray said with a slight smile.

"Quite," Ike mimicked the Englishman.

"Closing," the radio operator said. "Be in the center of town in a minute and a half."

The Rebels waited motionlessly. They were concealed in old buildings, on the rooftops, behind junked and ruined cars and trucks, behind packing crates and in alleys. They softly clicked weapons off safety and onto full auto. The Rebels would be outnumbered three or four to one, but that was something they were accustomed to; it had helped sharpen their fighting skills. They waited.

The lead Jeep in Willette's convoy swung onto the street. A man sat in the back seat, an M-60 machine gun at the ready. They were too confident, and that had led them into carelessness.

Ike figured Willette would be in the center of the column, for safety's sake, and he had figured correctly. The Rebels let the column stretch out before they opened fire at the front and rear of the column.

Willette's people never had a chance. They were more bully-boys than professional soldiers; only a few among their ranks had ever served in any hard military unit. And that worked against them. They did manage to trigger off a few wild rounds, which hit nobody. But the ambush was so expertly done, it lasted only a few moments.

"Cease firing!" Gray yelled.

Several Jeeps and trucks were burning at the rear of the column. One gas tank exploded, and that triggered a chain reaction among the last few vehicles in the convoy. The gas tanks blew, sending smoke spiraling into the sky. Debris rained down on the street, adding its crashing noise to the moaning and screaming of the wounded and dying. Willette stumbled out of a car, his hands raised over his head.

"Don't shoot!" he yelled, panic in his voice. "I surrender. I demand treatment as a prisoner of war."

Ike walked toward him, a coil of rope in one hand. "Oh, you'll get proper treatment, all right, Willette," he snarled at the frightened man. "The same goddamn treatment you gave those unarmed men and women and kids back at home base. You do remember all that, don't you?"

Willette threw up on himself at the sight of the rope in Ike's hand. A dark stain appeared at the man's crotch. "I was under orders!" he screamed. "I had my orders the same as any other soldier. Just like any soldier, I obeyed them."

"Shit!" a woman Rebel said, contempt in her voice. She spat at Willette's feet.

Willette glared at her. "You slimy fuckin' cunt," he said.

"You wanna swing, Willette?" she said with a grin.

Willette wiped puke from his mouth and cursed the woman.

She laughed at him.

Ike approached Willette. He stopped two steps from him and swung the heavy rope, hitting the man in the face. Willette's feet flew out from under him and he landed on his butt. His teeth clicked together and blood spurted from a bitten tongue. The rope had opened a gash on his cheek and bloodied his nose. Ike hooked the noose of the rope around Willette's dirty neck and dragged him down the street to a windowless store front. Willette was screaming and cursing. Each time he would get to his feet, Ike would jerk the rope and Willette would slam to the street to be dragged another few yards, howling and protesting.

Ike stepped up and inside, looping one end of the rope over a support beam. He hauled Willette up, until the man's boots were a full twelve inches off the littered floor. Ike secured the loose end of the rope and stepped out of the store, leaving Willette gagging and choking and slowly spinning and jerking. Ike did not turn around as he walked off. The act of hanging Willette would not bring Sally or the kids back to life, but it would ensure that Willette never committed another similar atrocity.

Only when the horrible gagging sounds had ceased did Ike look around. He looked at the swollen, blackened face of Willette. The man's bowels had moved and the stench was as foul as Willette's living character. Or lack of it. Ike spat on the concrete and walked back to his team.

Tina walked to Colonel Gray's side. "What do we do with the rest of the prisoners, Colonel?"

"Shoot them," Gray said.

*　　　*　　　*

First intercepted radio reports, picked up from walkie-talkies of the Rebels, indicated Sister Voleta's troops were getting pasted by the Rebels. Sister Voleta and her troops had been running hard, pushing their vehicles as fast as road conditions would allow. They now stood at the end of an old firebreak road just south of Angelico Gap, listening to the reports filter in. None contained any good news for Sister Voleta.

All the troops of the Ninth Order had discarded their robes for clothing more practical. Only Voleta wore a robe.

"We've had it," a man told her softly. "Those men who tried to take cover near Lake Nottely were either shot to death or burned to death."

"Barbarians!" Voleta spat the word. It did not occur to her that she had ordered the deaths of countless men and women and children by burning at the stake.

And the man reporting to her did not bring it up.

The man continued his depressing report. "We've lost contact with Captain Willette and his company. There are teams of Raines' Rebels working all over the area. Ben Raines—"

"I don't want to hear that name again!" Voleta shrieked.

"Yes, sister." The man bowed. He was faithful to the end, and the end was only moments away.

He opened his mouth to speak and Sister Voleta waved him silent. "I know, I know," she said. "I thought we were strong enough to defeat . . . that *pig*. I was wrong. I shall be big enough to admit it. Very well. We are not beaten. Far from it. We shall someday emerge stronger than ever. But for now, we'll head for the gap and the highway just north of it. We won't be able to take the vehicles any further. We'll have to leave them here and walk the rest of the way."

"Yes, Sister. I'll take the point."

"No, Lester." She put a hand on his arm. "You and a few others stay with me. I have a feeling about this."

"As you wish, Sister."

They walked straight into a deadly ambush. Ben and his people were hidden in the gap and chopped the men and women of the Ninth Order to bloody rags with machine gunfire. After only a minute, Ben called for a cease fire.

The Rebels picked through the carnage, gathering up all the weapons and ammo and usable equipment. They stripped boots from the dead and any clothing that wasn't ripped by slugs.

Sister Voleta was not lying among the dead and dying.

"That yo-yo got away," Captain Rayle reported to Ben. "I don't know how she managed it, but she did."

I'll have to contend with her someday, Ben thought. This isn't over. Her hatred for me is so intense, she'll keep trying to kill me, one way or the other.

I wonder if that baby was mine? he concluded. I guess I'll wonder all my life. Unless I run into him someday.

Ben walked among the dead and dying, picking his way carefully among the bloodstained rocks and brush.

Will this never end? Ben silently questioned the force that controls the destiny of every living thing.

Will those who follow me ever be allowed to live in peace? Must we, for the remainder of our lives, go constantly armed, forever doomed to wage one battle after another, simply for the right to exist?

He thought of Gale and muttered, "I wonder how many times so many Jews wondered the same thing?"

A cold rain began falling, chilling the earth and those who still lived upon it.

Is that your reply? Ben pondered, remembering the savage night on the motel balcony.

Ben stopped his aimless wandering along the battlefield and looked down, looking into the eyes of a man who lay dying at his booted feet. The man spat at him and cursed him, the hate within overpowering the pain within and without. His voice bubbled from a chest wound and the rain that fell into his open mouth.

"It ain't over," the man gasped his promise. "You won this fight, but a lot of us got out. They'll get you, Raines. And you'll die hard, I can promise you that."

"Why?" Ben asked.

"'Cause . . . 'cause America didn't work, that's why. You . . . said so yourself, back in '89. All we was tryin' to do was live our own way."

"But your society was based on a twisted religion from the mind of a woman so overcome with hate it defied normal thinking."

"Our right," the man gasped, blood, pink and frothy, bubbling past his lips.

Lung shot, Ben thought.

"We'll get you, Raines," the man once more

375

uttered the death threat. "I wish I could be there to see Sister Voleta burn you at the stake. Listen to you scream and beg for mercy."

"Why did you follow her?"

The man's eyes rolled back in his head and he shuddered several times, his boots drumming on the wet earth. His final reply was a sighing of air leaving his dead body.

Ben looked at the men and women gathered around him. His Rebels. His.

I've got to get away from this, Ben thought. These people must learn to cope without me. They have to do that, for future generations. I must leave. And not just for their sake, but for my own, as well.

Ben sighed. "Let's go home, people."

FORTY-TWO

Joni and George arrived at the slave camp just outside what used to be known as Perry, Florida just as the slaves were finishing with their former captors. It was not a pretty sight. Bodies were hanging from tree limbs, sprawled in death on the dusty grounds, and some had been staked out, spread-eagled naked under the sun, and covered with baby oil. The sun was slowly roasting them to death, in a most painful manner.

This was a much larger plantation, a combination cattle and farming operation, so there were almost twice as many slaves and almost four times the guards that had been at Live Oak. The fight had been savage and bloody, and the slaves, of all races and creeds and religions, had taken a number of casualties; but they had killed all the guards.

Joni introduced herself and George, asking, "How many more slave farms did Tony have, and where are they?"

"Four," the leader of the Perry group said. "But we only have to worry about two of them. At the plantations in Clarksville and up in Graceville, the guards won. They killed all the slaves. Just lined them up and shot them down." The speaker's name was Lou, a middle-aged man, but one who looked as though he had made his living as a stevedore prior to slavery. His chest was huge and his shoulders and arms padded with muscle.

"We've got to get to the rest of the plantations as quickly as possible," George said. "Some mercenary named Hartline is on his way down here."

"Sam Hartline!" Lou said, his face paling as he spoke. "Oh, God! That's a bad one. I remember him from three, four years ago. You're right. We've got to get rolling in a hurry."

Joni looked at the cheap wrist watch on her wrist. "Can we make it, Lou?"

"I think so, miss. We're pretty well armed all the way around and radio reports from the other two plantations indicated the revolt was on the side of the slaves. What do you have on your mind, Joni?"

"Linking up with Ben Raines."

Lou nodded. "I think that's a good thought, Joni. I was on my way out to the old Tri-States with a bunch of people back in '93 when we were ambushed in Iowa. Forced us to turn back. I always regretted we didn't make it."

"How long before your people can move out?" Joni asked.

Lou looked around him. "Give us an hour. You folks can get on Highway 27 and move on south until you reach Cross City. Wait for us there. Once we link up, we'll move against what's left of the guards at Chiefland, then head on over to Newberry. Do you know which route Hartline is taking down here?"

"Yes. Interstate 95."

"All right. Just as soon as we clear Newberry, we'll

take 41 up to the intersection of Interstate 75 and pour it on. That will take us right up to the ruins of Atlanta. You folks shove off. We'll link up with you in about two hours."

"You think we have God on our side in this one, Lou?" Joni asked.

"There is no God," Lou replied bitterly. "I gave up believing in that a long time ago. As far as I can tell, we've got only two things left to believe in."

"Oh?" George looked at the man.

"Ourselves and Ben Raines."

FORTY-THREE

Tony grinned at Ann. His grin was anything but nice. "I don't trust you, baby," he said. "I think you're up to something."

Ann said nothing. She crouched naked in the center of the bed. The knife she had stolen from Lennie was under her pillow, the blade open.

"I don't know what," Tony said. "But I'm gettin' bad vibes from you. So you and me, baby, we're gonna get it on one more time. Then I'm gonna give you to Sam Hartline."

This time, Ann could not prevent a hiss of fear and revulsion.

"Yeah." Tony grinned. "Hartline's gonna split you wide open. It should be interestin' listenin' to you squall."

There was nothing Ann could say, so she remained silent.

Tony checked his watch. A gold Rolex he had stolen years before. "Hartline ought to be back in two days. So you and me, baby, we'll get it on tomorrow for the last time." He grinned, exposing soiled and rotten teeth. "You rest up tonight, baby. 'Cause tomorrow, I'm gonna roll you over and take a whack at you from that direction."

He laughed and walked out the door, carefully locking it behind him.

Ann turned on the bed and looked at Peg and Lilli, "You heard him. I get it tomorrow. I got to do it tomorrow, or it'll never get done. Ya'll pack, and keep it light for fast travelin'. Spare shirt, jeans, socks and panties. Any food you might have hidden back. This time tomorrow, we'll either be free, or dead."

The girls hurried from the room. Lilli looked back. "Can I take one of the dollies, Ann?"

"Yeah," Ann said. "You can take one of your dollies."

"You gonna take one of your dollies, Ann?" Peg asked.

Ann shook her head. "No."

"Why?"

"'Cause I think, after tomorrow, I will have outgrown dolls."

FORTY-FOUR

Ben stood alone at the mass grave site. His face wore a grim expression.

"All this," he muttered. "For what? All these lives, snuffed out. For what?"

But only the silence of the grave greeted him. And graves do not speak.

Gale was surprisingly cheerful when Tina visited her while her father was at the grave site.

"You're pretty chipper today, Gale," she said. "What's up?"

Gale smiled at the young woman; they were about the same age. "Oh, I guess I'm just happy to be getting settled in one place. It's a nice house, don't you think?"

"It's lovely."

The home she had chosen was on the outskirts of what had been known as Dalton, Georgia. It was not a large home, for Gale knew Ben was probably only days, maybe hours, from taking off on his quest, and she didn't want too large a house to look after.

"Tell me the rest of it?" Tina prompted, taking the cup of tea Gale fixed for her.

"I'm happy because Ben is happy. Well, as happy as he ever is."

"Because he's leaving?"

"Yes, as odd as that sounds."

"I understand," Tina said. "Believe me, I do."

"I knew you would. When are you and Robert going to marry?"

"Probably never," Tina said matter-of-factly. "You know that marriage has become, is becoming, kind of old hat."

"One more long-accepted social institution gone," Gale replied with a smile. "Perhaps it's time for that."

Tina shrugged. "Who knows? Dad doesn't seem to object. Least he's never said anything about it."

Gale grinned at her. "How could he?"

Both young women chuckled.

"You going to live here all by yourself, Gale?"

"Yes. I'll be all right. You and Bob are right down the street. Ike and Nina have settled in a house right behind me. So I'm not afraid."

Tina finished her tea and rose. She said, "Lots of women would be pitching a fit right about now, Gale. They wouldn't put up with Dad leaving."

Gale shook her head. "Ben would never have chosen that type of woman."

"You're right. You know him pretty well, don't you, Gale?"

"Well enough to let him go," she said with a smile, and the smile was not at all forced.

FORTY-FIVE

How degrading! Emil Hite thought, as he shuffled along, carrying dirty clothes to the women to be washed. One day I'm king of the mountain, the next day I'm a fucking gofer.

"Hurry up with that laundry, you asshole!" one of the women squalled at him.

Just think, Emil pondered the frailties of being a god. One day they are groveling at my feet, the next day, they are shrieking at me like a bunch of fish-mongers.

Oh, woe is me! Emil thought.

"Get your stupid ass over here with those dirty clothes!" a woman howled at him. "And be quick about it."

Emil stumbled on the hem of his robe and the laundry basket flew from his hands, dirty clothes spilling out onto the ground.

Everybody started yelling at him, calling him the most awful of names.

Emil got to his knees and looked upward. "Why me, Blomm?" he said aloud. "Why me?"

One of his captors put a number twelve sized boot on Emil's ass and that put an end to any questioning of the Great God Blomm.

As Emil hurriedly picked up the dirty clothes, he saw, out of the corner of his eye, the young girl, Lynn, being led into what had once been Emil's house. She was giggling and simpering and allowing the man to touch her in the most intimate of places.

Lynn had been Emil's favorite. She gave great head for someone barely in her teens,

Oh, well, Emil philosophized. Easy come, easy go.

"Hite!" one very large lady squalled. "Get over here with those clothes, you stupid prick."

"Yes, Sister Hilary," Emil said.

"And knock off that 'Sister' shit, you phony," Hilary yelled in a voice that made Emil's head sting.

Bitch had a voice that would crack brass, Emil thought.

"And you better not wear yourself out, either," Hilary warned. "'Cause tonight it's my turn with you."

Jesus! Emil thought. And again, Why me?

Emil fervently wished he was back in Chattanooga, selling used cars.

FORTY-SIX

"Got a new truck for you, General," Colonel Gray told Ben. "My Scouts found this one up in Knoxville."

"Looks brand new," Ben remarked, as he walked around the Chevy pickup. No doubt about it, the truck was a nice one. Everything that could be put on a truck was on this one. It was a long wheel base, four-wheel-drive Chevy. The camper top was new and bolted down securely. The cab held enough radio equipment to transmit anywhere in the continental U.S., Ben reckoned. Bucket seats, with new clamps bolted between the seats for Ben's Thompson. The truck had two gas tanks and two spare tires bolted inside the camper.

"It is new," Dan said. "Well . . . the last model made, back in '88. My people found it in a private garage out in the suburbs."

"Uh-huh," Ben said. He wondered how many tracking devices Dan had hidden in and on the truck. Several, he concluded.

"We, uh—" the usually eloquent Englishman seemed at a loss for words—"well, we just thought you needed a new vehicle before you, ah, left us, sir."

"Thank you, Dan," Ben said quietly. "It is, ah,

common knowledge that I'm taking off soon?"

Dan nodded his head. "Yes, sir."

"I see. I won't be nursemaided, Dan."

"I know that, sir."

"But you'll probably send teams out to try and keep an eye on me, won't you?" Ben asked with a smile.

"Oh . . . probably, sir."

"Good luck, Dan."

The Englishman smiled. "Thank you, sir." He patted the hood of the truck. "Enjoy, sir."

As Dan was walking off, Doctor Chase walked up.

"Hello, you old goat," Ben greeted him.

"Old goat to you, too, King Raines," the old doctor fired back. "When are you planning to leave on your idiotic odyssey?"

"Soon."

"I see. Gale is not going with you, I hope."

"No. She's staying."

"Who are you leaving in charge?"

"Cecil. I'm going to call all the troops together tomorrow sometime and pin general's stars on Cecil's shoulders. I suggested I do the same with Ike, but he rather bluntly informed me he never wanted to be any type of fucking officer to begin with."

Doctor Chase laughed. "That sounds like Ike."

"While I'm gone, Lamar, I'm going to lay out the route for outposts. I discussed that with you. I'll be back next year and we'll start heading westward, setting up forts as we go. I think, Lamar, that is the only way we'll ever have a chance for any type of civilization."

"I agree. Well—" he cleared his throat—"you bastard, I'll miss you."

The two men shook hands.

Doctor Chase returned to the overseeing of his new clinic, and Ben walked to the quartermaster's new area and began drawing supplies.

"Be sure to put an old portable typewriter in with the other gear, Sergeant," Ben instructed. "And round me up several boxes of white paper. Good bond."

"Yes, sir."

As he left, Cecil fell in step with him. "You do plan on keeping in touch, don't you, Ben?"

"You know I will, Cec. But you're not going to run into any problems you won't be able to handle easily."

I hope, Cecil silently prayed. "I've instructed everybody to be in formation at 1200 hours tomorrow, Ben."

"Good."

Cecil still did not know what Ben planned to do at the formation. Ike had been sworn to secrecy. "You going to make a speech, Ben?"

"A very short one. I plan to be up in Kentucky by nightfall."

"Well . . . see you tomorrow, Ben."

"Tomorrow, Cecil."

FORTY-SEVEN

Tony Silver stood naked over the girl who whimpered in pain and fear on the bed. Ann was naked. The marks of the belt vividly crisscrossed her flesh. Tony tossed the belt to the floor and slapped her viciously across the face, rocking her head and bloodying her mouth.

"Bitch! I wanna know what the hell you're up to."

"Nothing, Tony," the child cried. "I swear it. Nothing."

"Then how come I don't believe you?"

In reply, Ann rolled over on her back and spread her slender legs. She watched Tony's face change and heard his breathing quicken.

Tony hefted his growing erection and smiled at her. "Come over, here, baby, and kiss this for me."

Ann scooted across the bed and put her small, bare feet on the carpet. Her right hand slipped under the pillow and gripped the handle of the sharp knife. When she looked up at Tony, he was slowly masturbating himself, his eyes closed.

Quickly she moved to him, and faced his hardness, one slender leg on either side of Tony's hairy legs.

He pushed the head of his penis against her mouth. "Suck it for me, baby," he said.

Ann gripped the knife with both hands and drove it into Tony's soft lower belly, just a few inches above his pubic hair line. She savagely jerked the blade upward, for she had driven it in with the sharp edge facing upward.

Tony made a low choking sound and opened his mouth to scream. Ann jerked the knife out and, using all her strength, drove the blade as deep as it would go into the center of his chest. The blade tore into his heart and Tony fell backward onto the carpet, dying soundlessly in his own blood.

Peg and Lilli came into the bedroom. They looked at the sight, no emotion at all registering on their young faces. They were survivors; they had seen far worse than this in their young lives.

"It's dark out," Lilli said.

"Get your stuff together," Ann said as she hurriedly dressed.

The girls raced for their slim bundles. Each girl had packed her favorite dolly inside.

All except Ann. She looked at her small collection of dolls scattered on the floor and shook her head. She looked at the blood on her hands.

"Too late for that," she muttered.

She picked up Tony's .38 snub-nosed Chief's Special and checked it as she had seen him do many times. All five chambers were filled. Ann knew something about guns, although she was far from being an expert shot.

Ann gave the knife to Peg with this warning, "Don't hesitate to use it."

Lilli darkened the lights and pulled back the drapes. "Only one guard, and he's clear down at the other end. No, wait! He's walkin' off down the corridor. He's around the corner and out of sight. Come on!''

The girls raced down the corridor and within seconds were on the ground level. Ann looked toward Patsy's room.

"You two wait for me down on the corner. Right over there." She pointed. "Go on. I got something to do. If I'm not there in fifteen minutes, you two take off. Head north. That's where Mr. Ben Raines is. Find him. Shove off!''

They ran and were soon out of sight in the dark night. Ann walked silently toward Patsy's room. She stopped once, to pick up a brick from the ground. She knocked softly on the motel room door.

The door opened. Patsy had only a second to register her shock at seeing the young girl before the brick smashed into her face, knocking her backward. She fell to the carpet, her face broken and bleeding. Ann hit her several more times with the brick, hearing and feeling her skull pop. She tossed the brick to the floor.

"Bitch!'' she said.

Then she was gone in the night, joining her young friends.

The trio headed north. Toward the Base Camp of Ben Raines.

FORTY-EIGHT

"We're too late," Captain Jennings told his commanding officer.

Sam stood in the middle of what was left at Live Oak.

"Yes," Sam agreed. "We'll drive over to Perry, but I have a hunch we're going to be too late to do any good over there, as well."

Had Sam not elected to take the interstate for faster traveling, and chosen the southern route instead, he would have intercepted Lou and his bunch of freed slaves just as they were pulling out from Perry. As it was, the two groups remained miles apart.

When Lou caught up with Joni and George at Cross City, they traveled on to Chiefland, only to find the battle was over. The slaves were victorious.

Now more than two hundred strong, the group traveled to Newberry. There, they assisted in mopping up what was left of Tony's guards, and without stopping to take a rest, immediately left, heading north on Highway 41. They followed that until it intersected with Interstate 75, and continued north, only stopping for refueling and bathroom breaks.

By the time Sam and his mercenaries finally reached what was left of the plantation at Chiefland,

Joni and George and Lou and the freed slaves were a full seventy-five miles up into Georgia. And rolling northward toward freedom.

Sam told his men to stand down and camp for the night. He walked to his communications van to call in to Tony. When he learned Tony was dead, and the three young girls gone, Sam chuckled. He relayed the story to his officers and noncoms.

Captain Jennings summed it up. "So now we got controlling interest of the only game in town, eh, Sam?"

"That is correct," Sam said, lighting a long, slim cigar. His men never asked where he got the cigars, and Hartline never offered any explanation, "Such as the game has turned out to be."

"Who killed Tony?"

"Who gives a shit?" Hartline replied, puffing smoke to the slight breeze that wound through the trees. He was thoughtful for a moment. "We can forget the slaves that were here," he said. "Come daylight, I want a full platoon to stay in this area, and start picking up anyone who comes wandering through here. Start getting these places back in shape. The crops are harvested for this season, so we'll have some months to rebuild. Fuck Tony Silver." He smiled. "I was going to kill him first chance I got, anyway."

FORTY-NINE

Ben pinned the silver stars of a general on Cecil's jacket. He smiled at the man and shook his hand.

"I wish you had warned me about this, Ben," Cecil muttered so only Ben could hear.

"If I had, you'd have run off and hidden," Ben replied.

Cecil joined Ben in laughter.

Ben turned to face his people, now more than three thousand strong, counting Abe Lancer and his mountain people and Dave Harner and his group from Macon. Ben lifted a bullhorn to his lips.

"There is a lot I could say, but I never liked long speeches. But let me say I am so very, very proud of you all. I'll be leaving in a few moments, heading out to at least start what I had planned on doing back in '88. That is to chronicle the events leading up to and just after the great war that brought this nation to its knees.

"I am leaving in charge a man I have the utmost faith in, General Cecil Jefferys. I don't want any emotional goodbyes. For I will be back. And when I return, I want to see permanent homes, schools, farms, and an orderly, productive society. You've all done it before, you can do it again. And you don't need me standing over you telling you what to do.

"Call this a small vacation for me. Just getting away from the office for a time. I'll see you people in about six months. That is all. You have duties to attend to, get to it."

Ben lowered the bullhorn, handed it to Cecil, and walked toward his new pickup.

The cheering behind him lasted for more than five minutes before Cecil shouted them down and sent them back to work. To rebuild something out of the ashes.

Gale was waiting for him at the truck. She smiled and said, "Well, Raines, if you're expecting me to get all mushy and sentimental, you're going to have a long wait."

"Heaven forbid, Gale. That would destroy my image of you."

"Uh-huh," she said dryly. She rose up on tiptoes and kissed him lightly on the mouth. "You take care of yourself, Ben."

"I'll do that, kid."

She slipped from his hands and walked away to where Tina was standing. Tina flipped her father a salute and Ben returned it. He got into the pickup, and drove off, heading north into Kentucky.

"You handled that rather well," Tina said.

"Damned if I was going to cry," Gale said. "One thing I learned about Ben, he doesn't like weepy women."

"Well, you can have a good cry when you get behind closed doors at your house."

"No," Gale said. "Ben wouldn't want that. I've got him growing within me, and that is enough. He'll be back. Whether to me, or to someone else, only time will tell. I think this, Tina: Ben is a man whose destiny is carved in stone. And he'll see that in a few months. He will see where his duty lies. And he'll come back. His destiny is not to wander the earth like a nomad, but rather to build, to bring order out of chaos, civilization out of anarchy, towns and cities out of rubble. He knows all that. He's just got to clear his mind. And when he does that, he'll be back."

Tina smiled. "You know him pretty well, Gale."

"Knew him," she corrected softly.

Both women looked up at the sounds of engines drawing closer. White flags flew from radio antennas on each vehicle.

James Riverson walked up. "The slaves from down south," he said. "They radioed us they were coming in."

"Survivors," Tina said.

"From out of the ashes," Gale softly said. "More men and women looking for order in a world gone mad." She looked toward the north, toward the now-empty highway Ben had taken. "Good luck, Ben."